Jeanne Savery

Runaway Scandal

Bev—
this one has a couple of really great old ladies showing us how to do it!
Jeanne Savery

Cerridwen Cotillion

What the critics are saying...

ꟹ

"***Runaway Scandal*** is a delightful, humorous, and yet surprisingly suspenseful tale about a very unconventional couple who have the audacity to be a love match in Regency England! […] If you are looking for hot love scenes they are not in this book but are implied with the couple sneaking off to be alone to satisfy one another. I think the romance and the implied sensuality of the couple is exceptionally well done. If you enjoy regency historical romances with strong and intelligent female characters, sensuality without the blatant sex scenes, humorous characters and plot twists, all with a touch of suspense, then I recommend this book!" ~ *Manic Readers Reviews*

"It would have been interesting to read how Tavie and Dominic met under the circumstance of their romance being a scandal." ~ *Night Owl Romance Reviews*

A Cerridwen Press Publication

www.cerridwenpress.com

Runaway Scandal

ISBN 9781419958069

Edited by Carole Genz.
Cover art by Lissa Waitley.

This book printed in the U.S.A. by Jasmine-Jade Enterprises, LLC.

Electronic book Publication March 2008
Trade paperback Publication September 2008

Cerridwen Press is an imprint of Ellora's Cave Publishing, Inc.®

Runaway Scandal

Prologue

June 1808

ꝏ

A fair number of weeks had passed since Lady Sarah Sands' graceless nephew descended on her son's doorstep with that trollop on his arm. Had he spoken the truth that day, he would have been forced to wed the redheaded shrew. His company alone was enough to compromise her. Still, there had been no report of his marriage. Just as Sarah had known, the girl was no better than the light-skirt she'd thought the chit to be.

Chit. That brass-faced bit-of-muslin must have been all of twenty-five.

But Sarah bided her time, wishing to be certain. When no marriage was announced, she was sure. This time she had the dissolute marquis just where she wanted him.

She ground her teeth. Old bitterness spread poison through her system. Under a benevolent God, she would have been born male and the heir. *She* would have been Marquis of Brightwood instead of Miles, her half brother. The closest Sarah had come was to marry the distant cousin who was his heir. But then her undeserving half brother's more than undeserving son inherited. Sarah couldn't bear the injustice of it all.

Revenge. She pushed aside past regrets for more positive thoughts. By the time she'd have finished telling the world of Dominic's latest devilment, he'd be snubbed by all. Ostracized. This time he'd gone too far.

Sarah reread the letter, her opening salvo in this renewed battle against fate.

Wednesday, 1 June, '08

Dear Aunts Elphinia and Alvinia,

It sorrows me to inform you of Dominic's latest damning action. My nephew is so lost to proper behavior he attempted to foist his latest bird-of-paradise onto me, in the guise of a woman in distress. He demanded I take in a harlot of the worst sort by claiming she was a governess, tricked and abandoned, and in need of a roof over her head.

I saw through that at once. No governess could have dressed so richly. A quickly totaled estimate of her attire came to no less than four hundred guineas. The cloak alone was worth over two hundred, lined, as it was, with sable. And her hat! No mere governess would have bought such a confection. Even if she might conceivably afford such a tonnish *style, a real governess would know it was not at all the thing. Far, far too dashing!*

Even you will agree that an attempt to push a woman of that sort onto one of his female relatives is the last straw. He has gone beyond the pale.

And so, dear Aunt Alvinia and Aunt Elphinia, you must finally admit your favorite great-nephew has utterly shamed himself, his title and his family. I rely on you to induce our world to show Dominic he cannot do just as he pleases. You can do so much more than I to punish him, as he deserves to be punished…

Sarah tasted wormwood. How galling that an old woman like Elf, a woman who had half retired from the polite world decades previously, still had more power in the *ton* than Sarah ever had. Oh, if only Dominic would take himself out of the world altogether!

"No!" Muscles tensing, Sarah sent a surreptitious glance over her shoulder. *I mustn't think that thought.* It frightened Sarah how obsessively it came to mind. "What I *must* do," she muttered, "and *instantly*, is decide how to end this letter, how to induce the aunts to do their duty. Yes, that is what I must do."

Lady Sands feathered the end of her pen against her narrow chin and scowled, searching for a way to end the letter lying on the desk before her. Nothing came to mind.

Dominic must be ostracized, got out of the way, no longer a constant irritant. He must be induced to leave for the continent. Or, still better, buy himself a commission in one of those regiments which, or so it was whispered, would soon be sent to Portugal under Arthur Wellesley's command.

Sarah looked down at her letter and read it through. "You can do so much more than I to punish him, as he deserves to be punished... More than I," she repeated bitterly.

It was *not* fair. A red haze filtered the light before Sarah's eyes but a smidgen of control remained. She knew her temper. If allowed free rein, it would destroy the careful tone of the letter. She must rid herself of it, quickly.

Footsteps scurried down the hall and Sarah's head rose, a vicious little smile forming. Her gaze glued to the open door, her hand scrabbled over the desktop. Her abigail Mary—arms piled high with newly ironed petticoats and chemises—stepped into view. Sarah's hand closed over something hard, something nicely fitting her grip and, in one smooth motion, she picked it up and threw it. The cup hit Mary's shoulder, cold chocolate spattering in all directions. The maid turned, her eyes tightly closed.

"Oh dear," cooed Sarah. "Did that nasty stuff spot those bits and pieces?" Sarah bottled up her glee at the ruination of all Mary's hard work. "You will have to do them over again, will you not? If you hurry," she added sweetly, "perhaps no chocolate will spot my things."

No warning was needed as to what would happen if a spot remained. Tight-lipped, Mary reversed direction, returning to the laundry room.

Another penance arranged for my maid, atonement for her sins, thought Sarah smugly. *Someday Mary will thank me of course.*

Sarah, her temper righted, reread the letter still again. Perhaps simply…

…to punish him, as he deserves to be punished. Dominic must not be allowed to forever go his length with no retribution. I believe you will see this to be true and will do what is necessary.

Your niece,

Sarah.

Sarah bit her lip, wondering if there were stronger words, less namby-pamby words, vicious words she would prefer to such blandness. She shook her head. It would have to do. If it were anyone but Elphinia, she could say more to Dominic's detriment, but it *was* Elf. Sarah sighed but then brightened. There would be further letters, those written to others less enamored, less besotted, with her dratted nephew.

As Sarah reached for another sheet of paper she thought of her ash-wood hunting bow. When she'd penned three more letters, she would reward herself. She could almost feel the smooth wood under her hand, feel the beat of her heart, almost smell the blood of some small creature, a woodcock or perhaps a hare.

Her hand shook as she dipped her pen into the ink.

Chapter One

ꟹ

"Are you all right, Alvinia?" asked Elphinia.

"I *think* so," said the second elderly lady.

Lady Elphinia Thornton, feeling bruised and achy, wished she could say the same.

The sisters knelt between the seats of the ancient coach, thrown forward by an unusually large bump. The road had worsened as they proceeded north, the stone with which it was surfaced broken into larger and larger bits. This last stretch was rougher than any so far encountered on their self-imposed journey of mercy.

Elf, as she'd been affectionately known by three generations of friends, tested her wrist. She hadn't, thank heaven, broken a bone when attempting to save herself. Next she resettled her new spring bonnet, a black one made of excellent straw, and grumbled softly as she realized the brim had cracked when it, and her nose, connected with the opposite seat. She touched said nose and concluded it had survived intact, its slender length neither twisted to one side nor swelling from the blow.

Having done all that, Elf pulled herself up from her knees and seated herself properly. She grasped the strap, which she'd been a fool to release. She'd not be so complacent again. Her free hand felt first one bony knee and then the other, rubbing them through the heavy bombazine of her traveling gown while, silently, she predicted the stiffening and pain to come.

Old bones, she thought, *are the devil.*

Having enumerated her aches, Elf turned to look at her sister who still knelt on the floor of the carriage.

"'Pon rep, Ally, you *are* hurt."

Lady Alvinia Thornton, her body as plump as Elf's was thin, bowed further over her arms, her hands clenched before her. She shook her head vigorously, a few strands of hair escaping the knot at the back of her head. It was her only response for another breath of time. Then, with much huffing and puffing, she struggled into her proper place.

Once she'd spread her skirts to her liking, she smiled at Elphinia, a smile as sweet as her nature. "I'm not hurt, Elf. It's just that since we were so fortuitously thrown into the proper position, it seemed a shame to waste it."

Elf's penetrating stare brought a faint blush to her sister's rounded cheeks. "Waste it?" prompted Elf.

"I prayed."

Elf turned to look out her window. She snorted. Softly. So softly she had some hope her more conventionally devout sister hadn't heard. It was *Elf's* belief that the good Lord helped those who helped themselves.

They had left the inn in Windermere early that morning and, later, threaded their way through the weekly market in progress in Ambleside. Beyond Ambleside, they'd followed the main road along the eastern edge of Grasmere but lost it just south of Lake Thirlmere. Now they were passing around that mere's south end, their long journey nearly at an end. To the west rose the sharp slopes of the Cumbrian Mountains. The beauty surrounding the travelers was incredible and constantly changing. One didn't wonder that the Lake District had become so popular in recent years—despite the roads.

"I thought it couldn't hurt," explained Alvinia.

"Hurt?"

"Praying. I mean, the situation..." Alvinia trailed off helplessly.

"Our great-nephew has been riding to the devil for years. And we've been on our knees asking help of the beneficent Lord for nearly as many," said Elf waspishly. "Given his latest excursion into scandal's realm, I've come to the conclusion he's past praying for."

"One must not give up on the poor dear boy, Elf. You've said that again and again."

"That was before he tried to foist a woman no better than she should be onto Sarah. There are limits, Ally, even to my tolerance."

"Oh no, Elf. Never say so." Ally shook her head, her smile gentle. "*You* would never give up. No, you never would."

There was complete faith behind those words and Elf bit her lip. She'd excused Dominic again and again, insisted he was merely sowing wild oats and that his time would come. The Thornton Blessing would turn him into a pattern card of respectability as was tradition. No Thornton heir married for wealth or position or status but for that least acceptable of *tonnish* reasons, a true and abiding love. Elf had believed that, when that time came, Dominic too would settle into a staid and proper existence.

The sisters had been raised in a generation not easily shocked and Elf recalled vividly the hawklike visage topped with white hair that had elevated her grandfather's looks beyond the average run of mankind. She also remembered the stories told about that particular marquis. His behavior had been *far* more shocking than Dominic's.

Elf had been certain their great-nephew, who looked exactly like the old gentleman, except his hair was not yet white, would follow the classic family pattern. The last three years had gradually eroded her faith. This most recent escapade was, without doubt, the folly that would tumble him beyond the realm of decent society. How had he dared?

"You know, Elf," said Ally, breaking into her thoughts, "I've been thinking about that letter from Sarah."

"Haven't we both. Would we, at our age, have attempted a journey of this magnitude if we were unconvinced of its necessity?"

"How true," said Ally and then spoiled her agreement by adding in a doubtful tone, "but *Sarah*, you know?"

Elf stiffened her already erect posture and turned from the waist. Her dark brown eyes met the sweeter, more innocent and more faded brown orbs of her sister.

"Sarah," repeated Elf thoughtfully.

"Yes. Remember how tiresome she was when last she visited, going on in that nasty way about how poor Dom tumbled from one scrape to another, dragging the name in the dust and that he didn't deserve to be head of the family. *And* how her son Owen was so much better suited to the role… Poor Owen. He would hate it, would he not?" Alvinia finished thoughtfully. She smiled as she observed the widening of Elphinia's eyes, the firming of her chin. "You *do* remember."

"Why did you not bring that up when we discussed whether we should dig into our bit of savings and suffer the torments of travel to see what we could do, if anything, to rescue Dominic from this latest folly?"

"I had not thought of it *then*," said her sister, again with unarguable simplicity.

Elf gritted her teeth and took tight hold of both the strap and her temper. It was not Ally's fault that she had not remembered. Ally always took the greatest care to believe the very best of everyone and would have put away any thoughts to the contrary in the darkest cellar of her mind. The miracle was that it occurred to her now.

Or perhaps remembering was the answer to her prayer?

Elf chastised herself instead. It was not *her* habit to gloss over the more negative aspects of a person's personality. *She* should have taken into account the source of their information. But what *had* she done? The moment she read Sarah's spiteful letter she immediately accepted it as truth. And, given

Dominic's well-advertised rake's progress, accepted that the rest of the *beau monde* would as well.

Elf halted in her mental tracks. The world *would* believe the worst of Dom, whatever the *facts* of the matter. So it was still necessary to discover the truth and the only way to achieve that was to confront Dominic. Since Dominic was fixed at Brightwood at this time of year, it followed that they too must travel north.

It is pleasant, she thought, *to come to the same conclusion originally reached but by a different route in an entirely different frame of mind. And thanks be to whichever guardian angel put the notion into my mind that I write Dom's godmother.*

The dowager Lady Matilda Clavingstone would keep an eye on things from the London end.

"I believe we have arrived, Elf."

"Have we? So we have." Elf stared at the wrought iron arch with the gilded rooster surrounded by the Latin words meaning "Our Dawning is Ever Here". Below the crest hung elaborate and tightly shut gates. Grumbling, their old groom-*cum*-footman climbed down and pushed aside the barrier, waiting until the antiquated equipage had passed through before closing the gates and climbing, not without more grumbling, back onto the perch beside the Thornton ladies' equally ancient coachman-*cum*-gardener.

Their way wound between banks of rhododendrons over which occasional glimpses of Thirlmere could be seen. The shrubbery left behind, the lawn was dotted with copper beeches, which would turn bright gold come autumn, giving Brightwood its name. Set on a gentle rise was an Elizabethan structure, the countryseat of Dominic Thornton, eighth Marquis of Brightwood. It had been built by the Thornton ancestor who did much to pad both his Queen's and his own coffers.

Piracy, legitimized by *letters of marque,* was the source of more than one private fortune dating from those far-off days when the Virgin Queen ruled. The Thorntons, through practicality and political *savoir-faire*, had managed to hang on to theirs—despite every generation having its profligate son.

It was more than two decades since Elf had last visited Brightwood. She gazed hungrily at the classic E-shaped mansion. "Oh, the fleeting years," she murmured, her thoughts uncharacteristically nostalgic. *How very long ago it was when Ally and I grew up under that roof.*

Eagerly, if a trifle anxiously, she searched the brick façade for changes. She found, at this distance anyway, there were none. Dom had done nothing foolish to change a structure that was, when all was said and done, perfection itself.

The well-raked drive curved slightly and, losing sight of the house, Elf bent to dust off her dress. "Ally, you have a spot on your skirt, dear. Right there."

"So I do." Ally too did what she could to make herself presentable and examined her sister. "Elf, your new hat!"

Elf removed it and glanced sorrowfully at the broken brim. She sighed and tossed it to the floor, putting it from her mind when she saw they'd nearly arrived. The heavily carved front door stood open to the pleasant summer day and the coach had no more than pulled to a jerky stop, giving the passengers one last shake, when Dominic's butler appeared. With his back stiff and his nose high, he approached the front of the coach. Words were exchanged between the coachman and the butler.

His lordship, it seemed, was not receiving but would, given who had arrived, be informed of that arrival. The butler stalked back up the steps.

"Oh dear." Ally worried her lip with small teeth.

"Ally, don't be a fool. Of course we will be received."

"But the butler seemed so very sure..."

"Dominic will not set *us* to the right-about."

The coach door opened, the steps put in place, but before the groom could help the sisters down, Dominic himself strode out.

"My loving aunts! What a surprise. The letter announcing your arrival must have gone astray."

"Don't be satirical, Dominic," said Elf. "You know very well there was no letter. Now give me your hand. Poor Harry," she waved at the groom, "must be even more shattered and exhausted than are we."

"If you didn't insist on retaining a coach which should have been retired decades ago, you might find travel less difficult. This boneshaker must have belonged to my grandfather."

Elf winced as she came down onto the drive and glanced up to see her great-nephew's brows dip even deeper, this time with unspoken concern. She sighed. She hated it when others became aware of the inadequacies of her aging body. It was bad enough *she* knew. She stood aside as Dominic helped Alvinia down and then, giving each old lady an arm, he escorted them up the shallow steps and in under the low-beamed ceiling of the central hall. He walked slowly. Although grateful she could pamper knees that were already stiffening, Elf was impatient of the need.

"Mrs. MacReady will show you to your rooms. Later, when you've rested, you will tell me why you have made this absurdly long journey."

Ally moved ahead and into conversation with the housekeeper but Elf hung back, meeting her great-nephew's gaze sternly. "Really, Dominic, you know very well why we found it necessary."

The dark brows dipped, the wings slanting higher in saturnine display. His scowl did not deter his relative one whit. She merely scowled in turn.

Dom's displeasure broke into a grin. "You do that so well, Aunt Elf."

"I've had decades more practice than you," she retorted.

He nodded but his smile faded. "To answer your question, I am unaware of any recent behavior on my part that would result in your arrival." He noted his great-aunt's deepening frown and added, "You will withhold your lecture, whatever it may be, until you've rested and refreshed yourself."

Dominic's hand swept in graceful invitation toward the stairs. Elf nodded, unwilling to argue with that particular combination of concern and arrogance. The lecture could wait. In fact, it would wait until she'd heard his story. Thank goodness, Ally had reminded her that Sarah always cried out against a providence that had not made her a man and the heir in her generation. Given Sarah's vituperative nature, Elf sometimes wondered if her niece didn't occasionally entreat the Good Lord to organize an early demise for the current holder of the title so that her son would inherit. The thought was absurd of course.

Inadvertently, Elf reached for the balustrade with her injured hand and did not repress a moan of pain at the mistake. Instantly, Dom was at her side, his fingers gently circling the arm she'd automatically jerked back against herself.

"What have you done?"

"Truly, it is nothing. We hit a rather large bump someway back and we were thrown forward. I strained my wrist a bit is all."

"A *bit*. It is swelling. Are you hurt elsewhere?" Dom sighed in exasperation when she shook her head. "Why do you insist on keeping that cumbersome coach when I have more than once offered you better? No, do not answer. Nor bother your head with my questions concerning your health. You will only say there is nothing wrong which a rest and a bath will not put right."

As Dom spoke, he swung Elf up in his arms, striding up the broad steps to the landing and turning to follow the path Ally and Mrs. MacReady had taken. Elf settled into his hold, putting her good arm around his neck. She chuckled softly.

"What is it *now*, oh-favorite-aunt?"

"Just that this is very pleasant. I assumed, oh, some years ago now, I'd never again feel the strong arms of a man around me."

"Would that have been when the late Earl of Winston died?" asked her irrepressible great-nephew.

Elf was long beyond blushing, so she didn't. "You are a scamp. I was unaware you knew of that, um, association."

"The whole world knew he was your devoted cavalier and *had* been since your unfailing light first broke on the social scene."

"Well," Elf tipped her head thoughtfully, "not *quite* from the first. I was engaged then to Lord Morganwaite. The *third* Lord Morganwaite that would have been. I believe the fifth now holds the title? My lord was brought home on a gate some days before our wedding." She tried for a doleful look that didn't sit too well on her sharp features and gave it up. "Ah, Dominic! What wonderful days those were. Yours is such a namby-pamby generation. You have no idea of the goings-on in my day."

"Not so namby-pamby I have not heard you found Morganwaite's unfortunate demise a pleasant release."

She giggled, as she had not for decades. "Dominic, wherever did you hear that?"

"From a little lady known to the world as Elf. She told me that pretending to be heartbroken was a wonderful excuse for not entering into another marriage contract. By then, if I remember correctly, you had enslaved Winston—despite the fact he was married to an exceedingly beautiful woman."

Elf sniffed. "Beauty is as beauty does. She was not a beauty. Ever."

Dom repressed a smile. "Here we are. Your old room, I believe."

Elf looked around and her eyes glistened with unshed tears, the arm around Dom's neck tightening. "It is exactly the same. How can it be?"

"Some years ago the original manufactory hunted out its old designs and made new material for the hangings. I believe it was necessary to have the rug copied by someone English as the French factory was not available, what with the war and all, but they managed a fairly good replica."

"I cannot believe it."

"My mother may be a perfect widgeon but even she recognizes what a jewel the centuries have made of Brightwood Hall." Dom slanted Elf a rueful look. "Not that my father would have allowed any change. Not so much as the color of the paint in the servants' hall, assuming Mother was so bird-witted as to suggest such a thing."

"Miles liked it just as it is. You may put me down now, Dominic. I'll rest and gird myself for that lecture you are to receive."

Dom's scowl returned but he placed his great-aunt on her feet gently. "I deserve no lecture."

Elf laughed. "So I presume. However the world will not agree. Sarah is seeing to that. Something must be done, Dom."

Dom's eyes twinkled wickedly. "It is done. Never mind. Here is Mrs. MacReady. She'll see to your needs and, when you have rested, come to the library where I'll await you." He paused at the door and spoke to his housekeeper. "See to that wrist. Ice, I think, and find out, if you can, if she has any other bumps or bruises. Remember, she will not tell you unless you become impertinently insistent!"

An hour later, Elf poked her head into her sister's room then entered. "You have gone to bed," she accused.

"Yes. I thought it for the best, dear."

"It is cowardly of you to order a tray in your room."

"Oh no, Elf. You will do much better without me. I have often noticed you get to the core of a matter much more quickly if I am not there tut-tutting and exclaiming and asking irrelevant questions. Besides, I look forward to a bed that does not swing and sway and bounce. I do not know how it is, Elf, but when we travel, even once we are snug in an inn, I never seem to rid myself of the feeling I am moving."

"I know just what you mean," nodded Elf, secretly agreeing she'd make more progress without Ally's help. She said all that was proper to her sister's comfort and left Ally to her tatting and thinking of her supper.

* * * * *

"I was beginning to wonder, Aunt-of-my-heart, if you'd decided to postpone this little discussion until tomorrow."

"Oh no. I am not so poorly as *that*." Elf nodded firmly, her brown eyes flickering from the pleasant, if unnecessary, fire to the delicate Queen Anne chair pulled up before it and on to where her great-nephew stood, dressed for dinner, a glass of, what looked suspiciously like, brandy in his hand.

Liquid courage? she wondered.

Elf tipped her head to one side and studied him. Earlier, when dressed in his buckskins, she thought him merely the handsomest man she'd seen since her grandfather passed on. Now, seeing him in pantaloons strapped tightly under feet shod in slippers, his beautifully tailored coat smoothed over a modest vest and all set off by an exquisitely tied cravat, she changed her mind. He was a modern-day angel, she decided. Then, noting the dark brows slanting in an aquiline fashion across his forehead, the piercing, deep-set, dark eyes and aggressive chin, she amended that to fallen angel. Dominic was made of the stuff that set feminine hearts beating. And had. Often.

"What may I serve you, Auntie Elf?" Dom moved toward a side table on which sat various libations. "Negus perhaps?" he suggested, eyes twinkling and tongue firmly in cheek.

Elf's look of loathing set him to chuckling. "What are you drinking?"

"Brandy, my love."

"That will do. It isn't some your grandfather put down, is it? I've no hopes it might be from your great-great-grandfather's stock of which I had my first taste. Ambrosia, Dom, I swear it."

There was no apology in his voice when he responded, "It is some my father laid down."

"Very well. We will see what sort of palate he had. I've heard rumors it was up to snuff and will be glad for an opportunity to test it."

Such socially proper preliminaries were to neither Thornton's taste. The young man and the old woman were alike in that they preferred a head-on confrontation. So Elf made no pretense of pandering to current fashions in propriety by asking the requisite questions concerning Dominic's health or that of his mother and sister—who was again *enceinte,* the baby due within the month. Instead, once seated with her glass, she started right in.

"Sarah wrote two pages of utter nonsense. *Two pages.* This from a woman who will not allow her servants to burn the wax-candle ends but finishes them off herself in the privacy of her own rooms. Such a pinchpenny! And yet she went to the expense of an extra sheet, afraid if she crossed her lines I might miss something. Ah! But there is worse. She will have written similar drivel to everyone she knows. I am here to discover the truth of the matter and I expect the exact tale, Nephew."

"May I know what she wrote?"

"You know what she wrote."

"I can make a good guess, I suppose," he said, his frown deepening.

"Come now, Dom. No procrastination."

"I am trying to decide where to begin. I suppose when I met the woman in question?"

"That seems a suitable point."

"She was sitting on a trunk with three bandboxes and two hatboxes piled nearby, all of them under a signpost at a crossroads. It was a rather cool day for the season and, from the look of her, she'd been sitting there for some time. Chilled to the bone, my beloved aunt, I am sure."

"Describe her."

"Hmm… Young but not in the first blush of youth. Dressed in well-tailored traveling attire covered by a discreetly trimmed fur-lined cloak. She'd removed her hat, which had three red feathers and a deep red, nearly black ribbon. Her hair was bundled up into a bun at the back and she was scowling more fiercely than any Thornton born, which is, you will admit, saying a great deal."

"That is a well-drawn picture." Elf tipped her head in the characteristic birdlike pose she adopted when thinking. "On the other hand, Dom dear, I do not believe you ever met your great-uncle Broward? No one could possibly scowl to the degree that man managed."

"I will concede you Uncle Broward because, as you say, I never met the man. He died when I was still in the cradle." Dominic sipped his brandy, his memories of his lady inducing a soft chuckle. "When I stopped, my lady in distress eyed my equipage—a perch phaeton, if you care to know—eyed the horses—a team of four excellently matched bays—and then eyed me. After that, she rose to her feet, stalked around the trunk and resettled herself, her back to me and her nose in the air. Needless to say I was intrigued."

"Of course you were." Elf nodded and sipped her brandy. "This is not the best brandy I've ever tasted but it is adequate." She sipped again. "Yes. Certainly adequate."

"I thank you on my father's behalf," said her great-nephew politely. Dominic stretched out his long limbs. His elbows on the arms of his chair and his glass balanced between the fingers of both hands, he crossed his ankles and cleared his throat. "I sent my groom to the horses' heads and descended to the ground, walking around to face her. I bowed politely and asked if I could be of service."

Elf waited while he sipped again and watched a tiny smile forming around the edges of his mouth—a mouth that was normally set in a sharply defined line. Elf's eyebrows rose at this example of softening.

"She denied I could be of any use at all and turned her head. I moved so I could again confront her and suggested that someone should help and asked for whom she was waiting."

"You are making a very long tale of this, Nephew."

"So I am. To shorten it, it seems she was employed as governess, by letter, with ticket sent on and instructions to come from the coach stop by carrier to this point where she would be met by a gig. She had spent two hours waiting for that last connection."

"Got her dates confused if there was any truth to her tale." Elf shook her head. "She was bamming you." Elf saw Dom hide a smile at her use of cant and corrected herself. "*Teasing* you. Dressed as you describe, she was a runaway or eloping or, far more likely, if Sarah was any judge of her age, someone's castoff piece of fluff."

"That is your considered opinion?" Elf nodded and he smiled. "Shall I continue?"

"Please do."

"I convinced her I'd no ambition to take advantage of her delicate situation and suggested I deliver her and her belongings to a nearby manor house where the residents could perhaps tell her how to contact her employer."

Elf's disbelief—resulting from the first part of his comment—was evident and Dom chuckled.

"You think I cannot convince a virtuous young woman I've no designs on her person?" he demanded.

Elf met his challenge by giving one of her own. "And had you none?"

"Wishing and willing are entirely different things, Auntie Elf, as we both know." He grinned at her reluctant agreement. Elf too liked to have her way but was resigned to not having it at *every* turn. "The lady was obviously gently bred, if a trifle nonconforming, and not for my taking."

"Nonconforming?" pounced his great-aunt.

"You demanded, I think, that I shorten my tale. The language used by my maiden-in-distress when first offered the use of my carriage to transport her elsewhere would have delighted you."

"Hmm." *Not,* thought Elf, *a well-brought-up maiden. Not by the bland standards of the present day, but a woman who becomes more intriguing by the minute.*

"Hmm, yourself," echoed Dominic. "Believe me, she was raised by all the conventions which have ruined every young lady thrown in my path by enterprising mamas. The training did not *take,* thank the gods. You would, dear Aunt, have approved her style. She rang a peal over me—and *not* in words allowed a lady with the slightest pretense of gentility." He fondled his glass and went on gently. "You see, dear Aunt, although I did not know *her,* she had heard of *me.*"

"Hmm." This time the sound was simply thoughtful.

"In any case, after my groom and I managed to raise her trunk into the box and tie her other belongings to various parts of the carriage, we proceeded to a nearby domicile. The squire's wife was a delightful woman who, shocked by my young lady's tale, quickly let it be known that *something must be done about that man*."

Dom paused for a response. "No comment?" asked Dominic. When Elf only blinked, he went on. "Later, to me, her husband was more forthcoming. The man in question has more than once *hired* a governess through the medium of the post for nonexistent progeny. The unwary governess is always younger than what is considered suitable by a careful matron and often desperate for a position. Needless to say, the governess always regrets accepting his offer, for reasons you are thinking and which therefore needn't be explained in detail. Since the man is also addicted to the bottle, the squire suggested he'd missed the appointment by being too foxed to remember it." Dominic emptied his glass, glanced at his great-aunt's, which was only half finished, and rose to add a further dollop to his own. "We were then faced of course with the problem of what to do."

"We?"

"My young lady and I."

Elf ignored the provocative phrasing. "Simple, I'd have thought. Give her the money to return from whence she came."

"Not so simple, my good aunt. I suggested exactly that but she refused. Most determinedly and quite vocally, she refused."

"Why?"

"I believe it was that occasion when she spun a tale about the younger son of the household who pestered her to the point she could not get on with her work." This time when he paused, Elf opened her mouth to speak but closed it without doing so. Blandly, he added, "I'd become somewhat suspicious by then."

"Not, then, a young lady at all." Elf spoke with satisfaction then remembered Sarah's accusations and frowned. Could Sarah have been correct for once?

"Get that out of your head, most beloved of my aunts. She is most definitely a lady."

"So what *did* you do?"

"I suggested taking her to Aunt Sarah." It was Dominic's turn to frown. "Such a buffle-headed notion and why it popped into my mind I do not know. I am not usually such a slowtop or given to air-dreams."

"No, you've always seemed the most intelligent of my relations. But the best of us can occasionally make a mistake. Am I to presume this happened near Sir Owen's home? Sarah lives with her son, I believe?"

"We were somewhat north of Nottingham. It wasn't above fifteen miles."

"So. You proceeded to your cousin's, where his mother presented you with an attack of the vapors followed by hysterics and, like a sensible man, you left."

"You forgot to mention the lengthy sermon delivered in the voice of a fishwife, which came, I believe, before she drummed her heels on the floor but after she shed tears over my misbegotten soul," said her great-nephew politely.

"So I did." Elf spoke with equal politeness and hid a smile behind her hand.

"In any case, Sarah was not the answer to our dilemma."

"What *was* the solution?"

"To tell the truth, I'd become a trifle tired of my lady's tales and her refusal to reveal her name. If I could only have discovered a name, I might have driven through the night, dumped her at her father's gate and driven off as quickly as my cattle would go." He sipped thoughtfully. "Then again, maybe not. Not once in our brief acquaintance had I found her boring." He chuckled at some memory. "Oh, Aunt, you would have delighted in the lecture she read our dearly detested relative. Aunt Sarah may have had reason for her hysterics, now I think on it. But then—ah! What an imagination my lady possesses."

"She prevaricated? Again?"

"Oh yes. At first it was diverting. I laughed through at least three versions, all of which must have been stolen from Minerva Press novels. None held water to the least degree." He waved a hand. "Veritable sieves, believe me."

"Which you pointed out to her?"

"Most politely." His mouth pursed for a moment. "The resulting row was not, er, pleasant."

"Yet you could not desert your lady."

Again that hint of a smile. "No. I try to finish what I begin. You know, my dear aunt, I wonder that I didn't think of *you*. Such a perfect solution."

"Of what, or rather *whom*, did you think?"

"My sister. She'd complained about the inadequacies of her current governess throughout the length of her last visit."

"So you set off for Deepenbrook?"

"Of course."

"Quite thirty miles, I'd think."

"Oh, at least thirty miles. It was only two or two-thirty, so it was not an impossible notion. Also, I have a very good team, Aunt-of-my-heart, which had been well rested at the squire's and more briefly at my cousin's. Yes, quite easily done before dark."

"And?"

"And *what*, dear Aunt?"

"And what changed your mind?"

"A combination of things." Dominic's brow wrinkled and a thoughtful expression formed his lips into a slightly pursed position before he explained. "First the right wheeler tossed a shoe which delayed us unconscionably. Then we managed to lose our way along a route pointed out by some jobbernowl lounging around the smithy. He swore it was certain to cut a good five miles off our journey. Then dark fell and," he sighed lugubriously, "no moon." He paused, his smile flickering briefly. "But there was a barn, you see."

"I hope I do *not* see." Elf made her voice as prim as possible but her uncowed great-nephew only laughed.

"If you are thinking I took advantage of my lady, then you had better think again." He raised his glass and watched the swirl of liquid. "You've forgotten, I believe, the existence of my groom?"

"So I did."

"You don't appear shocked, your sensibilities overset, my dearest Elfie. Nor do you seem about to go off into a swoon."

"I am certain you've settled things so that no wind of blame will touch the young woman's reputation, so I am not about to beat my chest and demand you marry the wench."

"Oh, I've settled it of course."

The softened look became so pronounced Elf felt a sudden qualm.

"Most agreeably too," he added.

"Dominic!"

"Hmm? You wish the end of my tale?"

There was another pause and again Elf watched that oddly sweet smile come into existence. Unnerved, she scowled the Thornton scowl and Dominic had the bad manners to laugh at her.

Before she could remonstrate with him, he explained. "I've already married the wench of course."

Chapter Two

Elf straightened. "Married! I've heard no word of this."

"If you had abided by your own fire, dearest-of-my-aunts, until tomorrow or, at the latest, the following day, you would have discovered the fact without the burden of a wearisome journey far from that, er, selfsame fireside." Dom settled himself more comfortably. "We just remembered to send off the notice to the papers, you see."

Elf bit her lip, wondering when and how they'd married. Then it occurred to her to wonder if he'd ever discovered the young woman's name. "I think you've left out a few bits. The last I knew, you hadn't a name for the chit."

Again that corner-tipping smile, which unsettled his great-aunt's mind. "Nor had I when I proposed." He looked up and met her eyes. "It didn't seem important, you see."

"Come now, Nephew. You would not bestow your name and title, to say nothing of the Thornton fortune, on a chance-met woman." She remembered that the heir always married for love. The Thornton Blessing—or was it a curse? "Or would you?"

"Why not? She is, I assure you, a lady. There was never any doubt of that despite what Aunt Sarah may have written you. My mother has been nagging at me for an eternity to wed and set up my nursery. I cannot count the number of tittering and blushing misses she's thrust to my attention. Well, here we had a lady in distress, a not unattractive lady, I might add. She absolutely refused to be sensible and return to the home from which, she finally admitted, it had taken much ingenuity and the devil's own luck to escape. So we came to a very pleasant and mutual decision to throw our lots together and solve our diverse problems."

He admitted this with an air of innocence that had his great-aunt muttering, "All my eye and Sally Pye." This use of rhyming thieves' cant for a lie drew a chuckle from Dom. Elf went on with something approaching sarcasm. "I am to suppose then that, with the rising sun, you set off north at a full gallop?"

"If you mean I lost all thought of the proprieties and suggested we turn our steps toward Gretna, you do me grievous insult," retorted her great-nephew with something approaching hauteur.

Elf sighed. "I did mean it. Please correct my thinking."

"We have a large and illustrious family, Elfie, former-love-of-my-life," he hinted. "Think what you'd have done."

Elf set her mind to the conundrum and, with a jerk of her head, looked directly at her great-nephew. She noted the twinkle in his eyes and chuckled. "Cousin Shute Barrington," she said firmly.

"I would not have the courage to refer to him in that informal way but, yes, our illustrious relative, the Bishop of Durham. As you know, his lordship is a fanatic for the proprieties. He produced a license as quick as a cat can wink and, later, did the honors of the marriage rite himself. And, before you ask, his daughter, Cousin Simpson chaperoned us before the wedding."

For a moment, Elf relaxed, convinced she'd hared north in search of nothing more than a mare's nest. Then another thought crossed her mind. "How long ago was this, Nevvy?"

"Now when was it?" Dom frowned. "What is today's date?"

Elf, her voice dry, told him.

"Ten June? Already? In that case, we've enjoyed three full weeks of marital bliss."

"And you have just now gotten any sort of notice to the papers? It is worse than I feared." Really angry now, Elf snapped her teeth together. "You thoughtless pup."

Dominic's brows drew together but he lifted his glass and waved it gently to and fro. "Following the wedding, one becomes rather, er, preoccupied. With other things, you understand?"

"*Following* the wedding? You fool, you bumbling idiot, you graceless, thoughtless pup." Elf repeated herself, too irate to think of something more derogatory. "There was not even an announcement of an *engagement*? You've set your wife up to face the slings and arrows of a cruel and insensitive, scandal-loving society!"

Dominic frowned more fiercely, disliking—as all do—to be told he was in the wrong. "Bedamned to society."

"Are you certain," asked his great-aunt sweetly, "the young lady has a similar attitude toward social ostracism?"

"You exaggerate." The frown turned to a scowl. "It would not go so far." His eyes met hers as he peered from under lowering brows. "Would it?" he asked rather helplessly.

"With Sarah fanning the flames before your belated announcement and your mother prostrate afterward? Vi will use every wile known to the female who loves her ailments, bewailing the fact she had no hand in your choice of bride. Between the two of them, they will raise an absolute storm."

Dom's lips firmed into an angry line as his temper flared. "There is nothing wrong with my bride."

"I assume you did, eventually, discover her name and style?"

"Of course."

"And might I too be made privy to it?"

"Of course."

Elf shook her fist in his direction. She'd have stamped her foot if she'd been on her feet but she was seated and her feet did not reach the floor. "Well?"

Instead of answering, Dominic rose and strolled toward a many-paned window where a high-backed chair faced the dusk-dimmed lawn. Elf watched in flustered embarrassment as he held out his hand and a young lady rose from its depths.

Drat the boy. What did I say or imply to the girl's detriment? How like the monster to let me go my length, unaware the chit listened.

As the couple approached, she studied the woman. Tall. Too tall for current taste, which insisted only petite and fairylike creatures qualified as beauties. But even so—or perhaps *exactly* so—a match for her still taller great-nephew? Red hair instead of the much-desired blonde, which, according to fashion, must endow the petite ideal. Quite outrageously red. *Defiantly* red. Part of it was tied up loosely on top of her head, long curls flowing down from the knot in a fire-lit flood of red.

Her gown was more simply decorated than was common amongst young women in these benighted days—an uncommon color too, a shade of pink Elf had never seen before. It was much to Elf's taste, not that she would wear such a modern mode at her age of course. The new bride held herself in a queenly way and, so far as Elf could judge, had nothing in style or manner to make her blush.

"Dear Aunt, may I present to you my chit of a wife, Lady Octavia Brightwood, formerly Lady Octavia Seldon, daughter of Mortimer Seldon, the sixth Duke of Rambourne." The young woman curtsied gracefully to just the proper degree. "You will call her Tavie, please, since she detests the name she was given at birth."

Only one name really registered. "Rambourne!"

"Just so."

"Oh my God, Dom, what have you done?"

"What have I done? Why, married the most charming and attractive young woman in all the world." He raised his wife's hand to his lips and kissed the tips of her fingers one by one—but his eyes watched his great-aunt warily.

"But *Rambourne*."

"Just so. No one," he stated with conviction, "will dare ostracize the daughter of a duke."

Silence settled over the small tableau. Dominic appeared totally unperturbed. Octavia's seeming composure was denied by the slightest of betraying trembles in the fingers Dom squeezed reassuringly. Elf, recalling past history—a story which had caused the most bizarre and longest-lasting scandal of the last decades of the eighteenth century, allowed herself the luxury of relaxing her tired spine and drooped back into her chair.

"Well, Aunt?"

"How can you suggest all is well?" she asked a trifle querulously. Her voice steadied. "Rambourne's daughter. Of all the young ladies in the kingdom, surely this one is she who most needed every care taken of her reputation. Oh dear."

The bride spoke. "I was very young when my parents divorced, Lady Elphinia."

Elf was glad to discover the lovely, deep voice was pure and well controlled.

"Surely," continued Tavie, "I cannot be considered responsible for the chaos my parents made of their lives."

"No, of course not," said Elf, forcing herself into her usual upright posture. She went on in her normal brisk tone. "I am so glad you realize that. And in any sensible society that would be accepted without question." Elf's exasperation was clear in her tone as she went on. "Or, if your father had had the sense with which he was presumably born and made you known to the *ton*, as he should have done when you came to an age to be presented, then it would not arise as a problem.

But isolating you as he did…" Elf shook her head. "Oh dear. Oh dearie me."

"I hate to mention this," said her great-nephew, in the tone of one passing on information for one's own good, "but you sound very much like Aunt Ally and it doesn't become you, my dear Elfie."

"Oh dear."

"Yes. Just that."

She looked up, her mind elsewhere. "What?"

"You are not the oh-dearing sort, my beloved aunt," he said in a kind tone.

"I'm not?" Elf realized he was teasing her. "Oh. Well, one saves certain words for when they are most needful, you know."

Tavie, reassured by her husband's calm, chuckled. "I do indeed. But the words I tend to save are not quite suitable to the drawing room. As I think Dom mentioned when telling our story."

Elf rose to her feet. "That is why I decided to reserve the most socially acceptable ejaculations for just such occasions. I never use them otherwise. Drat Sarah and her meddling," she added as she remembered the problems facing them. "Oh dear, oh dear." She looked from one to the other. "We cannot decide on the instant how to mend this situation but, given time, someone will think of something. Be assured I'll help in any way I can. I did hear the dinner gong, did I not? I find I am quite sharp-set," she said as she swept out the door and down the hall.

It is so long since I was last under this roof, she mused. *So many, many years. The memories! Oh, the parties, the long, lazy summer days…*

"Hmm, Auntie Elf."

Elf halted, turned. "Yes?"

"May I offer you my arm?"

Elf blinked. Something very nearly resembling a blush heightened the color in her thin cheeks. With all the dignity she could muster, she returned to where Dominic and Octavia waited outside the library door. Daintily, she placed her fingertips on Dominic's arm. The three of them strolled along in a companionable manner—in the direction opposite to that in which Elphinia had, in her preoccupation with the past, started out.

* * * * *

Lady Sarah Sands dropped the newspaper onto her eggs and stared, horrified, at the announcement. "Announcing the marriage of Lady Octavia," her tone grew shriller as she read, "daughter of his grace, Mortimer Seldon, sixth Duke of Rambourne, to Dominic Thornton, eighth Marquis of Brightwood on the nineteenth day of May. Officiating, his lordship, Shute Barrington, Bishop of Durham." Her voice rose to a shriek. "*Married*."

Sir Owen looked up from his book at the last word but quickly ducked his head and pretended to read. He wanted no discussion about marriage. All too often, it led to bitter recriminations as to why he himself had not yet chosen a bride and set up his nursery.

"He cannot be married."

Owen pretended he'd not heard.

"That date," she said, having reread the notice. "They have been married for at least three weeks." Sarah ground her teeth, remembering how she'd waited and waited for just such a notice. "Dominic actually married that trollop."

My cousin Dominic? Owen's ears pricked but he continued to appear absorbed in his book.

"She cannot be Rambourne's daughter. It is impossible."

She? Trollop? Of course such a person cannot be a duke's daughter. What is my mother thinking?

Sarah rose to her feet and leaned on the table, ignoring the greasy stain spreading across the page. "I don't believe it. It is a jest. A tasteless, thoughtless joke. Dominic cannot have married."

He cannot? Why not? Owen asked it aloud. "Why not?" Then he blenched. Now he was in for it. Why, oh why, had he opened his mouth?

"Your cousin Dominic? Married?" Sarah laughed, a harsh sound holding no humor. "That rake? That womanizer? So obviously a confirmed bachelor, one who would never wed? *Never*. He would not. He could not. He *must* not."

This time, Owen diplomatically nodded agreement although he didn't see why Dom wasn't free to marry whenever he wanted. Owen didn't wish to do so of course but perhaps, given the succession, Dom had come to the conclusion he must. Poor Dom.

His mother paced to the window and back to the paper. "The date. No, no. That woman! That soiled dove! She *cannot* be a duke's daughter." Sarah paced some more. "But Rambourne… *His* daughter would have the soul of her mother and, now I think of it, she had the look of that woman. But all that vulgar red hair!"

The trollop could be a duke's daughter? wondered Owen, confused. A comfortable solution occurred to him. *An illegitimate daughter of course…*

"Perhaps she was an illegitimate?" Sarah asked, echoing her son's thought, but then shook her head. "No, that won't hold water. Not if she was *that woman's* daughter. One could easily believe the worst of *her* offspring. And, yes, there was that resemblance—especially about the eyes and nose."

Lost in the pronouns, Owen asked, "Daughter? That woman?" He bit his lip. Would he never remember that silence was the best defense against his mother's tirades?

"Rambourne's divorced wife," she responded but otherwise ignored him.

Feeling reprieved from his own foolishness, Owen blinked and, determinedly, turned his eyes on his book.

Sarah returned to the paper. "I don't believe even Dom could do this to me," she said, tragedy dripping from her tone.

Owen looked up, gaping. He was so startled he once again forgot to hold his tongue. "To *you*?"

"To us then."

"I do not understand."

"No, of course you do not." Her bitter tone grated. "You have never understood what is best for you. If it were left to you, you would molder away here amongst your books and never give a care to your position. I will not allow it. Something must be done and, since *you* will do nothing, it must be me. The one who always does it all." She started for the door. "I will go to London."

Owen blinked. He really didn't understand what his mother had buzzing around in her contorted mind or why she felt she need do anything at all but, if she were to go to London, she would be out of his hair and he—and, incidentally, the servants—could relax from the excessively rigid punctiliousness she demanded of them all.

"London," she repeated firmly, her hand on the doorknob. "At once."

"Very well, Mother." Owen tucked his finger in the book to mark his place and rose to his feet. He too headed for the hall despite the fact he'd eaten only a fraction of his breakfast. "I will see to ordering the coach for you and hiring outriders."

"You will escort me."

"No," said Owen, calmly thoughtful. "I don't believe I will."

He bowed slightly, passed her by and exited the room before he became involved in an argument, knowing from past experience that his mother accepted a *fait accompli* but would fight to the last ditch to get her way if he allowed her the opportunity.

Owen hated arguments. All he wanted from life were his books, his library and the peace and quiet to get on with his studies. When his mother was in residence, as she was far too much of the year, she cut up his peace in a thousand irritating ways.

Two days later, Owen helped his mother into the coach and gave a hand to her downtrodden maid. He stood dutifully by, waiting until all was settled to his mother's satisfaction, and then ordered the driver to set off. He watched until the coach disappeared out the gates. She was gone.

Owen turned to his butler, the man having stood rigidly at attention until the moment the carriage disappeared. Their eyes met in silent communion. The two men turned together to enter the house, the one to immure himself in his study, nibbling from trays which would be brought him with suitable regularity, and the other to give orders that the household might, for the duration, relax—so long as no one stinted on their duties of course.

* * * * *

At Brightwood, the days passed in a delightful manner for two elderly ladies. Ally and Elf convinced Tavie they did not wish to be entertained, that the bridal couple was to pretend they were not there. Time enough to attack their problem when someone came up with a solution.

One day, Ally watched the newlyweds wander through the rose garden. She sighed happily. "Dear Elf. It is such a joy to see them as they are now. Young love traipsing through the flowers and bowers."

"More like living in a fool's paradise," retorted Elf. "But we'll bring them about. Somehow. Do stop staring in such a vulgar fashion, Ally. I wish to see the nursery."

On another day, as Dom and Tavie turned their steaming mounts over to a waiting groom and walked into the house, he questioned, not for the first time, the decision to leave their guests to their own devices.

"Dom, love, they are happy. It is not selfish to leave them alone." He didn't answer and Tavie shook his arm. "I assure you, it is true, my love."

"But they disappear around a corner just as I catch sight of them or into a room and shut the door just when I am about to suggest a game of whist. And in the evenings, we find them yawning over their dinners as if I did not know they *never* take to their beds before midnight. I believe they are reluctant to leave with nothing settled but refuse to intrude on the days of our idyll." He snapped his fingers as a new idea came to mind. "Perhaps they have attempted to intrude and we have been, shall we say, preoccupied?" His brows arched and his wife blushed prettily.

"Love, they are home for the first time in years." Tavie handed her hat and gloves to the waiting butler. "When Aunt Elf decides it is time for us to face reality, I am certain we will face it, will ye, nill ye!"

Dom too handed over gloves and crop and asked where his great-aunts might be found. Before Deblon could respond, the rattling sound of an approaching carriage drew them to a window. Pounding hooves churned the recently raked gravel of the drive and spurted it off in every direction as the equipage was driven at speed toward the door. Tavie's sun-touched skin paled beneath the few freckles she'd acquired. "Oh no."

"What is it, Tavie, love?"

"Reality has, I believe, descended a trifle ahead of schedule." She drew in a deep breath, straightened into queenly dignity and, from the side of her mouth, as if their guest were already within hearing, suggested, "Prepare yourself, my lover. It is my father."

"But I married you," he answered, barely moving his lips, easily falling in with her game. "How can he complain of that?"

Tavie groaned softly. "Believe me, he can and will." She dropped the act and said in normal tones, "I wrote him so he wouldn't worry, but..."

"You told him you were visiting your Miss Latimer."

"I love my governess and he knows it, but the announcement will have told him visiting her was a lie. The cat is out of the bag. I once accused him of wishing I should never marry. He very kindly explained that, once he was certain I'd not embarrass anyone by my behavior, he would choose a well-connected, well-behaved and strong-minded man to take care of me."

"So? I am well connected surely."

"Yes, and strong-minded but, really, Dom, do you think you qualify as well behaved? As meant by my father of course?"

As they spoke they watched two outriders gently extract from the carriage a sandy-haired gentleman, the slightest bit overweight and with one heavily bandaged foot. He carried his cane in one hand and resettled his hat with the other.

"Oh dear. As if things were not bad enough."

"What can you mean?" asked Dom.

"He is in the gout again," said Tavie, concern warring with the bubble of laughter she'd felt ever since first meeting Dom. She'd never been so delighted in her life as when she discovered her rescuer had the same irreverent sense of humor for which she'd been forever chastised.

A carrying chair was untied from the rear of the coach and, with much grumbling and a few words not often heard outside the stables, his grace was seated. His servants lifted him, chair and all, and started up the steps to where Deblon waited just beyond the open door, his nose in the air and, for reasons of ceremony, backed by two footmen.

"Out of my way." His grace shook his cane. "Where is he? The villain."

"He's in good form," said Tavie judiciously, but she trembled slightly.

Dom studied her face, which showed her inner conflict. "Tavie, love, you disappear. I'll welcome your father. Go now," he encouraged.

"The rake!" continued the duke. The chair was carried a few steps nearer. "Oh, the veritable monster of a man!" Rambourne's voice rose to a roar. "Where is he?" The gold-tipped cane came dangerously near to Deblon's nose.

Tavie, who had hesitated, threw her husband an apologetic look and fled, basely deserting him.

"Out of my way, I say." The chair swayed with the energetic waving of the cane. "Oh, set me down," said the duke peevishly.

"The Marquis of Brightwood is not receiving." Despite the cane that his eyes followed moving from side-to-side as the tip swung under his nose, Deblon didn't otherwise move a muscle.

"He'll receive *me,* the misbegotten ravager of innocence! What has he done with my daughter?"

"Daughter?" Enlightenment dawned. Or, more likely, Deblon, who was up to every rig, pretended it had. "Ah. Your grace. I apologize for not instantly recognizing you. It has been far too many years..." Deblon stepped to one side and, once out of reach of the cane, he bowed. "I will announce you at once."

"Never mind, Deblon. I am here." After checking to see that Tavie was out of sight, Dom moved forward to make his bow to Rambourne. "Welcome to Brightwood, your grace."

"Welcome? I am *welcome*? I don't believe you. What have you done with my daughter?" demanded the choleric gentleman once again, this time shaking the cane under Dom's nose.

"Wedded and bedded her," snapped Dominic, the temper he usually controlled so well disintegrating despite his best intentions.

"Wedded her, did you?" The cane lowered. "I don't believe it."

"The announcement appeared or you would not be here. If you did not believe it then why have you come?"

"To protect my baby from your evil designs," yelled Rambourne. "My baby. My daughter!" Rambourne's eyes started from his head. "My… Lady Ally?" he asked as she tripped up beside her tall nephew, a frown marring her usually serene face. "Is that you?"

"My goodness, Morty, what are you about? You are shouting to raise the dead. We've never had a ghost at the Hall, so perhaps I should not complain, since a ghost might be just the thing to give that last little touch of *je ne sais quoi*. Why are you sitting out here in the sun?" Her plump little hands fluttering, Ally urged his grace's servants to carry the duke forward. "Come in, do come in. Why, I don't believe you've changed a whit from when I last saw you."

"Nor you, Lady Ally." The duke turned into a jovial soul in the blink of an eye. "Nor you. Why, bless my soul. Dear me. Dear me. How delightful to see you again."

"There. That is better," soothed Alvinia as the duke was brought into the hall. "Now into the salon please. Careful. Do not bump that poor sore leg. Oh, you dear man, to have suffered so. Deblon, the very best burgundy. Instantly. And did not Cook bake up a batch of ginger drops this morning?" Deblon understood that was also an order.

"My goodness, Ally," said his grace, his eyes popping again, "all these years and you remember about the ginger drops?"

The bustling little old lady carried a footstool near and, holding a cushion intended for his back, hovered while his servants arranged the gout-ridden foot. She made shooing motions. "Now all of you. Go away. His grace needs peace and quiet after what must have been a most tortuous journey."

Dominic, taking the hint, backed out of the door and into his wife. She clutched at him, her body shaking, and, carefully, fearing she had succumbed to the vapors, he turned in her embrace and pressed her head to his shoulder.

"Shush, love. It'll be all right."

"All right?" A sudden spate of giggles overturned his belief she was crying. "All right?" she whispered. "Did you *see*? Did you *hear*? Why, he turned from a lion to a lamb in an instant. How *did* she do it?"

"My Aunt Alvinia has that effect on many gentlemen."

"But why did my *father* react that way?"

"That is easily explained," said Elf from the landing where she'd stood throughout the proceedings. "Your father, my dear, was part of her court. His calf love, which one never forgets. There was old General Amblesides, Sir Trumpington, Wilfred Massinggill the younger and Wilfred Massinggill the elder—such bristling between father and son you've never seen—and of course your father."

Tavie turned to face Elf. "But he must be twenty years younger."

"Oh no, m'dear. Merely fourteen or fifteen. General Amblesides was the eldest. He is long gone. Long gone. Wilfred the younger was the youngest by far. A mere stripling. He was a poet, which makes it understandable—or so I'm told," she said on a doubtful note. "They all doted on her. I once asked her why she didn't choose one and be done with it. She said if she could combine all their best points into one man she would but, as it was, she couldn't possibly disappoint the rest by choosing."

"That sounds like Aunt Ally," Dominic said with a laugh. "Do you believe it will serve?"

"Ally will soothe him, never fear. We'll leave them for half an hour." Elf frowned, her head tipped to the side, indicating she was thinking. "Was it your father who had a fondness for pickled apples? Does he still?"

With something resembling awe at the memory each old lady evinced for the little dietary foibles of someone they could not have met for a decade or more, Tavie nodded.

"Then I'll just have a word with Cook about luncheon. I think the two of you had best change into something more suitable. Riding garments are not unacceptable in the country of course but it might be wise to tog yourselves up in morning dress." She watched them look at each other, accept her perspicacity and, when they headed for the stairs, disappeared through the baize door to the kitchens.

"Dominic," said Tavie slowly, "my governess, who was something of a bluestocking—although she hid that from Father for as long as possible—once assigned me a slim volume by a Florentine by name of Machiavelli. Has it ever come your way?"

"Yes." He grinned. "Are you suggesting it might have influenced my aunt?"

"I wonder."

Dom chuckled and led her on up the stairs. "Don't be naïve, my dear. It is really too bad Machiavelli has been dead all these years. My aunt Elf," he said with simple pride, "could write a book which would teach even that Italian master of deviousness a thing or two."

Chapter Three

Ally fluttered and hovered until His Grace of Rambourne held a glass of jewel-colored wine and a small table was placed "just so" for the ginger drops. Then she brought close another stool for herself and settled her skirts around her. "It has been such a long time, Mortimer. I quite thought you had forgotten your oldest flirt."

"Not old, my dear lady. No, no. Never old. Why, you and your sister are quite my youngest friends," he responded gallantly. "What a surprise, finding you here." At the thought, he frowned. "Now I remember. That devil is your nephew, is he not?"

"Great-nephew," corrected Ally. "Our dearest relative. So kind and always so attentive to our comfort. Never does he drive north or south but what he stops in Cheltenham to see us. He brings delicacies from London or, if coming from Brightwood, fresh fruit or game to add to our rather mundane meals and always he tells us the gossip and knows just what we like."

The duke snorted. "Rake and wastrel. That's more like than the picture *you* draw!"

"No, no." Ally's fluttery personality was submerged by her need to make her old friend understand. "Merely your average Thornton heir, my dear Morty. Surely you know our history? Each generation thinks the next is going to the devil and each generation eventually settles down with the one and only love of their life to live happily ever after. Why, dear Dominic proposed to your daughter before he knew her name! A proposal from a Thornton heir happens that way. Always.

Suddenly they are certain and nothing will stop them from achieving their ends."

"He kidnapped her. He stole her away from me." A confused look spread across the duke's plump cheeks. "What I cannot understand is how he could have done so. You do not know how carefully I have guarded her."

Oh, don't I just, thought Alvinia with a touch of exasperation unusual to her softhearted nature. As was her habit with such thoughts, she pushed it from her mind. "I believe that is not quite the way of it," she soothed, picking up the plate of biscuits and offering it to her old beau on the rather obscure theory that, if his mouth was otherwise occupied, he couldn't very well say any other silly thing. "In fact, dear Tavie had run away from you before they met. Dear Dom rescued her from what might have been a most distressing situation if the villain had not, for one reason or another, delayed picking her up."

"Villain? Villain? No. No. Your nevvy is the only villain I know."

This time, Ally refilled his glass before offering more biscuits. "Now, dear, you are not listening. You are to let me speak and you are not to interrupt. Do you hear?" she asked, shaking a finger at him with delightful sternness.

The duke, already very nearly as smitten as he'd been decades earlier, promised, reluctantly, to listen and not to interrupt. Thereupon she told a simplified version of all Elf had told her.

"So you see, Morty, far from being the villain of the piece, dear Dominic saved her from ruin."

"Saved her *for* ruin." A morose expression settled his grace's features into the picture of patient acceptance. "She will ruin herself and him as well and if it is true they are wed, it is too late to save him."

Ally fluttered her hands, much distressed. "*She is not her mother.*" The duke tried to speak but Ally, this time shaking her finger in earnest, rushed on. "You have done your best to see that she *is* like her mother but, praise be, you failed."

"Her overabundant spirit! Her temper! Her unwillingness to be led by older and wiser heads! Oh, how can you say she is not like her mother?"

"Because she has far more intelligence and far more heart than that poor dear lady ever had. She and Dominic will be very happy and contented and will produce a quiver-full of little Thorntons and all will be well." Ally sighed. "That is, all will be if we can smooth over Sarah's nasty gossip and the fact Dom's mother will not be happy about the situation."

"See? I said it would be a disaster."

"No, no. Or, if so, then only because your treatment of your daughter has complicated things beyond belief." The duke huffed but Ally didn't let him interrupt. "Elf has a plan, you see." Ally's smooth forehead furrowed at the thought of Elf's "plan" which, boiled down to barest bones, was nothing more than to get Tavie known to the *ton* as quickly as they could.

"Elf is here too?" asked Mortimer, his mind once more diverted.

Ally stared at him. The notion she and her sister might, for one reason or another, be separated was beyond her comprehension.

"Yes, yes, to be sure." He nodded. "Of course she is here. Didn't think. Well, well, if the scamp had the sense to call in you two to set things right then perhaps he has more in his cockloft than I'd thought."

Ally, very sensibly, didn't contradict his conclusion.

The duke sipped his wine. "Very good burgundy, this," he said inconsequentially, holding it up to the light to study its color.

Ally prematurely breathed a sigh of relief. "Yes. The Thorntons have all been blessed with an excellent palate. One will never find a bad wine in their cellars. But we'll need your help. Dear, dear Mortimer," she touched his knee gently, "you must promise to help or all will be lost."

"Lost? All lost? But of course it is lost," he said, once again falling into his former dismal attitude. His eyes flickered to Ally's expression of mild disgust. "Isn't it?"

"No, of course it isn't. It merely requires a *soupçon* of resolution. Just the tiniest bit of backbone. All will be well, I promise."

Ally said a silent prayer, asking to be excused for promising a result she could not really guarantee. After all, she had doubts of her own. The truth was not always enough. And allowing the *ton* to find out for themselves how delightful Tavie was appeared to be the sum total of Elf's plan, which seemed far too simple to solve such a complicated social dilemma.

"Well, if Elf has a hand in it, I must be wrong. I will do as she suggests of course."

"Good."

Ally and Mortimer turned at the explosive intrusion of sound to see Elf framed in the door. Behind her, waiting to enter, were Dominic and Tavie.

"The first thing you must do is congratulate Dominic on his lovely wife and give the bride best wishes. And you will do it gracefully and sincerely, Mortimer Seldon. That is the first step," ordered Elf tartly.

Cowed, His Grace of Rambourne did as suggested.

* * * * *

Lady Sarah Sands looked at the friends sitting around her table in the salon of her son's tidy, little London house. "I tell you it is true, my dears." Sarah nodded her head so vigorously she very nearly spilt her tea. "The chit is a brass-faced hussy. *Just* like her mother. Would you believe she had the nerve to tell me to my face I was an unchristian woman who would do better to mind my tongue? I was never so insulted in my life. Red hair as well," she added with a grating titter. "You know what *that* means."

Three of Sarah's oldest acquaintances listened, two of them avidly. Miss Ralston and Miss Toller, like identical puppets, lapped up each word along with rather stale bread and weak tea and tut-tutted with the expected sympathy. The third, Lady Matilda Clavingstone, a roman-nosed dowager, swallowed the whole with rather more skepticism, all the while hoping their miserly hostess would be more generous than usual with the cake, set just out of reach in the middle of the table.

With narrowed eyes, the dowager asked, "You say he told you he found her abandoned along the road? That she'd accepted a post as governess but had not been met?"

"That is the tale with which he tried to fob me off but one look at her and one could see that whatever she was, she was not a governess. She was far too richly dressed." Sarah stifled lingering jealousy for that fur-lined cloak. "How he could have thought me so stupid as to believe such a Banbury tale I cannot say."

"But you have since discovered she is Rambourne's daughter," stated Lady Clavingstone. "The girl Mortimer Seldon has refused to present," she added in explanation to the other ladies who turned their heads from one speaker to the other like a well-trained chorus. "Of course her costume would be rich," her ladyship reminded Sarah.

"Oh, indeed. If she *is* Rambourne's daughter."

"You would suggest Lord Brightwood was tricked?" Matilda mulled over the idea and shook her head. "I don't believe it. Not into marriage."

"My dear Matilda, what else can it be? Surely you do not believe a duke's daughter would be found in such a compromising position."

"You are, in your skitter-witted fashion, becoming quite jumbled." When Sarah's lips thinned, Matilda hurried to elaborate. "If she was his mistress, then he knew she was no Seldon and would not have married her. Also, whatever else one may say about Brightwood, he is a gentleman. He would not attempt to settle his bit o' muslin on the family."

Sarah could see her plan falling into ruin and wished she'd not invited Matilda to today's effort to blacken her nephew's reputation and spoil his marriage. She rushed into speech. "But think of her mother. Perhaps the chit led him on and when he discovered who she was, he could not think what to do and hoped to put a good face on it with that ridiculous tale of abandonment."

Again Matilda turned the notion over in her mind. Ponderously, she admitted, "I must agree there is something smoky about the whole, Sarah. And don't turn your nose up at a bit of cant."

"I tell you, this Octavia Seldon—"

"Thornton," interrupted the hawk-faced Matilda.

"Must be just as wicked as her mother."

"I don't see that," contradicted Matilda.

Sarah, wishing more and more she had not invited Matilda, sighed. Unfortunately Matilda was her only friend to move easily in the first circles. She'd expected Matilda to spread the tale where it would help the most. Usually Sarah clung to that friendship with every means she could find but, for once, she was becoming quite irritated with Matilda. "What do you not see?"

"I've never understood why a child should bear the weight of her parents' indiscretions."

"Then explain why her father has seen fit to hide her away and let no one see her," ordered Sarah, a sly note of triumph in her voice. "There must be something wrong with her."

The puppets nodded vigorous agreement.

"More likely," sniffed Matilda, unconvinced, "a caprice of old Rambourne's. You know what he is like." She looked around the table and added, "Or perhaps you don't." She'd remembered that Sarah, despite her title, only managed to live around the fringes of the *ton*. "He's a bumbling old fool of the first order."

Sarah tittered. "Really, Matilda. Rambourne is a duke. You are not to say such things."

"Why not?"

Sarah blinked. *Why not*? Good heavens, was her old friend so foolish? "Because," she explained, "he is a du—"

Matilda interrupted to mimic. "Because he's a duke? It makes no difference what a man's rank is. The rank doesn't make him other than he is. And Rambourne is a fool. I suspect, now I think on it, that he *feared* she'd take after her mother and proceeded to keep her so close and under such a watch it drove the poor girl mad."

"*There*. You do agree something is wrong with her."

The wide-eyed listeners practically drooled into their cups. *Mad, was she?*

Deciding her parsimonious hostess was deliberately ignoring the cake, Matilda rose to her feet. "You are the fool, Sarah, if you continue to spread such silly rumors. I will write to Elf and tell her what you are up to."

"Don't you dare. Oh, how could you say such a thing? I am not a fool. I am only telling what Dominic tried to do and describing that hussy for what she is, which is *far* less than she ought to be."

"No, you describe her as you hope she is."

"You were not there." Sarah wrung her hands. *Oh, why did I invite Matilda?* "You don't know what it was like. I tell you I was insulted under my own roof. And then he *married* her. Oh, it was spite. Just spite. He'd do anything to keep my poor Owen out of the succession. I wonder if that poor girl knows what he has in mind." Sarah tittered as a new thought took root. "He'll have her *enceinte* before the summer is out. And he'll see she stays with child, over and over, for years."

"Sarah, you have become confused again. Just who is the villain in the piece? Your nephew who will turn the poor, dear innocent into a brood mare or the light-skirt who trapped your nephew into marriage?" Matilda waited for her friend to stop gobbling at such forthright words. "I must go. Do not," Matilda glared at the other two guests, "spread this sort of tale all over town."

"Oh, do go away. You have no sympathy. No sensitivity. You do not understand."

"I understand you mean to make life as difficult as you can for the pair. It is not nice of you, Sarah. I wonder why I put up with you."

"Ooohhhh..."

Sarah, prone to falling into hysterics for nothing at all, proceeded to do so again with somewhat more reason than usual. After all, Matilda was her best ticket to *tonnish* affairs and she had no wish to lose it.

Matilda pursed her lips, stalked to the bellpull and yanked once. The housemaid who responded was told to find Sarah's woman. As soon as the abigail arrived, Matilda, not waiting to see how Sarah went on, departed.

Sarah recovered as soon as her newest enemy was gone and, basking in the sympathy of her other friends, actually brought herself to cut and serve the cake.

It was not, thought the more perspicacious of the guests, *really worth the wait*. Nor did she believe all Sarah had said about the new marchioness. On the other hand, her bread and butter—in the form of invitations to dinner—was based on the gossip she could relate, so she would not let truth stand in the way of this new tale.

Later, the guests waited to follow the housemaid out. "I know," said Sarah with well-feigned innocence, "that I may depend on you not to tell a single soul what you've learned today. It was merely that I had to tell someone of my terrible experience."

"Of course we won't," promised the one mendaciously. The other nodded her agreement—having qualms about committing herself, out loud, to such a lie.

Sarah smiled gently. Perhaps Matilda would not cooperate but these two were panting to get on to their next call in order to relieve their stuffed budgets of the newest scandal.

* * * * *

Dominic's London butler threw open the double doors to the largest salon of the Brightwood townhouse and announced Lady Clavingstone. Matilda entered and peered around. "Where are you? I cannot see a thing. Heavens, Violetta, what is the meaning of this?"

Matilda groped her way through the darkened room to the windows, banging her ankle on a low stool on the way. Reaching the heavy velvet drapes, she flung them back, raising clouds of dust in the process. Matilda sneezed. Dominic's mother, it seemed, did not oversee Dominic's London servants as she should.

"Ohh," moaned the dowager. "As you love me, Matilda, do close those drapes. My head. My poor, poor head."

"Violetta, my dear, you are not ill." Matilda sighed, thinking it was too bad of her acquaintance to be forever falling into Cheltenham tragedies.

"My boy. My poor, poor boy. My poor deluded son."

"Your son has made an advantageous marriage and you moan about it?" Matilda put all the scorn into her voice that she could. "You should be crowing with glee. The Rambourne fortune will go to Octavia. Not the entailed property of course, which must fall to the heir, a distant cousin, but you know Rambourne will cut up a very warm man and you can bet an abbey his personal fortune will go to his daughter."

"Fortune," said Violetta, her voice dripping disdain. She sat up, trailing scarves and shawls around her. "How can you speak of fortune? *That woman's* daughter has trapped my son."

"Octavia's mother willfully ruined herself. Once Georgianna had done so, so thoroughly she could no longer deceive herself, she went on to enjoy her life amongst the *demimondaine* excessively—or so I've heard. She is dead now and what that old history has to do with Octavia, I don't know or wish to know."

"I never liked her."

"You have met Octavia?" Matilda stared down her nose, noted her hostess's confusion at the question and understood. "Oh. You mean her mother. You were jealous of course. She was prettier than you and she was delightfully charming. If she'd had a modicum of sense to match, she'd have been a paragon. Since you seem to have very little sense yourself, you do not value that as you should." Matilda frowned, another memory rising from the well-stocked larder of her mind. "I also seem to recall you lost Rambourne to her. Which, if you were not such a widgeon, you would admit was no loss. You did not love him."

"Matilda, you should not speak to me like that in my own drawing room." Violetta spoke in failing tones, lying back as she did so, her hand pressed to her chest. "Oh, my palpitations."

"Fiddle."

"You don't know what it is to have an undutiful son. You don't know how worrying, how debilitating, to watch your dear departed husband's heir run on his way to ruin. You do not suffer from a poor head and a weak heart and—"

"And a surfeit of humbuggery," interrupted Matilda. "You know there is never a thing wrong with you when you *wish* to do something. You only ail when you prefer not to exert yourself. *And exert yourself you must.* Sarah is doing her best to raise a scandal that is pale and uninteresting in the normal way but which, given that poor girl's mother, may lead to misery, which is something neither your son nor your new daughter-in-law deserves."

Violetta sat up again. "She deserves anything. How dare she marry my son out of hand with never a word to me?" She went on in dramatic tones. "To learn of one's only son's marriage through the medium of the society columns in the newspapers! Do you continue to insist I have no reason for my pain and unhappiness?"

Matilda snorted. "Didn't write you, is that it? Oh, that scamp of an idiotic boy!"

Violetta turned her head away. "You would not think it humorous if it were your son."

"No, I don't suppose I would. But knowing Dominic, I suspect it didn't cross his mind. He likely only thought of notifying the papers when the notice column was, for some totally unrelated reason, brought to his attention." Matilda rose to her feet. "You will do what you can to scotch Sarah's mischief, will you not?"

"I do not see why I should do any such thing."

"Pout all you will, Violetta, but remember that any harm Sarah does to his wife will reflect on Dominic and on yourself as well."

"Sarah does not lie." Violetta refused to meet Matilda's eyes. Instead, she mangled the corner of one of her shawls between nervous fingers into a mass of horrid wrinkles.

"No, but she twists the truth to serve her purpose."

"Oh, go away." Again Violetta reclined, the back of her hand pressed to her forehead. "I am much too unwell to deal with Sarah. You are Dominic's godmother. *You* do something."

"I mean to. I'll write Elf of course." Matilda thought a moment. "Perhaps Sir Owen will lay aside his books and come to town. I'll write *him*. Someone must stop that woman from spreading her poison."

Violetta sat up so quickly she nearly fell from the settee. "*Not Sir Owen*!" Matilda nodded and Violetta groaned. "Oh no. He will come here. I have never liked that boy. Such a bore. So sadly lacking in dash—"

Lady Clavingstone forbore to point out it was exactly that quality in her own son that Violetta so often deprecated.

"I have never understood why Sarah dotes on him so. He will cut up my peace in some way. He always disturbs me with his prosy ways and his lectures and going on and on about how I must do this and must do that."

"You mean the boy knows right from wrong and he forces you to do something you do not wish to do. Something you know very well you *should* do."

"Oh, go away. I am ill. So ill and no one cares. Oh, Miles? Why did you die and leave me alone like this? Ohh."

Again Matilda pulled a bell rope in someone else's house and again she asked that her hostess's maid be sent in. When that rather awesome woman arrived, Matilda ordered a measure of hartshorn be prepared. For her beneficent efforts, she received a glare from Violetta.

The latter preferred to manage her own ailments.

Matilda suppressed a desire to chuckle until she was shown from the house. But humor faded quickly as the situation returned to mind. Something must be done and done quickly or Dominic and his bride would face a scandal that would require years to overcome. Her ladyship wondered if, after writing Elf, she should pack and join the young couple at the Lakes.

No. It would not answer. Someone must be in London to squash the rumors Sarah managed to insert into the *ton*. And since Violetta had decided to let things run their course to revenge herself for Dominic's neglect, it seemed Matilda must do it.

Matilda liked her godson. What was more, she trusted him. If he married Octavia Seldon, then the girl—young woman, really, given what her age must be—would be worthy of his notice. *And* worth any effort.

Drat Sarah Sands! She would not stop at talking. She would write people who had left London now the season was winding down. So it looked as if she too would be forced to write a few letters.

Matilda sighed. She much preferred almost anything to taking up her pen. But she, at least, did not shrink from doing her duty. She plotted. A lightly humorous account of Sarah's obvious jealousy and Violetta's pretended megrims, inserted—carelessly of course—in the midst of whatever trivia came to mind. That would do.

Once home, Matilda began her chore. The first letter was to Elf. It merely verified that Sarah was behaving as badly as expected. The second, also brief but to the point, was to Sarah's son. Matilda urged him to come to London and take Sarah in hand. Those two letters completed, she ordered her butler to see the epistles taken directly to the General Post Office on Lombard Street and, with a sigh of resignation, returned to her desk to begin the first of the many newsy letters she must send to old friends.

* * * * *

Silence descended around the Brightwood salon. From long windows, one could see the sun on lawns that stretched down toward the lake. Dominic cuddled Tavie closer and Ally smiled to see it. The duke, however, frowned at the unsuitable public show of affection, but he'd just been roundly scolded by Elf and didn't quite feel able to hand out a lecture of his own, lest she think that too outside of enough and lecture him all over again.

Elf had not minced words and Mortimer wished for time to himself so he could think up a whole handful of good arguments in his own defense. Elf had not allowed him to say a word. Worse, she read her lecture with his daughter sitting there listening. It was too bad of Elf and so he would tell her—once he'd had time to assimilate all she'd said and find the holes in what seemed, on the surface, a very logical argument. Surely he had not been so very much at fault. He'd wanted to protect his beloved daughter. How *could* he have been wrong when all was done out of love for the girl? His grace shook his head.

"Well, Aunt, you've read each of us a splendid lecture," said Dom.

Mortimer brightened very slightly when he recalled he had not been alone in suffering Elphinia's scorn. His daughter and new son-in-law had also come in for more than a few blunt words.

"So," continued Dom, "having that off your chest, do you think you might explain what to do about this desperate situation you foresee?"

"You think I am painting too dark a picture, do you not, Nephew? But you do not understand the depths to which Sarah will sink in her desire to forward Owen's claim."

"Owen, as he knows, has no claim."

"When there are no males in direct line, a male to inherit must be found through a cadet line. That is Owen."

"He'd be the first to denigrate the notion he was ever likely to inherit. Or to wish it."

"Of course he would. He is perfectly happy barricaded in his library and doing whatever it is scholars do. That won't stop Sarah from becoming a complete nuisance. You may believe the letter she sent to Ally and myself was only the first of many she wrote."

"Oh, letters."

"Yes, *letters.* Describing your new wife as a hoyden and forward and pert and very likely worse." Elf ran Sarah's letter through her mind. "*Much* worse. She will remind each correspondent of Tavie's mother's outrageous behavior and then point out that the girl's father would not have kept her close if nothing were wrong with the chit, implying, I don't doubt, that a strain of madness ran through her mother's family. By the time you take Tavie to London this autumn for the little season, you'll not be received."

Mortimer groaned. "Do you really believe that is how she will see my keeping my precious girl safe?"

"How else?" asked Elphinia, overly blunt in her irritation.

Tavie's hand shook where it lay in Dom's grip and he pulled her nearer. "We won't go to town," he said and, reprehensibly, nuzzled at his wife's ear before whispering, "We'll stay here where we are happy."

Tavie, her whole body trembling, spoke softly but firmly. "No, Dom. I know from reading the court news and society columns how much you enjoy the season. You have always gone to London and you must not forego your pleasures because I intruded into your life. I will stay here. No one will ostracize *you* if *I* am not there."

The duke nodded, thinking it a very good plan.

Ally shook her head so vigorously four pins, a comb and three locks of hair fell down her back. *She* thought it a terrible notion.

Elf, speaking for both of the sisters, said, "Very generous and totally absurd. You, Tavie, will enjoy the London scene as much as Dom—balls, soirees and routs. The opera and the theater. All those things you have yet to experience. We must simply see that you are *not* ostracized. People must discover for themselves that you are a delightful young woman and that you and Dom have made a love match. As a first step, and the last if we are lucky, we will hold a house party here at Brightwood. It will end with a ball. Summer is upon us and the

Lake District is flooded with visitors. We will discover who is already visiting the area and send invitations to others to come to stay at Brightwood. Your particular friends, Dominic, and yours, Mortimer, and do not tell me you have none because I know you do. *That* is the first step."

Tavie blenched. "I am to play hostess to a houseful of strangers?"

Elf nodded. "You will do it very well."

"Oh yes, my dear," said Ally, reaching to pat the young woman's hand. "You have made us so very comfortable, I know you will do so for everyone. And," she added knowingly, "I know the very person to tell us who visits the district." Ally turned to Elf. "Miss Porson, Elphinia dear. She still lives in Grasmere, I believe? *Just* the one to know everyone's business, do you not agree? We must invite her to tea."

"Why, Ally, such genius," enthused Elf. "You have provided the solution to a teensy problem which has been plaguing me. I could not think how to make up our guest list when we didn't know who already visited the region. Yes. I will write a note immediately and a groom will ride to Grasmere and await the answer. I will tell her we'll provide a carriage for her." Elf paused to shake her head. "Miss Porson. Why did I not think of her? I do not know how someone so nosy, with so few family connections and still less money, has become so totally acceptable everywhere."

"We are at your disposal, Aunt," said Dom lazily. He looked around. All were busy with their own thoughts. "Are our deliberations ended?" There was still no response so he rose to his feet, pulling Tavie up with him. "Since we have finished, we will be off now and join you later."

"Where are you going?" asked the duke.

Ally shook her head, tut-tutting. "Dear Morty," she said in a hushed voice, "you don't ask newlyweds such a question!"

Dom laughed. "In this case, dear Aunt, the answer is unexceptionable. I am teaching Tavie to drive and the carriage must have been waiting ten minutes if not more. I will inform Deblon you'll need a groom, Auntie Elf, so that your invitation may go off at once. We'll see you later."

His arm around her shoulders, he walked his bride into the hall and, after orders to Deblon, out into the watery sunshine. He cast a knowledgeable eye to the scattered but gathering clouds and predicted rain before teatime. The carriage was, also as predicted, awaiting them and he helped Tavie onto the driver's seat, but she immediately slid to the far side.

Dom cocked a brow at her and she blushed. "What is it, Tavie?"

"Remember when I said Elf would let us know when the honeymoon was over?" He nodded. She looked at him with sad eyes. "I think, Dom, we've been told."

He compressed his lips into a stern line and jumped into the driver's seat. "Let her go, Joe," he told the groom and wished he'd a pair of high-steppers before him instead of the elderly mare with which he'd been teaching Tavie. "I do not see why we need to change anything. Not yet anyway. Not until the guests arrive, I mean."

"Dom, I'll have piles of work if we are to have a house party. There won't be time for…for…"

"Tavie, love, are you crying?" He pulled to the side of the drive and looped the reins. "Not my Tavie!"

"No." She wiped her eye with a glove-covered finger. "Dom, I wish I'd known what an Ishmael I am. I'd never have married you and subjected you to all this scandal. I don't want *you* suffering because *I* am an outcast. It isn't right. I very selfishly let you go ahead and make the arrangements for our marriage and didn't *think*."

"Tavie, you widgeon, if you *had* thought, would you have guessed there would be such a fracas?"

Tavie raised her eyes to his, hers glittering with unshed tears. She blinked and he smiled. Slowly, she straightened. "No." She frowned. "How could I? I am indeed a widgeon!"

"Yes, you are," he said, teasing her, and added, "You could not have known. You did just as I did." She looked a question and he smiled gently. "We fell miles into love and didn't care about a thing but ourselves. Now we have to pull our chestnuts out of the fire and, with everyone's help, we will. Believe me?"

"I have to. I won't believe the love I feel for you could harm you."

"Good girl. Now what did you say about the honeymoon being over?"

She straightened fully. "Oh, that much is true, Dom. I see you've no notion at all of what must be done. Why, just to begin with, think of all the rooms to be prepared."

"How long does it take to order Mrs. MacReady to prepare them?" he asked in a dry tone of voice.

"Dom! Oh, Dom," she laughed a rueful little chuckle, "if it were only that simple. Oh dear, I do not wish to give up our idyll."

"Nor I."

"But we must."

"Only temporarily then," he warned. "I won't allow you to escape me for long, Tavie, so see to it you get those rooms prepared as quickly as you can."

Tavie's delightful laughter broke free. "You ignorant man."

"There's more?"

"Yes."

Dom sighed. "Don't tell me. I fear I'll discover it soon enough. Now since you believe you'll be too busy to find time from now on, do you not think you should take the reins for today at least?"

Tavie nodded, her sunny nature coming to her rescue. Scandal, after all, had not yet run away with them. She would enjoy every instant still remaining of their golden honeymoon days.

Chapter Four

ꟹ

Miss Porson lifted her teacup, her bright, birdlike gaze darting around the salon. She had nearly fallen all over herself when the invitation to Brightwood arrived. So timely too, what, with all the whispers circulating about the marquis' secret marriage and the fact no one knew a thing about his bride, except of course all those delightful but not really believable things that troublemaker, Lady Sarah Sands, had spread.

But where, wondered Miss Porson, *is the bride*?

Lady Alvinia was conning the list the three old ladies had drawn up and Lady Elphinia was asking if their guest wished more tea.

Miss Porson gave a guilty start. "Yes please." She extended her cup and saucer.

It would be too bad if she had made this journey and spent well over an hour at Brightwood and was forced to leave without even a glimpse of the young couple. The door opened and Miss Porson straightened, her sharp eyes curious and her nose very nearly twitching with interest. But it was only an older gentleman who limped toward them across the Axminster carpet.

"Dear Morty," said Ally, laying aside the list and rising to her feet to go to him. "Oh dear. Your poor foot is still troubling you, is it not? Miss Porson, have you met his grace, the Duke of Rambourne? He has come to help celebrate his daughter's nuptials."

Mortimer bowed over Miss Porson's hand. He wished he'd remembered the old biddy was expected so he might have avoided her company. Little old ladies had made his life more than merely miserable back in the days of his own scandal. "Good day, Miss Porson. Pleased, I'm sure. Delightful weather, is it not?"

"Duke of Rambourne? The new marchioness's father? How delightful to meet you." The narrow nose twitched harder and Miss Porson, drawing in a deep breath for courage, voiced the question that had been plaguing her since her arrival. "And just where *are* the happy couple?"

"Newlyweds, you know," said Ally with something near a sly chuckle. "Dear me, Miss Porson, one should not ask where newlyweds are to be found."

Miss Porson turned red, mortified by Ally's suggestion. The blush deepened when the door opened and, *finally*, Dom and Tavie entered the salon arm in arm, laughter on their lips.

"Oh, there you are, my loving aunts. And your grace," Dom bowed slightly toward his wife's father. "And who is this delightful-looking little lady? Why, Miss Porson! I did not recognize you. How do you manage to become younger each time I meet you?" He drew his wife toward their guest.

"None of your honey, Dom," said Ally in a teasing tone. "Why, you might make dear Tavie jealous, might you not? My dear," she said to Tavie, "do come meet an old friend of Elf's and my youth. Miss Porson..."

Miss Porson had risen to greet the duke and bobbed up again to meet his daughter. She was astounded by the bride's height. "Such a tall young lady," she murmured.

"So right for my very tall nephew," returned Ally with evident pride.

The talk became general and, although Miss Porson waited almost breathlessly for evidence of any of the traits Lady Sands had mentioned, she discovered only a very well-brought-up young woman who also appeared to be a very happy young woman. In fact, the way she looked at her new husband was the most shocking thing about her! It was not *comme il faut* to actually love one's husband. Worse, if she were any judge of the matter, the marquis was equally besotted with his marchioness. Brightwood had much better control of his features of course but he couldn't hide his feelings from Miss Porson, who could read the faintest clue.

A love match, concluded Miss Porson. *Will not Lady Sarah Sands be upset by the news?*

Once they'd waved goodbye to Miss Porson, Elf said, "That went very well, I think."

"Oh yes," agreed Ally, nodding her head several times. "She cannot wait to get home and write Sarah, telling her how wrong she is about our dear Tavie."

"Do you think she will?"

"Yes. Poor Sarah will be so upset. Because she will remember and know that Miss Porson will visit everyone with whom she has the least acquaintance and will tell them about taking tea with the new marchioness and what a delight she is. So we must hurry, Elf dear, and get out invitations. A soirée as soon as possible perhaps? And of course the house party and ball."

"A soirée? Why?"

"Because, Elf, knowing Dominic as we do," said Ally, "do you believe he will remain so perfectly behaved for much longer? He will do *something* to put up the backs of his neighbors and that will reflect badly on his wife. So I think it best to organize everything as quickly as possible."

"Hmm. I suppose it is possible," answered Elf, "that Dom will get on his high horse about something. He has gotten himself married, however, and if he runs true to form, he will be a pattern card of propriety from now on."

Dom, who had been listening to them, growled softly.

"Dare we chance it?" asked Ally a trifle hesitantly.

His expression grew grimmer.

Elf laughed. "No, I do not think we will. We begin work on the invitations immediately."

Dom bowed punctiliously, first to one great-aunt and then to the other. Then he deliberately turned his back on them. "I see you and I are not wanted, your grace," he said to his father-in-law. His ears were tinged from embarrassment because only a few weeks earlier his great-aunts' fears more than likely *would* have been realized. "Your grace?"

"Eh? Eh?" With Miss Porson's absence, Mortimer had settled himself before the small fire and ignored all around him. "Not wanted you say?"

"The ladies are to plan a ball and will do better without our presence," Dom explained.

"That is quite true," said Ally in a kind voice. "I think the two of you might be better occupied elsewhere."

The duke, as obtuse as usual, settled more deeply into his chair. "Quite comfortable right here, my dear."

"Why do not you and I adjourn to the library?" hinted Dom, repressing a chuckle at Tavie's despairing glance. "We can have a little chat before dinner," suggested Dominic. "Actually I would like the opportunity to talk to you."

Tavie's father, a trifle put-out at having to move himself but unable to ignore such a direct suggestion, struggled to his feet, Ally cooing and coddling and helping as much as she could.

His grace's mind began functioning in the process. Once Dom's great-aunt handed him his cane, he straightened himself to his full height, such as it was. He nodded his head, a judicious nod, accompanying a thoughtful look in his eye. "Yes, yes. A little talk," he said. "Settlements and all that. I understand you. Don't know why I didn't think of it before now. Not that anything can be settled until we have the solicitors in of course but we should get some idea where we stand."

Tavie, alarmed, rose to her feet.

"Not you, Tavie," said her father testily. "Nothing to do with you."

Tavie met her husband's eyes, found them twinkling and decided to agree rather than set off a scene by asking whom it *did* concern if *not* herself. Besides, another argument was to be avoided when they were about to begin the work she'd foreseen.

At least, she thought, brightening slightly, *no one can ruin our nights.*

Over the next few days, Elf and Ally were agreeably surprised to discover that Tavie, although totally without experience, knew exactly what was expected of her.

Both were impressed. Ally said so.

"I had the dearest governess," Tavie confided. "If I am lucky and have daughters, I hope Miss Latimer will be available to teach them. The difference will be that, unlike my father, I *know* she is a terribly bluestocking and it won't bother me a bit."

"I should think not if she does half so well by them as she did by you, my dear," responded Ally with a fond smile.

* * * * *

Dom stepped into their room from his dressing room and moved silently to where Tavie sat at the dressing table. Her head was bent, revealing a graceful length of neck, and her tongue pressed to her upper lip as she concentrated on buttoning one tiny button after another at her right wrist.

"The very devil to do it left-handed, is it not?"

"Dom!" She looked into her mirror and smiled.

"If you would ask one of the maids for help, you'd have less trouble," he mused. His hands moved from her shoulders to the buttons at the back of her dress, buttons Tavie had managed, with great difficulty, to do up.

"I told you I found it rather fun doing for myself. Up until I ran away, I never gave a thought about how one managed one's hair or how one kept one's clothes in decent order. I didn't know how much work my poor maid did for me."

"At least I have convinced you someone should care for your clothes." He slipped the top button out of its loop and moved down to toy with the next.

Tavie did up the last button at her wrist and looked at his reflection. "What you *said* was that you'd not put up with me taking so much time away from you. I thought it remarkably selfish of you."

"Did you?" He slipped the second button.

"I did. Why, how could you know I *wished* to spend all that time with you?" she teased.

"Oh, I don't know. Somewhere I got the idea that you didn't mind *too* much." The third button went and Tavie's dress slipped down one shoulder, calling her attention to what he was doing.

"I begin to understand," she said in a dry voice, "what you mean when you say that I'd not have so much trouble dressing if I had a maid."

"Hmmm?" He bent to do completely un-innocent things to her shoulder with his mouth. "Should I stop?"

"You know you should."

"But should I *stop*?" he asked again, the stress a bit different.

Tavie giggled. "I think Cook has begun setting dinner back all on his own. For three nights running, we've been late getting down for it."

"I've a notion we will be late again." The fourth and fifth buttons went easily and then, tempted by the expanse of skin he had exposed, Dom's hands went to her shoulders. He let them drift down to where her breasts were half exposed by her chemise. "Oh yes," he murmured. His voice slurred. "Definitely..."

Some time later, he helped her back into her gown, did up the buttons at the back and then suggested he go down so it wouldn't look as though they had been doing...whatever it was they *had* been doing.

Tavie blushed but, picking up a brush, nodded agreement.

Instead of going directly down to the salon, however, Dom tracked through the halls until he arrived at Elf's room. Despite his preoccupation with his wife, he had not been unobservant the afternoon Miss Porson visited. He was still shocked by the avid way that little lady had stared at Tavie. Since Elf had also begun being "late" for dinner, aware that if she went down at the usual time she must pretend ignorance until the young couple appeared, he expected to find her in her room. He was not disappointed.

It was she who was surprised to find him standing there. "Dom?"

"Dearest of my aunts, may I have a word with you?"

Elf stood back in invitation. Dom strode in and crossed to the windows. Elf finally asked, "What is it, Dom?"

"I've been thinking about all you've said, Aunt. At first I thought you must be exaggerating that Tavie could be involved in a serious scandal. Then Miss Porson..." He swung around. "Aunt, I apologize for disbelieving you." He turned back to the window. "That's only part of it though."

"It is?" she asked when he didn't continue.

"I received a letter today."

"From?" Elf stared at his stiffly held shoulders.

"A *friend*." He said the word in a funny tone.

"A friend?" she mimicked.

Dom swung around, a grim expression hardening his features. "I very much dislike anonymous letters, Elf."

"I should think so." When he didn't speak, she asked, "This one *was* anonymous?"

"Oh yes. I realize I erred but I was so angry I followed my first impulse, which was to burn it. I couldn't believe the filth, words I never speak, let alone write."

Silence followed his revelation and neither moved for a long moment of time.

"Dom, will you be advised by me?"

"That is why I am here, Aunt. I've no notion of how to deal with it."

"Don't ignore it, thinking it a tempest in a teapot." Elf's hands tightened one around the other as she remembered the last time, twenty-five or thirty years ago, when she'd been involved with such a person. "That's the first rule. Writers of such letters are deeply disturbed people. They will spiral up to worse behavior if not satisfied by the damage their letters do. When the next arrives, as it will, bring it to me. I have a large correspondence and there is a chance I will recognize the writing."

"It appeared to be disguised so that is not likely." The grim look became grimmer. "What do you mean, worse?"

"If they get no reaction, no response, the writer will try something new. Was it all against Tavie?"

"No." A muscle jumped in his jaw. "I came in for at least as much vituperation as she did. There was also a tirade against Tavie's mother."

Elf nodded. "You must be careful, Dom. Very careful."

"But I cannot possibly have an enemy who hates me so. Elf, is it perhaps that Tavie has an admirer who is jealous that I married her?"

"That's a better notion than any I've had." Surely Sarah had not become so obsessed with the idea Owen might inherit that she had become unbalanced!

Or had she?

* * * * *

Sir Owen climbed stiffly from his carriage and looked up and down the street. He hated London and avoided it whenever possible. Now, thanks to his mother's antics, he'd been obliged to leave his comfortable country home and, since he was a very poor traveler, suffer nearly three days on the road. Having done that, he must now face the woman that duty required he call mother. Owen sighed and squared his narrow shoulders. He'd order her things packed and take her home. But once home, it was too much to hope, even then, she'd cease attempting to harm his cousin Dominic and the new bride. What to do once they were home was a problem, but surely taking her away from London was the first step.

If Lady Clavingstone was to be believed, and her letter was both literate and pointed, his mother had already done more than enough. Because she was making such a nuisance of herself, he must suffer another long trip and, reaching Brightwood, apologize for his mother to Dominic and to his cousin's new lady. It was outside of enough. His own mother had no better understanding of her only son's needs or of his wishes than to cut up his peace this way.

And so he'd tell her.

That was, he scowled at the still shut front door, he would if anyone ever answered his groom's knock and allowed him entry to his own house. He motioned to the groom and the man beat with the knocker more loudly and, this time, more determinedly.

The door opened and a pert little housemaid, stuffing what looked like a duster behind her back, peered out, her eyes widening at the sight of the tall, well-set-up groom. "Yesss?"

"Sir Owen has arrived."

"And who, pray tell, might Sir Owen be?" She flirted her eyes at the groom.

"Sir Owen who owns this here house," said the groom sternly.

"Never heard of him," she answered, fluttering her eyelashes and flashing such a look at the poor young man he grew red about the ears.

"Where is Merrywood?" asked Owen, approaching the steps.

"Oh." The maid wiped her free hand on her apron and put it behind her. "Didn't see you standing there. Old Stiff-rump—" she blushed even as she smirked at Owen's scowl, "Mr. Merrywood, I *should* say, collapsed. The missus, Lady Sands, I mean, said we'd do very well without a butler, so you see…"

"Where is my mother?" asked Sir Owen sternly.

"Mother? Oh, your *mother*." The maid lost only a trifling bit of her natural insouciance. "She's still in her room, Sir Sands."

Owen ignored the fact the maid hadn't proper knowledge of titles and how to use them. To him, it wasn't important.

"'Tis very early, you know," the girl scolded, her irrepressible eyes flirting with *him* this time. She curtsied. "Sir Sands," she repeated a trifle belatedly.

Or was it important? The chit needed a setdown. "The correct form of address is Sir Owen," said Owen. "Am I to be kept standing on my own doorstep forever?" Owen, whose temper was placid and not easily roused, could, when angry, become quite formidable. This latest outrage on top of his being required to travel was making him very angry indeed.

Hurriedly, the maid backed up and Owen stalked into the hall. The groom went to help the coachman unload the baggage since it was clear no footmen would appear to do work that was properly theirs.

Not that there was all that much. A small trunk and two boxes were all. Sir Owen would find it an insult to be thought a dandy. Not that anyone *would* suggest such a thing. At home, the butler performed those duties that would normally fall to a valet, such as pressing his coats and removing dirt from his leathers after his occasional rides and the knife boy blackened his boots quite well enough for Sir Owen. So, all in all, perhaps it was understandable the maid did not recognize, in the modestly dressed gentleman at the door, the owner of the modish house in which she worked.

"Where is Merrywood? In his rooms?"

"Mr. Merrywood was sent away."

"Merrywood was *what*?" roared Sir Owen.

"M'lady sent him away." The maid was either very brave or very foolish for she repeated sullenly, "Said she had no need of a butler."

"Merrywood was not her servant to dismiss."

"Oh, my head. What is this ruction? Why can you not be quiet?" Sarah's voice turned flat. "Oh…Owen." Sarah, halfway down the stairs, bit her lip and clutched tightly at the railing.

"*Where is Merrywood*?" Again Sir Owen roared and his mother blenched. "You will tell me. Instantly."

The shock of seeing her son where he'd no business being, faded. "Do lower your voice," said Sarah, rallying. "You will have all the house privy to our business."

"I wish to know immediately where I may find Merrywood."

"You do not *need* to find him. He is too old and ailing to be of the least use. I sent him away."

"I know that. *Where has he gone*?"

"But, dear," Sarah's eyes widened in confusion, "how should I know where a useless old man has gone?"

"Madam, one day you will go too far. You," he pointed at the maid who was staring, wide-eyed, at mistress and son, "is there anyone in this benighted house who can tell me where Merrywood has gone?"

"Mrs. Merrywood perhaps?"

Sir Owen sighed. "Yes. It is conceivable his wife will know where to find her husband." He waited, impatient, looking at the maid. "Well?"

"Well what, sir? Er," the girl batted her eyes, "hmm, Sir Owen?"

Owen pressed his lips tightly together, attempting to control his temper. "Why," he said with strained patience, "have you not yet gone to get me Mrs. Merrywood?"

"Oh." She stared. "Did you want her?"

Owen raised his eyes to heaven, sighed deeply and growled at his parent, "Can you do no better than this when hiring servants? Or is it another example of your well-known parsimony you waste money on such as her?"

"You've never understood how it is with money, Owen," said his mother petulantly.

"Are you still here?" asked Owen, rounding on the maid. "Why have you not gone to get Mrs. Merrywood?"

"Because she ain't here…Sir Owen," she added belatedly.

"Where—is—Mrs.—Merrywood?"

"Why, doin' the shopping of course," said the maid, blinking. She was understandably confused that he didn't know and, since he did not, decided he must be something of a slowtop. "I tol' you it was early for house calls, didn't I now?"

Sir Owen raised his fists to heaven and shook them. "This is not a house call, you idiot child. I *own* this house. I *live* here."

"Really, Owen, you should not shout at the servants. Besides, you are making my headache worse. I do not know why you are here." Sarah's tone was peevish.

"I came to take you and your meddling ways back home where I can keep an eye on you. But now I must find out what chaos you have perpetrated in my house and set things to rights before we may leave."

"Meddling ways?" said his mother. "*Meddling ways*! I haven't the least notion what you are going on about."

"You have done your best to upset my cousin Dominic and make me a laughingstock and I must suffer, as you know I *do* suffer, by traveling all over England to set things right. While I do that, you will write all your friends telling them that you are sorry to have said such ridiculous things as I'm told you've said to everyone you know and—*Mother, where are you going*?"

Sarah continued up the stairs, her nose in the air. "I will not stand around to be berated in public and lectured like any schoolroom chit. Particularly not by one I've known since before he was in nappies. If we are to argue, we will do it in private as in any reasonable household. And you!" She turned at the top of the stairs to glare down at the maid. "If you dare to say one word of this to anyone, I will see you gone from here and given no character and you know what *that* means." Sarah, much on her dignity, turned and disappeared down the hall above.

Sir Owen sighed. For once, his mother was correct. If only she didn't rouse him to losing his temper. If only she would learn to accept her lot in life. More to the point, accept that *he* accepted *his*. In fact, accept that he *preferred* his current position to the one she would wish on him. He sighed again. "Is it too much to ask in an establishment run by my mother that breakfast be served?"

"Well, I don't know." The maid frowned. "Lady Sands says she don't eat breakfast while in town so she don't think no one else need eat it either."

Owen closed his eyes tightly, forcibly reining in a temper newly roused by still-another example of his servants' ill-treatment. "None of you are allowed breakfast?" he asked quietly, wanting to be certain.

The girl blushed and didn't quite know where to look.

Interpreting that to mean they *did* eat even if they'd been ordered not to, he nodded. "I see Mrs. Merrywood is her usual sensible self." The baize-covered door at the back of the hall opened and Sir Owen glanced that way. "And there you are now, Mrs. Merrywood." Sir Owen relaxed slightly, a smile forming for the bouncy, little, gray-haired, apple-cheeked woman who had been housekeeper here since before he was born.

"My dear Master Owen, or I should say," she went on, curtsying as she spoke, "*Sir* Owen. You poor, dear man. I know just how you'll have suffered, bounced and jolted and very likely with damp sheets when you stopped for the night. Why are you standing here in the hall? You come along and I'll have you your breakfast ready just as you like it in no time at all and, by then, your room will be ready and you can have a bit of a lie-down and then you will feel more the thing." She beamed at him.

"Mrs. Merrywood, I will not move an inch until you tell me how Merrywood is and where he is and just why you did not let me know the goings-on here?"

"Merrywood is fine, Sir Owen. Just old age catching up with him. It's past time he retired, and so I told him when he complained about being put out to pasture as it were." Mrs. Merrywood soothed her employer, all the time urging him toward the parlor in which the family dined. "He's living with our daughter now. The one who married the publican in a good way of business, you'll remember? And I think, in a year or two or so, I'll just go and live with her too."

"But I haven't seen to properly pensioning him off," complained Owen. "Surely you knew I wouldn't allow either of you to retire until I made proper financial arrangements?" Sir Owen sighed and, because she was a trusted retainer, added, "I do not know why my mother is the way she is, Mrs. Merrywood. But I hope you know I do not approve of the way she behaved toward Merrywood?"

"Of course, of course." His housekeeper was rather embarrassed by his frankness. "We knew you'd make all right. Once you knew. Now you just sit yourself right here," she soothed, "and I'll be back before the cat can blink with your breakfast."

Two hours later, Sir Owen left his bedroom, feeling very nearly right as a trivet, and went to face his mother. "Mother, you will be packed and ready to leave in the morning. Since I am in town, I will see to a few other things I have been putting off but you must not think that excuses your behavior. It does not. How dare you do anything which would put my friend to the blush?"

"Friend? Friend! Dominic is not your friend." His mother hunched her shoulder and turned away.

"He is my friend. We like each other very well."

"If he were truly your friend, he would have had an accident in one of those awful races in which he drives or he would have fallen when indulging his ridiculous penchant for climbing in the Fells or when in Scotland. It is too bad of the French for making it impossible for him to go to Switzerland. I understand fatal climbing accidents are common in the Alps." She noted Sir Owen's widening eyes. "Why are you looking at me like that?"

"I see I have been entirely too indulgent of what I thought was merely an innocent wish to see your son in shoes which would not fit. I do not *wish* to be Marquis. You must be mad to think it."

"I am not mad." Her voice rose, becoming shrill. "It is not mad to wish your son to take his rightful place as head of the family. It is not mad to wish to see him cut a dash at *tonnish* parties. It is not mad to assume that, given his profligate ways and total lack of care of life and limb, Dominic would take himself out of the way of your advancement!"

"Have you no care at all for *my* wishes or *my* interests?" asked Sir Owen sadly. "It is all for yourself you wish to see me active in society, a way of life that interests me not and for which I am totally unsuited."

Sir Owen's sad expression drew from his mother a slight but only momentary pang of guilt. The boy simply did not understand. If only she could make him spend a season at his townhouse, make him attend the routs and balls and those delightfully *tonnish* entertainments contributing gaiety to the season. He, as an eligible bachelor, would get many such invitations—at which point her altruistic thoughts veered back to her true interest—and those invitations would include herself of course.

Sarah didn't understand why *tonnish* hostesses so often left her off their lists but now was no time to puzzle that out. Owen was the problem. He must see what he was missing. He would put away his dusty tomes with which he'd very likely ruin his eyes and his health. And he would discover a young woman whom his mother could tolerate. They'd marry and have children, especially a son who would dote on his grandmother and who would not grow up to be bookish as had her slowtop of a son.

She studied Owen and closed her eyes in pain. "You had better see a tailor now you are in town. It is between seasons so it would not take long for one to replace your wardrobe with much more stylish apparel. Weston would be the best. Have you lost weight and I not noticed? I swear that coat is so loose you could shrug into it without help." She tittered at the thought.

Owen blinked. "But of course I can. That is how I prefer my coats. I'll not waste time on a tailor but I must see my solicitor about pensioning off Merrywood. You did not treat him well, Mother."

"Oh, do not concern yourself over such as him. You go on and on about trivialities. How is one to treat a servant after all? As if they were your best friend?"

Her titter was less easily ignored. Owen found it particularly offensive.

"You are so droll, Owen."

"You are a heartless woman."

Sarah's mouth dropped open and her eyes widened. "How dare you?" she shouted at him. "I am your mother."

"Yes. I have often wished you were not."

Sarah blinked, shook her head and decided she could not have understood him.

"Good day to you, madam. You will be ready to depart in the morning."

"I will do no such thing."

Owen paused by the door and turned to look at her. There was a firmness of purpose she'd not before seen and a sorrowful look she didn't understand at all.

He waited until he was sure she paid him her full attention. "Mother, if you have not packed your belongings, I care not. With or without your trunks, *you* will leave tomorrow." He waited for a response but when he saw his mother was working herself up for a bout of hysterics, he opened the door and walked away.

It was not a craven act on his part. It was, as he well knew, the *only* way to make his mother give over her tantrums—which she *did* do just as soon as she realized she had lost her audience.

Sarah rang for her long-suffering abigail. It was so satisfying to have a maid who could not leave her service and who would do anything at all she was required to do. Sarah, aware her maid had once borne a child to the master of the household in which she then worked, never hesitated to use that knowledge for her own comfort. That Mary had not wished to submit to Lord Besselmite was of course irrelevant. Sarah had not hired the woman because she had a forgiving nature or charitable motives but because the girl was far better trained than any Sarah would normally have hired. Well-trained abigails were expensive—or in disgrace, as was Mary.

At first, Mary was happy to have any work at all. It had been years of course since the abigail had felt the least bit grateful, but that did not bother Sarah in the least.

"Pack," ordered Lady Sands. "It seems I must remove to the country. Sir Owen requires my presence there."

"Yes, my lady."

Mary could not quite repress the fact she knew, as did the entire household, that Sir Owen had given his mother a scold.

Sarah's eyes narrowed. "I think you should also rip out the seams of my lilac taffeta and sew them up again. It is a trifle tight. You should have it done in time for dinner this evening." That would teach the girl to be pert.

Mary clenched her jaw. "Yes, my lady."

"Don't forget the packing, Mary," said Sarah in a sweet tone. "You will have no time this afternoon to get into trouble, will you?"

Mary drew in a deep breath and held it carefully before letting it out slowly. "No, my lady. Certainly not."

"Very well. You may go." Sarah smiled at her maid's rigid back. Oh yes, it was a delight to have such a well-trained maid. And one who would not answer back and who would do exactly as she was told. After all, it was only by retaining her place with Sarah that Mary could send money to the farmer in whose home her son lived.

*****

Meanwhile, several streets away, another lady found herself in a far different mood. "Sir Owen? Oh no. I cannot see my nephew. Tell him I am not in," said Violetta, Dowager Marchioness of Brightwood, in die-away tones to her butler.

"But you are in, Aunt," said Owen who followed on the butler's heels. He trod into the darkened room. "Why do you not open the curtains? It is an unusually beautiful day outside." He bashed his shins on a low stool but, with no more than a word or two under his breath, went on to throw back the drapery. He sneezed. And sneezed again. "There," he said when he'd recovered, "is that not much better?"

"No, it is not," said Violetta crossly. "I have a headache. And I know you are about to make it worse."

"Aunt, you know I would do no such thing. I must escort my mother home." He blenched at what he was about to promise but duty, he reminded himself, was duty. "I will then return to London to escort you to Brightwood." He couldn't travel with his mother and Dom's mother together. The two women fought continuously when together. His stomach, however, gave him qualms at the mere thought of all those extra miles. His jaw firmed. He knew his duty and he *would* do it.

"Escort me to..." Violetta raised a hand to her forehead. "I knew you would cut up my peace. I told Matilda you would do so." She groaned. "I cannot possibly travel to the Lakes. It is too far. The roads are too bad. Besides, I hate the country and am never well there."

Owen's brow creased. "Are you certain you have that right, Aunt? You have not been out of London for quite some years now. It seems to me you are never well *in* London, so how do you know you might not improve by a change of air? Very likely you will find it beneficial."

"Owen, you are not going to talk me into leaving my home. I am not well, I tell you."

"But you must, dear Aunt. It is for Dominic."

"Dominic does not care a farthing for me, so why should I care for him?" Violetta pouted, pulling her shawls around her.

"I do not understand you," said Owen, honestly bemused. "He has always spoken of you with much affection."

Sir Owen had a bit of difficulty telling the difference between warm affection and tolerant humor since he had no sense of humor himself. Violetta was similarly handicapped but was aware, from her point of view anyway, that Dom's "affection" took strange twists.

"My dear aunt, it is essential you come. Only by taking you to him do I believe I may counter the ill my mother has done him. Aunt, may I ask you a question?"

Violetta, unconvinced of the state of her son's heart, glared at him. "You will, whether I will it or not."

Owen, single-minded, ignored the hinted-at aversion. "Is my mother quite, er, completely, er—" His tone dropped to a whisper. "Er, *sane*?"

Violetta blinked, unsure she'd heard correctly. "Sane?" she asked cautiously, wanting clarification.

"Or is she perhaps just a trifle, well, insane? Not ready for a place in Bedlam of course, but should I see she is, er, watched?"

Violetta rose to a sitting position, forgetting her affectations. "Why, my poor boy, what makes you believe she is mad?"

"Not *mad*! But she persists in the delusion I should be head of the family, which is, in itself, a mad idea. Moreover she is often so very cruel—er, I mean *thoughtless*." He thought of the outrage he'd felt that morning. "She turned off old Merrywood without telling me and made no provision for him and *that* after more than five decades devoted service to the family. And, now I think of it, I occasionally wonder about that maid of hers. The poor girl often looks quite ill."

"Maid? You mean Mary?"

"Is that her name? I do not pay much attention to the female servants, you know."

Violetta did know and had, on occasion, wondered what it might indicate about her nephew. "I believe Mary is a charity case, Owen. She once served in Besselmite's establishment." That was said in a repressed tone and was adequate explanation even for the unusually obtuse Owen.

Owen's eyebrows rose. "I see." He digested that. "But charity? My mother?" he asked doubtfully. "No, no. There must be another motive and I will have to exert myself to discover it." He sighed deeply, wishing he were still innocently occupied within his beloved library and unaware of any of this. "Is there no end to it?" he asked in a sad tone as he rose to his feet. "Now speaking of exerting myself, I can return by the middle of next week assuming I do not pamper myself. You'll have time to prepare for our travels. Do not concern yourself about carriages and all that. I will speak with your coachman. Aunt," he added, alarmed, "do not do yourself an injury!"

Violetta had risen to her feet and shook her hands in the air. "I am not traveling to the Lakes."

"But you must." He stared at her.

Slowly Violetta collapsed back against her many cushions and tugged peevishly at her scarves and shawls, arranging them around her. She sighed.

"Aunt, you must see it is imperative you go."

"What I see is that you will give me no peace until I agree to do so… I will be ready. Remember, I will not travel on a Sunday so you must think where we will stay over." She seemed to wilt. "Now go away."

Owen rose and bowed.

"Oh," she added, "before you leave me, I would appreciate it if you would pull the bell cord. I am far too weak to get up and do it myself."

"Weak, Aunt?" he asked as he maneuvered around the furniture crowding the room.

"You have made me suffer palpitations with your demands." Violetta waved a languid hand, laid the back of it against her forehead and turned away her head. "You always make me suffer palpitations," she said, her voice faint.

Owen chuckled. "Such a delightful sense of humor, Aunt," he said, proving, once again, that he had none. "What a jest, pretending to be sick. The way you go on, why, someone outside the family, who did not know you, might believe you were really ill!"

Chapter Five

"Domini!" sang a tenor voice.

"Domino!" yelled a deeper.

Elf stopped her progress down the steps to the hall, halting on the third from the bottom. Silhouetted in the open door were two men, the sun behind them, making it difficult to distinguish who they were. She glanced around for Deblon or at least a footman but saw neither.

In chorus came, "Dominic, old man!"

"We've come to see the camelopard," added the shorter figure. He went on in a somewhat quieter tone. "Oh, oh. Bert, look. It's dear old Elfie!"

"My love!" said the deeper voice. A blond giant strode toward Elf. He reached for her and lifted her into his arms, smacking kisses on each of her cheeks.

"Impertinent," said Elf, but there was no anger in her voice.

"Are you going to marry me?"

"Gudgeon."

The epithet didn't appear to bother her captor, perhaps because there was no heat behind it. He smiled down at her.

"Put me down," demanded Elf.

Bert shook his head. "No, love, I don't believe I will. Having got you," he said in dramatic tones, "I believe I will hold you until, at long last, you agree to wed me."

"You'd be in a pickle if I said yes," suggested Elf, suppressing a desire to laugh at Bertram's antics.

"No, no. You do not understand," he scolded gently. "Must marry. The Ancestor insists. But never seen a lady to match you, dear, *dear* Elfie." Bert gently settled the little old woman more comfortably and Elf, freeing an arm, put it around his neck. "There now. I believe that will do. We'll be comfortable for as long as it takes you to say yes."

"This could get quite embarrassing, you know, if it goes on long enough." Elf allowed herself a chuckle at the faint reddening across Bert's cheeks as he absorbed her suggestive words.

"Oh my." The second man's quizzing glass swept up to his eye and was directed toward the back of the hall. In a laughing voice, he asked, "Is it the camelopard? It doesn't look like a strange, long-legged, spotted quadruped to me."

Elf and Bert looked at Geoffrey Martin. Geoff pointed his glass toward the new arrivals and returned the instrument to his eye. Bert turned. Elf, willy-nilly, turned with him.

"Elf, love," Bert said in a sad voice, "I have discovered a serious flaw in my character. I am fickle. Elfie, my first love, my dear one, you do understand, do you not? Oh, do say you understand?" As he spoke, he strode toward Dom and Tavie, set Elf carefully on her feet, and dropped to one knee. Hand to heart, the other flung to one side, he stared up at Tavie. "Marry me!"

Tavie giggled.

"Is it the camelopard? They have very long, er, limbs, I am told." Geoffrey's gaze drifted down Tavie's length and he nodded. "Yes, I believe that checks. The incredible beasts are also purported to have excessively long necks so that, I've been told, they may eat the leaves from the tip most top of tall trees. Bert, would you say this delightful creature has a long neck?"

"Her neck is perfect," said Bert solemnly.

"Yes, I think so too. I don't believe that checks at all. And spots. Bertie, camelopards have large spots, do they not?"

"Yes, Geoffrey, I have heard they have spots. Rather large, reddish-brownish blotches actually. And before you ask, no, there's not a single spot."

"Oh dear. It is not then the camelopard?"

"What are you two idiots blithering on about?" asked Dom, attempting, with little luck, to stifle a manlier version of the giggles that Tavie attempted to hide behind both hands.

"It is only what Lady Sands is said to be saying." Geoffrey, his eyes wide in pretended innocence, stared at his old friend, hidden meaning transferred with the look.

"Among other things," added Dom's other friend *sotto voce*, also meaningfully.

"Aunt Sarah?" All desire to laugh faded but Dominic forced one anyway. "Is *that* what she names you, my dear?" He looked down at Tavie. "Ah well, you know, my love," he said thoughtfully, "she is such a squab of a woman and quite obviously she did not like looking up at you, so perhaps it is not so surprising?"

Elf's mouth hardened into a line, not at all like her usual firm, but sober, expression.

"Well, well," Dom continued. "Tavie, love, I suppose I must introduce you to this pair of idiots. The buffoon there before you on his knee is Bertram Montague, Viscount Darling. Our friend with the oversized eye—"

Geoffrey, at this unsubtle reminder, shoved his quizzing glass behind his back.

"Is the more or less Honorable Geoffrey Martin."

"Marry me," intoned the giant at Tavie's feet.

"I can't. I am already married to Dominic."

Bertie sighed. "Isn't it just like the man? I do not see why he should have all the luck. Do you," he asked hopefully, "have a sister just exactly like you? One who might like to marry me?"

"No." Tavie restrained a laugh and answered with grave, if false, solemnity, "My father says one of me is one too many as it is."

"I am very sorry to be rude but the duke hasn't a notion what he is talking about."

"Are you certain, Lady Brightwood," asked Geoffrey gravely, "that you would not care to go back to that roadside where Lady Sands claims Dom found you and have one of *us* discover you? Instead of that oaf with whom you have had to make do, I mean?"

"I am quite happy with the way things turned out," answered Tavie with equal gravity.

"Well, there it is. Sorry, Bert. I tried."

"Yes. I'll just have to go back to Elf." So saying, Bert was suddenly, and surprisingly gracefully for such a big man, on his feet. He returned Elf to her former position in his arms before she could evade him. Assuming of course she'd have wished to avoid him. "Say you'll marry me."

Elf pretended to frown and, although held high against his chest, crossed her arms. "I'll never marry a fickle man. If you wish to stay here, as I assume you do, you will release me so I may inform Mrs. MacReady of your arrival and have rooms prepared for you."

"Oh dear, I should have thought of that," said the suddenly contrite, brand-new mistress of Brightwood.

"You have had no opportunity, Tavie, to think of anything. Put me down, Bertram."

Sad-faced, Bert put Elf back on her feet. "I see I must resign myself to bachelordom."

"Dear Elf," said Geoff, ignoring his friend's joshing, "we have settled ourselves at the inn. It is Dom's honeymoon after all." There, he'd made the expected verbal sop to convention. "We would not *think* of intruding." This last was utterly mendacious.

"Much anyway," added Bert, irrepressible as usual.

The thought of course *had* crossed their minds and they had argued the point all the way from London.

"Nonsense," said Tavie, taking on the role of hostess. "You are only anticipating the event in any case. Dominic, have the invitations been sent off?"

"Deblon," Dom asked the butler who, belatedly, came into the hall, "has the mailbag been carried to the post house?"

Deblon bowed to the young men. "Welcome to Brightwood, Lord Darling, Mr. Martin. Mrs. MacReady is preparing your usual rooms." He turned to Dom. "The mail needn't go for another hour, my lord. Is something to be added to it?"

"No. To the contrary, I have something I wish removed. If you please, Deblon, would you find the invitations directed to Geoff and Bertie and take them out? Whoever takes the pouch in is to collect my friends' valets and all their gear from the inn. And pay off the tab, whatever it may be."

"Very good, my lord," said Deblon over the demurrals made by Bert and accepted the coins shoved into his hand by Geoff. He bowed and exited the hall.

Twenty minutes later, the four young people were settled in the library. Bertie drank off a glass of burgundy and sighed. "Oh, much better. Do you think I might have another?"

"No, you might not," admonished Geoff. "You wish to make a good impression on Dom's wife, do you not?" he finished, speaking from the side of his mouth in a scolding fashion.

"Oh." Bert pretended chagrin. "Forgot."

Tavie giggled again. Her eyes sparkled and her hand tightened around Dom's. She hadn't been so entertained in years. Perhaps never. "I think one more wouldn't hurt your reputation."

"Ah! A maiden after my own heart."

"Not a maiden," hissed Geoff. "Not anymore."

"Forgot," said Bert in morose tones.

Geoff opened his mouth to add something more but, noting Dom's rising temper, realized he'd gone too far. He sent an apologetic glance first to Dom and then toward Tavie who pretended she hadn't a notion what his sly comment meant. "I wonder if maybe I should go cover myself with sackcloth and ashes," murmured Geoff. He shook his head. "No, that would only compound my error by drawing attention to it. My lady, forgive me?"

"For what?" asked Tavie with grave solemnity.

"For discovering too late what an ass I can be." Geoff sighed, but whether it was for his gaffe or for the sudden realization their relaxed bachelor days, when one could say anything that came into one's head, were over, he kept to himself. "An utter ass."

Bert looked surprised. "No, no, runt, you were always the brightest of us."

Geoff lifted his quizzing glass, his hideously magnified eye glaring at Bert.

"Why are you angry?" asked Dom. "It wasn't an insult. Worse, it was true."

The moment hung in the balance, the long-hated nickname versus the compliment. Then Geoff chuckled. "Yes. I was forgetting, was I not? Bert is all brawn. You have all the looks. But I am far and away the brainiest of us and that will be an advantage on into our dotage. Poor Bert's muscle will fail and he'll become a stooped and trembling old man. Dom's looks will fade, poor fellow, and he'll be as ugly as the rest of us. But I!" He struck a pose. "I will continue to have brains no matter how elderly I become."

Tavie turned her head into Dom's arm, her body shaking in an attempt to stifle laughter. Gently, Dom lifted her chin and looked into her dancing gaze. He smiled. "Oh yes, love, that is the way I always wish to see you. Happy and full of joy and so very, very lovely."

"Here. What's this? What do we see?" Bert shook his head, attempting to hide his laughter with a scowl. "Oh no, Dom, it will not do. Think of the old tabbies."

"A love match," sighed Geoffrey. "But, Bert, we knew it would be a love match. At least I presume you love our friend as much as he obviously loves you?"

"Oh, ever-so much more, I should think," said Tavie, suddenly finding it easy to maintain a solemn face.

"Then that's all right." Geoffrey raised his glass to Tavie and drank off a bit.

"It's fine when it is just ourselves," objected Bert, "but you don't think it will do when they are out in the world, do you?"

Dropping all affectations, Geoff tapped his quizzing glass against his chin, pensiveness falling over him like a cloak. "I think maybe it will. In fact, I think it is the only way."

Dom sent a puzzled look toward his suddenly solemn friend. "The only way to do what?"

"Squash those rumors your much-disliked aunt is spreading."

"Oh dear." All the sparkle left Tavie's face. "Dom." She jerked at his sleeve until he looked at her. "I think my plan is the best after all. Do find Deblon and we'll burn all those invitations. You may go off to London with your friends. I will be perfectly content awaiting you here. Really. You didn't *wish* to marry yet. You know you did not. If you had not found me, you'd be as free as you ever were to follow your pleasure. You must go on to London by yourself." She managed to hide all but the merest hint of wistfulness.

"Such an earnest young lady. Dear lady, do you not know that we will not allow the *ton* to hurt Dom? So, since hurting you means hurting Dom, we will not allow anyone to harm you."

"Thank you, Lord Darling, but…"

Further speech was impossible in the uproar from three healthy and outraged male voices. Finally they sorted themselves to just Dom's. "My love, these are my friends. You will please us by calling that two-legged mountain," Bert was inches taller than Dom and a bit broader, "Bert or Bertie. And the runt there—" Geoffrey was several inches shorter than Dom, well proportioned but a slender, dark-skinned, dark-haired man. "That is Geoff. We have had no formality amongst us since the first time we rescued poor Geoff from tormentors. Which," he added thoughtfully, "was more years ago than I like to remember."

Tavie tipped her head to one side in unconscious mimicry of Elf. "Is there a story, Dom?"

"Not really. It is just that Bert and I cannot abide a bully and Geoff, here, really *was* a runt in our school days. Just the sort to bring out the worst in the meaner of the bigger boys."

"What Dominic is saying, my dear," explained Geoffrey, still a trifle touchy about his lack of inches, "is that I came to my full growth rather later than most boys do. They protected me physically, while my quicker mind kept them from the switch the Latin master wielded with such frenzy."

"Ah, I see. A mutual-benefit society," said Tavie.

"I freely admit that I benefited," said Dom, smiling.

"Me too," said Bert.

"Now," said Dom, "it is time for my wife's driving lesson. You've never seen a lighter pair of hands. Do come see how she has progressed."

"How will we know if she has progressed since we did not see how she began?" objected Bert.

"You will say she is a nonesuch and no nonsense!"

"No, no," said Tavie, the lighthearted feelings returning as she enjoyed the new experience of being surrounded by three attractive males, one of whom she loved to distraction. "I am the merest whipster. But I think I have aptitude," she admitted, nothing shy about her, "and you must see if you agree I may someday become at least a tolerable whip."

They strolled onto the front steps and down to where a tilbury stood, the placid mare between the shafts. Dom helped his wife into the seat and joined his friends, who were complaining about the animal hitched to the simple carriage.

"Here now," objected Dom, "you do not expect me to endanger my wife by using *my* horses when teaching her, do you?"

"No, yours are too spirited, but *such* a plodder, Dom? Have you nothing in between? There can be no more life in that excuse for a horse than…than in a sheep."

"I believe you are blinded by good training into thinking obedience is docility. Take the circle by yourself, love, and show these gentlemen what you have learned."

Tavie bit her lip. Dom no longer touched the reins but he had always been beside her—just in case. Dare she try it by herself? She glanced at his friends and back to Dom's encouraging smile. Putting her chin in the air, she gave old Sugar the office to start.

Dom watched her, eyes narrowed for just a minute. He relaxed as he perceived he had not erred in his judgment Tavie was ready to go it alone. "Now then, Geoff," he said quietly, "give me chapter and verse. What is going on?"

"You would not believe some of the stories making the rounds. Most are not believed but one has some basis and is whispered more than the rest. Tavie, it is said, must be mad. It is suggested it came through her mother's family. Why else, the tattlers ask, should the duke have kept her locked away for so long?"

"Damnation."

"That's the worst. A counter story, put around by I know not whom, is that Lady Sands resents the possibility of an heir between Owen and the title and is blackening Tavie's character in revenge. That is easily believed by anyone who knows the family. Since I heard another to the effect your mother is irked you married without her blessing and is sulking, I doubt *she* started it. Most rumors are discounted but nevertheless circulated with the greatest enjoyment. You are well liked, Dom, but you are also envied."

"Why would anyone envy me?" asked Dom, mystified.

"Ah, what it is to be so modest," scoffed Geoff.

"Yes, he'll be taking himself off to a monastery next," added Bert.

"No, he won't, Bertie. Just married. Mustn't forget that."

"Cut it out, you idiots. This is serious. What am I going to do? I won't have the *ton* hurting my Tavie."

"Two minutes in her company and no one could believe she is insane. You'll need to introduce her." Geoff snapped his fingers. "Wasn't a house party mentioned?"

"Yes. I do not know the whole of the guest list but among others it includes at least a couple of government types, solid Tories, thanks to the duke, at least one of the top society ladies," he pursed his lip, "Lady Sefton, I believe, thanks to Elf, and a number of young marrieds, thanks to yours truly. As well, my dear fellows," he warned, "a few young ladies with mamas panting to see them wed."

Bert groaned but Geoff wasn't bothered by the news. Everyone knew he wasn't hanging out for a wife and, with his lack of title and modest fortune, he was not such a prize he need worry about entrapment. He chuckled at Bert's glum expression.

"The worst are the relatives Elf insisted I am required by common decency to include."

"Including the loathsome Sarah?" asked Geoff.

"I do not believe so but that won't prevent her arrival if she gets wind of the affair."

"How true. And Owen?"

"Oh, he's invited but I don't mind Owen. In his quiet way, he can be a very interesting addition to a group. No, just the odd bunch every family has tucked away and ignores when possible." Dom had every intention of ignoring them during the house party too.

"Owen is *interesting*?" asked Bert.

"Owen *is*. Am I not correct, Geoff?"

"Yes."

Bert's brows climbed his forehead.

Geoff explained, "His range of knowledge always surprises me."

"You go ahead and be surprised. I'd rather not find out," Bert replied.

"We understand," said Geoff. "And we certainly don't want you straining that excuse for a brain which resides under your skull, so you just take it from us. Owen is an unexceptionable young man and welcome anywhere he cares to go. The fact is he doesn't care to go."

"Quickly, bantam," said Dom. "Tavie is almost back. Is there anything else we can do?"

"You know rumor is the hardest of all evils to combat. We can only show the world Tavie is," he raised his voice slightly as Tavie pulled to a stop beside them, "already an outstanding whip. You do very well, my lady."

"If I cannot 'my lord' Bert, you mustn't 'my lady' me," she retorted with a smile. "But thank you for that totally undeserved compliment." Tavie drew in a deep breath and, eyes glowing, spoke to Dom. "I did it. I did it all by myself." She grinned a wholly unladylike grin of triumph and won Dom's two friends for life. Dom moved closer, reaching for her, and she threw herself off the seat and down into his arms.

"I really did it!" she said again, hugging him. "I cannot believe I did it."

"So you did, love." Dom smiled over her tousled head.

His friends beamed too, equally proud.

* * * * *

Several days later, Tavie and Ally were up to their ears in lists. Tavie knew her duty and did not complain but, oh, how she wished she might be riding, enjoying the rare sunshine while out with the men.

"Now you have finished those menus," said Ally to Tavie, "I'll check with Mrs. MacReady that she has in stock all she will need. She's an efficient housekeeper so I doubt a thing will be required but one must always ask."

Tavie sorted through the piles of notes and raised astonished eyes to meet Ally's. "We seem to have done all we can do for the moment, have we not? Since Dom isn't back, perhaps I'll write a letter to Miss Latimer. She was my only friend for so many years and I have not written for over a week. This is the first moment I've had free in ages. I won't be long, however, if I am needed…"

"Just see you are not long." Ally laughed. "Dominic has had several words to say, as it is, about the hours you spend on work for the party." Her plump features contorted into a wryly humorous expression that sat oddly on her pleasant features.

"Men!" Tavie chuckled. "They know nothing at all about the effort required to organize a party of this size. It took forever just to decide whom to put into which bedroom. Thank heaven you and Elf know all those quirks about each guest's particular requirements. I'd not have known who must not be placed near some other person and how so-and-so must be given a west-facing room and all the rest. And then we had to do it all over again when Alvanley changed his mind and decided to come and we needed, for him, the bedroom into which we'd put the Seftons. I still do not see why Alvanley required that and no other room."

"It is quite simple, dear. That is the only room that still has an unconverted powder room. A servant will be ordered to sit in it each night to check that Alvanley doesn't start a fire when he stuffs his candle under his pillow or knocks it off the bed table onto the floor. Yes, both are ridiculous methods of putting out one's candle but he will not desist. You'll find, however, that he is a very witty man—oh, quite in the line of Brummell—and helps liven up a house party, so no one objects to his little eccentricity."

"Is he of an age with Dom then?"

"Beau Brummell and Alvanley are slightly younger, I believe, but age has nothing to do with their invitation. They are of the bow-window set. Dandies, my dear… *The* dandies," added Ally at Tavie's obvious confusion. "They set fashion for all the rest. Our Dominic dresses well and follows the restrained style introduced by the Beau but he would not like to be thought a dandy. A famous Corinthian is our darling Dominic. Of course Dom is acquainted with the dandies, despite not wishing to be one."

Tavie digested that before she asked, "But Alvanley is not my father's friend either, is he? I don't see why he was invited or, come to that, why he accepted." Along with any number of others, thought Tavie, all of whom might be thought to have better things to do.

"Oh well, camelopards, you know," said Ally and winked, her chubby face wreathed in smiles. "Everyone wants to meet the camelopard! Besides," she sobered, "the fact is everyone knows everyone else. House parties are rarely restricted to only those with whom one is particularly intimate. Such a bore that would be. No leavening, you see, to lighten the other ingredients."

Tavie laughed at the little joke but the laughter faded as Ally shut the door and left the young bride alone. Alone and forgetful of the letter she'd meant to write.

Camelopard. It was funny when Geoff made such a game of it. He and Bert were Dom's closest friends and of course they'd wished to see the woman Dom married in such an odd way. But it became less than funny when a person of Alvanley's stature was willing to undertake the difficult journey to the Lakes just to meet the newest scandal to titillate the *ton*.

Made nervous by her cogitations, Tavie laid down her pen and walked to the window, automatically stopping before she got too close. She looked toward the stables and saw the three friends approaching. The sight distracted her from the upsetting train of thought and she smiled to see them.

Tavie hadn't smiled or laughed so much in the whole of her life as she'd done since Dom insisted on removing her from the side of that road. The weeks since they'd met had been the happiest she'd ever known.

But what had her preceptress repeated so often? *Don't tempt the fates, girl,* was one of Miss Latimer's favorite sayings. Tavie's morose mood returned. That was exactly what they'd done, was it not? Living happily from minute to minute, day to day? And not a thought for the future? Was that not tempting fate?

Dom, she was certain, hadn't yet thought about his reaction if their guests snubbed her. He'd be furious. She knew that instinctively. She understood because she had something of a temper herself. The question that worried her was how he'd behave, what he'd do. The coil of nerves she'd been pushing down and pushing down since Elf's first loving scold sprang up, making her feel slightly ill.

Dom waved. Tavie released the catch and pulled the window in. "Have a good ride?" she called before glancing down. The distance to the ground disturbed her and she stepped back.

"Not at all," he responded.

Having lost her train of thought, Tavie had to recapture her question. *Not* a good ride? "You *didn't*?"

"Come, love," he chided, "how could it be good when you were not there?" Dom grinned up at her.

"Ah." She relaxed and smiled. "I see. You think to butter me up with such palavering ways. You don't want me to suspect the truth, that you didn't give me a thought all the time you were off enjoying yourself."

Bert looked at Geoff. "She wants to be puffed up in her own esteem," he said in the tone one used to explain something. "*You* are our most fluent palaverer, Geoff."

Geoff pretended outrage. "How dare you suggest that anything I might say to our Tavie would be mere flummery? Why, she is such perfection there is no way I can flatter our lady."

Tavie's laugh rang out. She tried some of the cant phrasing she'd learned since their arrival. "You are a complete hand, Geoff. You'll turn my head with such flimflam."

She turned her eyes to Dom and their gazes locked. As if drawn, he walked off the path and toward the house. Her hand, white-knuckled, clenched around the frame and Tavie leaned toward the window as he neared so that she could keep him in sight. There, against the wall, clung an ancient vine and, almost before she could gasp out her disapproval, Dom had climbed up beside her first-floor window.

"Dom, you idiot." She felt moisture under her arms. "Get down before you fall."

"No. Give me a kiss. I've not had a kiss for hours."

"Here? Now?" She tried to make her voice light and hide how worried she was.

He nodded. "Here. Now."

"With them watching?" she whispered, still forcing herself to meet his mood.

"Bert, Geoff, turn your backs. I want to kiss my wife."

Obediently, Bert and Geoff turned and, equally obedient, Tavie leaned forward and held his chin between her fingers. Her mouth touched his lightly before she stepped back to where he couldn't reach her. "Now get down from there," she scolded in a more revealing tone. "Please, Dom. If something were to happen to you, I don't know how I'd survive it."

Dom found himself surprised by the emotion behind those words. It occurred to him that loving Tavie implied a concomitant responsibility. He must be careful not to rouse worry or concern, do nothing that would cause her pain. He climbed higher and stepped onto the windowsill, then down into the room. He took her into his arms, holding her close.

"I didn't think, love. I'm sorry," he apologized, although it was for the wrong thing. "You couldn't know I've climbed those vines since I was old enough to realize what a shortcut they made between the house and the outdoors into which I escaped whenever I could. I know which vines can be trusted and which cannot." He looked deep into her eyes. "Forgive me for frightening you that way?"

Tavie, long ashamed of her fear of heights, found she could not explain her weakness and, by doing so, give him a disgust of her. She nodded, gave him a peck on the cheek.

"Good. Then give me a real kiss," Dom demanded.

"Only if you'll promise you'll not forget it is almost time for lunch as you did the other day and also remember that you need to change out of your riding gear."

"Hmm. I do smell a bit of the stables, do I not?"

Tavie wrinkled her nose in agreement.

"How about coming up to our rooms and helping me change?" he asked, a sly note to his voice.

"Hmm. What an intriguing notion," responded Tavie, trapped in his suggestive gaze. Her caution concerning lunch was already fading from her head.

"Let us go. You can give me that kiss you owe me when we get there."

"But, Dom," she mumbled some time later, the sound of the gong intruding through the sensations holding her in thrall, "we mustn't forget lunch. Again."

"Food?" Dom asked, bending over her where she lay on their bed, staring into her eyes. "Tavie, love," he asked, "are you really hungry for *food*?"

And what could she say? It was an entirely different appetite her spouse roused and it needed satisfying urgently. Besides, she thought, snuggling against him, she'd ordered the bowl of fruit and tin of biscuits kept in the sitting room for just such occasions.

* * * * *

Sir Owen, sighing, clutched his aching head before speaking. "Aunt Violetta, I know how bad the roads are. I know, because I too find traveling a curse. Do you think yourself the only sufferer?"

Since Violetta didn't admit that anyone but herself was allowed to suffer, she certainly did think herself the only one. It was really too bad of Owen to drag her across the countryside like a piece of luggage. She moaned.

"Very well. We will stop at the next inn, although I believe it would be better to push on." A louder moan met his words. "All right, all right. I see how it is. Your head aches and you are tired. We will stop." He pounded on the roof and the guard bent down to open the trap. Owen passed on the new orders. "Really, Aunt, you've become more of a nuisance than my mother. Once, you were the happiest of creatures, the most fun of any of my relatives. I often wished you were my mother, but now I don't envy Dominic at all. You, with your aches and moans and groans and complaints, are quite as bad as Mother, although in a different way of course. I sympathized with your loss of a beloved spouse but most people grieve for a year or two and that is enough. You, young as you are, have made a vocation of it and frankly, Aunt, you've become a dead bore."

"Ohhhhh…" Violetta hadn't a notion how to reply to such plain speaking. She hated Owen. She hated his words. "Be still," she shrieked and then groaned as a sharp, stabbing pain thrust through her head. "I will not listen to such impertinence," she whispered shrilly, her head clutched between her hands. The trouble was, she had listened. What was worse, what he said made sense. She was harming no one but herself with her megrims. And *boring*? She'd never been boring in her life…

The coach hit a particularly bad rut and both Sir Owen and Lady Violetta groaned, for each really did have the most awful headache. Mutual suffering, however, did not put them into charity with each other and, as the next few days passed and they drew nearer and nearer to Brightwood, what little rapport they'd once had disappeared.

So did Violetta's briefly held resolve to put aside the role she'd taken up at her husband's death—that of the perpetual invalid.

* * * * *

"Now what?" asked Dominic, hearing a row in the hall. He excused himself to his great-aunts and Tavie and moved toward the salon door.

It swept open and, draperies fluttering around her, an elegant turban framing her face, his mother flung herself into his arms.

Tavie wondered who the still attractive, middle-aged lady might be, but only for an instant.

"Oh, my dear, *dear* boy. How horrible for you. What a drastic sacrifice. Oh, my child, you should have come to me. I would have saved you—"

Violetta's words filled Tavie with horror and the sick feeling only grew worse.

"I would not have let that terrible family trick you into a disastrous marriage. Oh, my dear son! How I have failed you."

"Mother!" said Dom, a Thornton scowl indicating his anger. "You are making a fine cake of yourself. Behave!"

The dainty figure clutching his arms blinked. "How dare you!" She shook him, although it had no visible effect. "I suffer the company of your abominable cousin and the rigors of travel all the way north to this outlandish place, and why? For no reason but to come to your side in your hour of need! You dare suggest I make a cake of myself? Oh, you ungrateful wretch."

"Mother, I am very much in love with my wife. You will welcome her as she deserves to be welcomed or you will leave."

Putting on the airs of a tragedy queen, Lady Brightwood, or, as her new style must be, the *Dowager* Lady Brightwood, collapsed onto a well-upholstered tête-à-tête—*after* of course ascertaining its whereabouts.

Dominic walked away. Vi opened one eye a trifle, saw her graceful swoon was not only ignored by her son, for whose benefit it had been staged, but that she was being studied by two pairs of old, but obviously interested, eyes and the blank gaze of a young woman whose well-controlled expression she could not read. Violetta sighed and gave it up. Straightening her skirts around her, she seated herself properly.

"Well," she said, "if I must be insulted under my own roof I suppose someone had better present me to the trollop."

Tavie gasped, her skin losing all color. Ally reached for her hand and patted it.

Dominic, who had nearly gotten himself under control, rounded on his heel and stalked back to his mother. "Speak of my wife in such words ever again and I will never again speak to you."

"Don't be foolish, Dominic. Of course you would put your mother before your wife." She half closed her eyes and assayed another insult. "Such a wife!"

Rightly setting Tavie's rigid spine and tense features to the growing tension between son and mother, Elf rose to her feet. She placed herself between Dom and his mother. Dom stared blindly through his great-aunt and it required her fingers on his face to bring her his attention. His rigidity softened slightly, although his fists were still curled into knots and his back stiff with outrage.

Quietly, Elf told him not to be a fool. "Don't you see she is dramatizing herself to be interesting? Ignore it, Dom, and take your wife away. Your mother is upsetting Tavie excessively. With you gone, Ally and I can deal with Violetta. Don't doubt it. Besides, I believe Vi intimated that Owen escorted her and you should see to his comfort. Traveling makes him ill. It was a true sacrifice, his escorting your mother here."

As Elf spoke, the stiffness gradually left Dom. His hands unclenched, his face cleared of temper and he reached for Elf and hugged her. "How would we go on without you?" He held out his hand. "Come, love."

"Yes," said Octavia in a high, choked voice, "I must consult with my housekeeper." Keeping her eyes locked on Dom's, her shoulders stiff, she walked, with none of her usual grace, to where he waited.

Dom led Tavie from the room and into the hall where he turned her into his arms, ignoring the servants who rapidly effaced themselves, except for Mrs. MacReady and Owen, who found himself quite embarrassed by this public display of affection.

"I am so sorry, Dom," said Tavie. "So very, very sorry."

Dom pushed Tavie a little away and looked into her face. "Now what sort of nonsense is running around that beautiful head of yours?" he asked.

"To be the cause of a quarrel between you and your mother is outside of enough. To cause a family to be torn apart, it is terrible. I am so sorry."

"I'll believe you a lovely widgeon if you go in that way. My mother and I have agreed on very little since my father died. She took it as a personal insult, you see, and has made life difficult for everyone around her ever since." A movement drew Dom's gaze across the hall. "Ah! There is my cousin. Owen, I know you must go to your room to rest, but will you meet my wife first?"

Putting his arm around her, Dom led Tavie across the hall to where Mrs. MacReady stood by the stairs.

Owen, already up a few steps, returned to their level. "I am," he said, "very happy to welcome you to the family, my lady. Later, when I feel more the thing, I wish to apologize to you and Dom for my mother's treatment of you."

As she noted the greenish pallor to Owen's skin and the dark circles under his eyes, Tavie's compassion was roused. "But not now, Sir Owen, you poor soul. You are in such obvious distress. The blue room, Mrs. MacReady?"

The housekeeper nodded.

"I will take Sir Owen up myself while you prepare one of your excellent tisanes, which will help." Tavie turned her attention to Owen. "Do come along, Sir Owen. Travel sickness is so wearing but we'll have you right as a trivet in no time. You'll see."

Tavie, very much herself again when she saw someone else suffering, put her arm through Owen's and, talking soothingly, led him up the stairs.

Dom smiled at Mrs. MacReady who smiled back. Slowly, they grinned at each other. Owen had had a decidedly bemused expression on his face. Octavia Thornton, *née* Seldon, the new Lady Brightwood, had made yet another conquest.

Dom had great faith she'd win over the whole of the *ton* in the same delightful manner—just by being very much herself.

Chapter Six

"Well!"

"Yes, Violetta, we believe Dominic chose very well. Now come down off the ropes and behave yourself just as your son suggested."

Vi ignored Elf's advice, suffering, as she was, from a strong sense of ill-usage. "Really Elf. How could that…that…scandal's daughter suggest she needed to talk to *her* housekeeper? Mrs. MacReady is *my* housekeeper and *has* been for decades."

"Oh no," said Ally. She shook her head, her expression solemn.

"No! What can you mean, Aunt Alvinia? You know…"

"What Ally means, Violetta," interrupted Elf, "is that Mrs. MacReady belongs to the Hall. She was Dominic's housekeeper before his marriage and therefore, now they are wed, she is Tavie's. You must not pretend, even to yourself, it is not so."

Violetta arranged herself in an attitude of tragedy, making excellent play with scarves and shawls. "I am to be thrown from my home! I am to be exiled from all security! I am to be left alone in my old age, haggard and ill, and forced—" She stopped, glaring at Elf. "How dare you laugh at me?"

"Tell me, my dear, when did you last visit the Hall?"

"It is the *principle* of the thing," responded Violetta with dignity. "How dare my son, with no notice to me, with no notice to anyone if I have the right of it, get himself married? And to *such* a one. A beanpole! Such vulgar hair! Red. I will never live it down. It is such a scandal."

"Only if you make it one."

Violetta blinked. "If *I* make it one? How can you say so? I have had nothing to do with it."

"And there's the rub, is it not? You presented to your son's notice one eligible, but boring, young lady after another and, quite rightly, he never gave one of them a second look. He has found his own wife and that you cannot forgive, is it not so?"

"I am not such a selfish beast! If I thought for one moment such a gangly girl—*girl*? Why, she is quite old. Quite definitely on the shelf. Most definitely not suitable to take *my* place—" Vi looked guilty at this show of jealousy. "Where was I? Oh yes, I am not selfish. If I thought she would do for my dearest Dominic, I wouldn't say a word." Vi dropped her self-righteous pose as she continued. "However, not only is she far and away outside what is thought beautiful, she is a Rambourne." Her voice dropped to a conspiratorial level. "Do you know she has never been seen in society and she is all of five-and-twenty? Explain to me, if you can, why a father would hide away his daughter from all contact with the *beau monde* if something was not seriously wrong with her."

"Because," said Elf impatiently, "her father is a fool. It had nothing to do with the girl at all."

Violetta thought about that. "But Sarah said…"

"Sarah too is a fool," interrupted Elf. "I begin to think the whole world is populated by fools. I didn't use to include you in that category, Vi, but these last few years you've given me cause to wonder. This idiotic posturing of yours has gone on all too long. I wouldn't mind if it were true grieving for Dom's father but you are simply feeling sorry for yourself."

"Not you too! Can no one understand my loss?"

"My dear," said Elf kindly, "we understand very well. But *five years*?"

Violetta sighed, her mouth drooping. "It is as if it were yesterday." A tear trembled on her lashes.

"I remember how much your husband loved life, Vi," said Elf, projecting an understanding Ally recognized as real but exaggerated. "Would *he* approve of the way you are going on?"

Slowly Violetta's eyes widened. She stared at Elf. "Oh dear." She rose, her gaze on something no one but herself could see. As if sleepwalking, she crossed the room and disappeared through the door.

Ally's mouth dropped open. "Whatever is the matter with Violetta?" She stared at the empty doorway.

"Is it possible," said Elf, nearly as surprised, "that I actually pierced that self-pity she has been indulging far too long? Losing Miles was a terrible shock but her reaction to it has become nothing more than habit. Perhaps when next we see her, she'll have improved." Elf thought about that and shook her head. "Or perhaps it will take a few more scolds. We should have taken her in hand long ago, Ally. We are much at fault to have let her go on like this for so long."

Ally agreed. "Do you think she'll accept Tavie?"

"Oh yes. Not at once of course. Her feelings were seriously hurt by Dom's negligence in not immediately informing her of his marriage. You will agree that, in that, he did not treat her well, thoughtless boy that he is. But she'll come around."

Ally bent nearer her sister and they put their heads together. "If that is the case, and with Morty complacent, surely we can—"

"Yes," interrupted Elphinia. "*If* we can make our puppets act properly, throwing away the tragic airs of a wronged mother and the *rodomontade* of an overly protective father. If only one could force one's actors to speak their lines. It is so difficult when one knows best, to see all thrown away by one's cast of characters and only because they refuse to speak as they ought."

About halfway through this speech, Violetta walked back into the room. "You are putting on a play?"

Elf jumped guiltily. "Vi, you startled me out of my wits."

"We can't put on a play now so you didn't make one bit of sense, Elf. Not a whit. What," asked Vi, "were you discussing?" Violetta looked suspiciously from one sister to the other. She crossed her arms and tapped her foot. "I want to know what you and Ally are about."

Elf sighed. She'd been caught and knew it. Offense, she recalled, was the best defense. "Do you truly wish your son's marriage surrounded by scandal and gossip?"

"No, of course I don't." Violetta obviously meant that sincerely.

"Then, my dear, you will behave as a lady and *not* be unfriendly to your daughter-in-law."

Violetta regressed. "That red-headed doxy!"

"She is a delightful young woman who will make Dominic just the wife he should have. She is not a *light-skirt*, as you very well know."

"But Sarah—"

"Sarah is a jealous old cat who would find ill in the behavior of a saint. That is, she would if the saint were associated with Dominic. You know she wishes to see her Owen in your son's shoes. It doesn't suit her book that Dom has married and will, in the course of things, produce an heir. Sarah is being her usual spiteful self."

Violetta's eyes widened. "I hadn't thought of that."

"No. You didn't, did you?" asked Elf on a note of triumph, conveniently forgetting to admit that she too had to have it pointed out to her.

* * * * *

Later that afternoon, Violetta drifted down the stairs, a shawl, its ends tied in knots, trailing from one hand and one or two diaphanous scarves floating around her in the breeze of her passage. She halted on the landing when she saw the hall was occupied. "Your grace! *You* are here?"

Rambourne raised his head, his craggy brows coming together. "Well, where else would I be?" he asked in a testy tone.

"Oh! I knew it!" Violetta raised one arm and pointed her finger at the duke. "You and your daughter tricked my boy into this scandal of a marriage. You planned it! You—"

The duke, very nearly as in love with dramatics as was Violetta, interrupted. "Nonsense," he shouted. "It was your son who ran off with my daughter. My precious jewel. My dearest delight. He stole her away from me with nary a word or a by-your-leave. The monster! My poor innocent kitten to be in the hands of that reprobate son of yours..."

"Foolishness! *My* son rescued *your* daughter from dire peril!"

Rambourne opened his mouth to retort but, since he was tiring of a scene not of his making and couldn't argue the truth of that point, he closed it and sighed. He stared up at Vi for a moment and found himself surprised at her ethereal loveliness. "That's the tale they've settled upon," he said more rationally. "I suppose it will be best if we agree to believe it."

Violetta, however, was not yet ready to give up the delightful pastime of giving vent to her emotions. "How dare you? If my son says it was so then it *was* so. He would not lie."

"If we must continue arguing, do you suppose you might come down here?" asked his grace, his tone irascible. "I'm getting a crick in my neck."

Violetta took a better look at the duke. He was much as she remembered him from when she'd set her cap at him during her first season—and lost him to another. His figure had thickened but only to the point of giving him a distinguished look. He still wore his clothes with an air, although, because he spent so little time in society these days, they were out of fashion. His sandy-colored hair was white at the temples but that too added to his attraction. He limped a bit and leaned on a cane. She wondered if he'd had an accident—then noticed the soft slipper on one foot and guessed, accurately, that he suffered from gout. The cane, she decided, topped as it was by an ornately carved ivory ball, enhanced the sense of hauteur rather than detracting from it.

Vi tripped down the last steps, draperies fluttering, and raised her hand.

Taking it, the duke bowed over it, the whisper of his breath touching her fingers. *Oh yes,* thought Violetta, her heart beating faster. *He is still one of the most attractive men I've ever met. Even though I loved my Miles to distraction I'd be a ninny if I were not aware of it.* But she allowed none of her thoughts expression in her face.

Rambourne held his arm ready. "Shall we," he asked, "see if there is a fire in the small salon, my lady?"

"That would be pleasant." Violetta batted her lashes at the duke. Looking away, she blinked, this time thoughtfully. *Am I flirting with his grace? But my life is over. I swore it when Miles died, did I not?*

Still, there was that bit Elf had said. Miles *would* scold her dreadfully for wasting her life upon her couch. She must think about that.

But not now. Not when Rambourne stared down at her in such a bemused way. What fun! Was it possible his grace might still be brought up to scratch? Twenty years later—well, thirty—oh, all right, she admitted, but only to herself, *thirty-five* years later.

Although why do I wonder about this when it isn't as if I would accept him if he did propose?

She'd never remarry. That went without saying. One could have only one such love in life, and to marry for less? Oh, it wasn't to be thought on…

Or was it?

* * * * *

Elsewhere, ice in her gaze, Lady Sarah Sands confronted Owen's butler. "I did not ask if it were *possible*. I ordered a carriage be ready for my departure early tomorrow morning."

"But, Lady Sands," said the butler, forgetting his dignity so far as to mop his brow. "Sir Owen demanded all his carriages be overhauled while he was away. Even that old coach his grandfather stopped using. They are dismantled to one degree or another and putting one back together by tomorrow is simply not—"

"You will cease making excuses and see that a carriage is available. That is all."

The butler removed himself to the hall where the housekeeper waited, a frown on her brow. "It is as we feared," he said. "She is not to be balked."

"Sir Owen will not be pleased."

"Sir Owen will understand I've done all I can to thwart the lady. And I don't mind telling you, I did not like the look in my lady's eye. It bodes ill for me."

"She cannot give you notice to leave. Only Sir Owen can do that. So what *can* she do?"

"If I knew, I could be on guard. Perhaps she will push me down the stairs as she did that tweeny who displeased her. Who knows what that one might do? Well, I've work to do and I'd guess you do too," the butler finished on an austere note which attempted to hide his unease.

Sarah, listening at the door, smiled a malicious smile. So her son *had* told the servants she was not to leave the estate? She'd thought as much when her every request for a carriage was denied. She'd have a few words to say to Owen when next she saw him. He must learn his mother was not to be treated with such disrespect. After all, one day she would the Marchioness of Brightwood.

Sarah had long ago dismissed from her mind the fact that she would *not* acquire the title if her son were to inherit. Whatever the conventions, she would, de facto, adopt it. She might never be marquis as she *should* have been, but she could and would be marchioness.

And that butler? How right he was. Someday she'd be revenged on him, but not now. That could wait. Years if necessary. She would have revenge for all the petty slights and more serious insults she'd received over the years. If only she'd been born, as she should have been, a man. Then there would be no problem, no insults, no need for revenge.

But revenge of every sort could wait. She had more important plans, ones that must be put into effect immediately.

Now where was that sinful Mary? Her maid had her work cut out for her if they were to leave in the morning.

* * * * *

Tavie stared out the dark window at nothing in particular. Dom, Bert and Geoff had gone off earlier that evening, leaving her with the parents and the great-aunts. She had escaped as soon as she could and come here to their private sitting room. Now, while munching an apple in quite hoydenish fashion, she stewed in a very un-Tavie-like manner.

The date for the arrival of the first of their guests was approaching and the nearer it came the more nervous she grew. Not that anyone guessed. Self-control had been bred into her and what she'd inherited from nature had been perfected by her beloved governess. Not even Dom guessed how worried she was.

True, her mother-in-law seemed to have accepted her graciously—after that first soul-destroying meeting. Tavie tipped her head. Rather humorous really, if one could be objective. What an actress. The great Mrs. Siddons, who was the same age as Violetta, would take second place to such incredible competition, or would if it were not ineligible for a *tonnish* matron to take to the boards. Ah, but what a loss to the theater it was! Tavie chuckled at the notion.

She shook the thought away and went onto another. *Dom.* How she worried about him. He was happy. Now. That was unquestioned. But when he discovered what the *ton* thought of her? When he came to understand how far to the fringes of society she stood despite her birth, or perhaps because of it? Scandal's daughter Dom's mother had named her… But why should a divorce, decades-old, still be of such interest? It was confusing indeed.

Could Dom continue to love her if his world refused to accept her?

Tavie chided herself for sounding like a whining little martyr. It would never do to succumb to self-pity, but how hard it was to retain her usual optimism when her whole life was in the balance.

Dear Elf believed their plan the right one. She had the family's best interests at heart. But were those Tavie's interests? What if Elf failed in her effort to promote Tavie as a perfectly normal and acceptable member of the *ton*? Especially since she was not.

Not, thought Tavie, her ire rising, *that I am a harlot!*

That was the detested Sarah's suggestion, as reported by Violetta. Dom had raged until Bert and Geoff had teased him out of it, showing him the funny side. Why could *she* not see the humor?

Elf did.

And Elf believed the house party would show the bride to the *ton* in the best light, introducing her in an informal country setting rather than the stultifying formality of the autumn's little season. But perhaps Elf was wrong. Perhaps it would be better to be lost in a London crowd? Elf insisted not, that the rigid rules governing society would allow no one a chance to know her as an individual and the rumors would persist. Especially with the despicable Sarah fanning the flames.

Thoughts of Sarah brought Owen to mind. Poor Owen. He wanted badly to apologize and Dom simply refused to allow it, telling him he was not responsible for his mother's venom. It wasn't kind of Dom and she must remember to point out that Owen would feel much better if only she and Dom let him get it off his chest.

Tavie heard Dom coming and smiled.

"That's how I like to see you, love," came the deep, caressing voice of her husband. "Smiling and relaxed and enjoying the good things the world offers," he said, unaware of her real feelings. "May I have a bite?"

Tavie looked down at the apple she forgot she held. She swung on around to show him more than her profile, her smile deepening. "I did not expect you until much later, my love. Was the cockfight not worth the bother?"

"I don't know how it is but any occupation which I cannot share with you has become a dead bore. Can *you* explain it?"

He strolled on into the room, removing his coat and cravat and tossing them onto a convenient chair. He unbuttoned the sleeves to his shirt and pulled at the ties holding together the front, revealing a deep vee of hair-roughened chest.

Tavie giggled. "You have a rather limited view of what occupations we may share, do you not?"

His eyes narrowed in amusement. "I do not believe you'd have enjoyed the cockfight, my dear."

She laughed outright and put her hand in his. He tugged her into his embrace, taking the half-eaten apple with his other hand and tossing it out the open window. Their gazes locked for a long moment. Then, slowly, he molded her closer, leaning slightly as she rose on tiptoe—and their mouths met. The kiss was long and sweet and, when it broke, Tavie laid her head onto his shoulder, reveling in the feel of him.

"We have never talked about children, Dom."

"*Our* children," he said with quiet satisfaction. Suddenly he pushed her away and stared down at her, consternation plain in his face. "Tavie, are you telling me—"

"No," she interrupted him, laughter in her voice. "No. I just wondered how you felt about them," she clarified. "I don't want my children raised as I was, Dom."

"None of that half-an-hour-at-teatime. Not for us, my love. We will watch over them and play with them and love them. Will that do?"

She nodded. "It isn't," she said, explaining what she feared was a misconception on his part, "that my father didn't love me or pay attention to me, Dom. He did. But he didn't *trust* me."

"We'll trust ours. How many should we have?"

"That's another thing. I want lots of children, Dom. I don't want them lonely." She didn't add *as I was*.

Dom nodded. "I have a much younger sister, so I was raised alone. She is increasing again and cannot come, so you'll meet her another time. As for our children…lots of children sounds just right." He frowned suddenly and pushed her to arm's length, his eyes running down her form. "That is," he added, a worried note creeping into his voice, "as long as having children doesn't harm *you*." He clutched her close, his heart pounding against her cheek. "Tavie, I could not bear it if I lost you. I'd rather do without any children at all than lose you in childbed."

"Shush. It isn't the thing to admit this, Dom, but I learned about childbirth by helping a woman in distress. She had been a decent woman but was seduced by some wastrel and thrown aside when she became pregnant. Miss Latimer and I found her in extremis in a spinney when we were out riding. It was too late to go for help and we did what we could for her. Dom, it was terrible. She died and the baby lived only a few days. It frightened me."

"I should think so. How old were you?"

"Only thirteen."

"How distressing." He studied her serene features, confused. "You do not seem particularly worried now."

Tavie chuckled. "My governess was enlightened. She took me to the woman who did most of the midwifery in our area. The midwife talked to me, explaining why that woman died. Starvation and lack of will to live, mostly, and then she looked me over to see if she thought I'd have difficulty." Tavie grinned widely and posed, turning her hips from side-to-side. Her face flushed with embarrassment but her eyes were twinkling at what she was about to say. "Dom, that old witch just snorted and told me I was built like a cow and would have no difficulty at all."

Dom frowned, ignoring her laughter. "But did she *know*? The devil. I wish you had not made me think of this. Now I'm worried."

"If it means you will not make love to me anymore, I'll wish I'd not broached the subject. I was curious how you felt about children because, if you were the sort who banished them to the nursery with nannies, never to be seen or heard, except for that half hour at teatime when there was no company, then we'd have had to have a few words on the subject," scolded Tavie, trying to tease him out of his suddenly somber mood.

Dom studied her for a long moment before he set his mouth to hers. He made love to her that night with more tenderness than ever before.

When he cuddled her close and drifted into sleep, Tavie hoped that she was *enceinte* with their first child. *Never would a child have been conceived with such love,* she thought and slid into sleep herself with a smile on her lips.

* * * * *

Another day passed in peace, except for one thing. Tavie caught bits and pieces of conversation between the men, words that set off flashes of worry in her mind. Late that evening, Dom didn't come to bed when expected, so Tavie redressed herself and returned to the main floor.

She consulted with Deblon who was on duty in the hall then sent him to bed. "You'll have long days during the house party and should not be waiting up on selfish beasts who haven't the consideration of most infants."

"My lady, you know that is not true."

Tavie felt her cheeks warm at the mild scold. "Perhaps not, but you are not needed. Go to bed, Deblon. That's an order."

Deblon, knowing she was correct about the tiring days to come, stifled his conscience and went. Tavie, after a raid on the kitchen, joined the men in the library.

Horror grew as she listened to the excitement with which they discussed plans. She looked from Bert to Dom, to Geoff and back to Bert and tried to interrupt. "But—"

"We'll need packs. *Packs,*" Bert repeated when Dom did not immediately add it to his list. "Don't forget the time we left the packs at home and had to make it only a day's climb."

"And food. Lots of food," said Geoff, reaching for the last of the bread and ham Tavie had brought as an excuse to join them.

"Leave it to you to remember food," teased Dom.

"But—" said Tavie, looking from Dom to Bert, to Geoff and back to Dom. Again she was interrupted before she could voice her thought.

"The weather is perfect," enthused Bert, his exuberance uncontainable.

"Yes." Dom spoke solemnly. "I talked to old Minton. It will hold for the rest of the week. He is almost never wrong."

The other two nodded just as solemnly. The ancient shepherd had a reputation.

"But—" Tavie looked from Geoff to Bert, to Dom and back to Geoff.

"We'll only need two good days," added Bert, interrupting Tavie still again.

"Yes. Two days. Then we must be back for the party." Dom sighed at the thought.

"But—" Tavie spoke loudly, and this time she jerked at Dom's sleeve.

"Tavie, why are you clutching me like that?" asked her husband, removing her fingers and checking if she'd left a crease. "My valet will have a fit."

"No one will let me get a word in edgewise. Is it truly your intention to climb Helvellyn?"

Dom looked bewildered. "Isn't that what we are discussing?"

"I guess it is," she said in a rather small voice.

"Tavie, we climb something every summer. It is a custom we have," said Geoff kindly. "So what is the problem? Don't you want Dom away from home right now? We thought it a good time since you've so much work preparing for everyone's arrival and we won't be interfering with it, you see."

She knew it would be rude to answer his question honestly and debated the wisdom of asking the question worrying her half to death. Then she blurted it out in spite of herself. "But isn't it dangerous?"

"Of course not," scoffed Dom. "We've done it any number of times."

"Dom, don't lie to her. Of course climbing can be dangerous, but not terribly so, if one is trained and not foolish," soothed Geoff. "We are experienced, having climbed from an early age and Helvellyn isn't a particularly difficult climb. Also, we aren't stupid so we always take an even more experienced guide."

"Not a guide."

"Of course he is a guide."

"Well, that too, but Taggert, he's a friend," insisted Dom.

"Yes, Taggert's an old friend," repeated Geoff and added smoothly, "He taught us all we know about climbing and he acts as guide to others."

"But Helvellyn…"

"Just because it is the third highest mountain in England doesn't make it more difficult, Tavie," Bert explained in another attempt to soothe her obvious agitation.

"Third highest?" Tavie gulped. "Oh dear."

"Now see what you've done, you thick-wit. She didn't *know*," Geoff groused at Bert.

Tavie shuddered. "I've heard such stories. Falls and fogs…"

Dom pulled her close, suddenly understanding that she was frightened. "Do you want me to stay home?"

She swallowed. It was exactly what she wanted but could not admit.

"I've an idea," said Bert before her silence became obvious.

"Idea? You?" hooted his friends, taking advantage of tension-reducing laughter.

"Yes. *Me*. I get them every once in a while. Just because I don't go spouting off about them the way Geoff does, does not mean I never have any."

Everyone chuckled at his pretend outrage and soon, unable to keep up his stern expression, Bert laughed as well.

"What is this great notion?" asked Tavie, turning so that she leaned comfortably against Dom's chest, his arms around her.

"Why not take Tavie too?"

"Take Tavie? Up Helvellyn?" Dom's and Geoff's words mixed.

Dom, his voice rough, added, "Don't be ridiculous."

Bert's cheeks reddened. "Well then, not Helvellyn. Of course it is too difficult for a novice. But we could choose something easy and begin teaching her the way of it and then she won't be so upset when we go on to harder climbs."

"You know, Dom, amazing as it is, I think Bert actually has an idea there. What do you think, Tavie?" asked Geoff. They all turned to stare at her.

Tavie looked from one to the next and back again. "Me? Climb?" She shook her head. Her voice squeaked. "A *mountain*?" She shook her head even harder.

"Why not?" asked Bert. "We've a hundred from which to pick."

"We'd choose a simple day climb," said Geoff. Bert nodded agreement while Dom scowled at the notion.

Noticing his friend's expression, Geoff soothingly added, "And we'll take Taggert along because he's a better teacher than any of us."

"There are a hundred mountains?" asked Tavie, attempting to distract the three men from the insane notion she might actually agree to climb a mountain.

"Over a hundred mountains actually," said Geoff. "So far we've climbed sixty-two. It is our goal to climb them all. We'd pick a new one for this climb, except we are short of time and new ones take more planning. Besides, we've climbed all the near ones."

Tavie couldn't speak for shock. They wished to climb them *all*?

"We could start her on fell-walking," suggested Bert. "That way you'd see results faster," he explained to Tavie.

Tavie drew in a deep breath. They took it so much for granted. If only she didn't have this knot inside whenever she thought of Dom going into danger—and *such* danger!

Tavie had discovered at a young age she was uncomfortable looking out her bedroom window, never mind over the battlements of the oldest part of her father's castle. Even thinking about it made her feel nauseous. *No.* The heights involved in mountain climbing weren't to be thought of at all. Not for her.

Slowly she shook her head. "Thank you for thinking of me. But there is the house party and the ball and all those things one cannot do until the very last minute." She swallowed and said what she knew must be said. "You just go along and enjoy yourselves. I'll be too busy here to even notice you are away, let alone worry about you."

"Truly, Tavie," said Dom, his arms tightening around her, "there is no reason to worry. Taggert knows every crook and cranny of these hills."

Not eased, exactly, but hoping to hide that she was still upset, Tavie smiled and moved away. "I'll just go on up to bed now and let you get on with your planning." She sent a flirting look over her shoulder at her husband. "I only came down because I was lonely."

Dom grinned at her. "You came down," he accused, "because curiosity killed the cat." He approached her as he spoke. "Now you know we are not carousing or gambling and haven't sneaked in a village wench—"

Tavie reached to lightly box his ears. "I'll return to bed before this conversation deteriorates beyond what is proper for my innocent ears."

"I'll be up in a moment," Dom responded, following her out into the hall and closing the door. He kissed her warmly. "Oh yes, love," he whispered in her ear, the heat of his breath doing delightful things to her insides. "I'll be up in no time at all if you'll just give me another like that one."

Instead of the requested kiss, Tavie gave him an impish, very suggestive look and, after a moment, he blushed, the flood of blood in his cheeks evident even in the dim light of the few candles still burning in wall sconces. Tavie chuckled, proud of herself for having, for once, caught him in an unintended, but exceedingly salacious, double meaning. *Up* indeed! She'd come a long way from the slightly frightened and exceedingly naïve woman he met along the roadside.

Repressing her satisfaction, Tavie kissed Dom lightly and extricated herself from his arms. "I'll be waiting for you to be *up*," she said, swishing away from the swat he halfheartedly aimed at a particularly appropriate part of her anatomy.

Tavie waited by the window in their sitting room. She stared across the dark lawns that rolled down to Thirlmere, the water a silvery gleam in the starlight. To the east lay Helvellyn, near enough one could see it on a clear day. Tavie shuddered. She didn't want Dom climbing mountains. She knew she'd worry every instant he was gone from her. But was she the sort of woman who would tie her man to her apron strings? Was she to disallow him the freedom to *be* the man with whom she'd fallen in love? How terrible that would be.

He *was* a man. And he was *not* foolish. And he was set on besting Helvellyn, something he'd proven he could do. She had to let him go and she must not let him know how she feared for him. Unconsciously, her back straightened and her head came up. The answer to her problem had already been voiced. She too must learn to climb.

She would learn to enjoy it too—even if it killed her.

Hmm, she thought, *perhaps that was not the most felicitous of phrasing.*

Moreover, thank heaven, it was a plan she could not immediately put into effect since the party preparations required her presence—but just wait. Her shoulders squared to stubborn straightness and she continued planning with self-induced bravado.

Tavie had not managed to convince herself that she too would be going to London in the autumn as Elf insisted was the case.

So.

When Dom took himself off for the autumn season, she would have a talk with the guide, Taggert. She would explain her fears to him, swear him to secrecy and, with Dom gone, the guide could begin schooling her. But even the thought of actually doing it had Tavie swallowing. Hard.

Luckily, just then, she heard steps in the hall so, as the door opened, she put aside all thought of her ever climbing anything higher than a footstool and turned with a smile on her face. She'd not willingly allow Dom to learn of the fear his hobby induced in her.

* * * * *

Two days later, very early in the morning, Tavie stood, straight-backed, on the front steps until the climbers, followed by a couple of footmen burdened with their supplies, disappeared beyond the trees by the lake. When they were out of sight, she hurried to her sitting room. Dom had indicated where, along the tree-lined shore, was an unseen dock and boats. He, Bert and Geoff would cross the lake to where Taggert and his ponies would meet them. If she watched from her window, she could track them a bit farther. The day was slightly overcast and the air hazy and she was unable to see Helvellyn, even through the telescope Dom had set up in the window. Her last sight of the trio would be while they were on the water.

After an interminable interval, the boat appeared. It rode deep in the water, laden with three grown men and their supplies. Tavie kept her eyes glued to the slowly moving dory, a new worry in her mind. Was it overladen? Would it overturn? Sink? She ignored the knock at her door, didn't allow it to break her concentration.

Then the door opened. One could hardly ignore intruders who rudely entered even when not invited to do so. She straightened from behind the telescope when Violetta's voice shrilled behind her.

"How dare you allow my son to go into such danger?"

"Danger? They assured me there was none," lied Tavie, forcing her features into a mask of innocence before turning to face her mother-in-law.

"You are not stupid. You know better." Vi flounced on into the room, her draperies whipping around her. "But you don't care. You don't deserve a man like my son. You don't—"

"Lady Brightwood…" Tavie corrected herself, stumbling over the name she'd been urged to use. "*Vi*! None of that is true." Tavie had quickly learned it was best to interrupt such tirades before her mother-in-law got well into her stride.

The older woman had the grace to look a trifle chagrined. "I am so upset I do not know what I am saying. But you should not have allowed it," she added, contradicting her implied apology.

"How could *I* forbid it if *you*, his *mother*, were unable to do so when he was much younger and still subject to parental discipline?"

Violetta dropped onto the chaise lounge, shawls dripping around her drooping figure. She pulled one, then another closer and shivered. "His father was proud of Dom's climbing. I could convince neither they should leave such stuff to men like Taggert but they told me I was ridiculous and went climbing every chance they got. And every time word came of lost climbers or hikers, off they'd go with the rescue teams. Peers of the realm! What business was it of theirs that some fool lost his way or hurt himself?"

"I cannot believe you mean that, Vi."

"Why can I not? I do mean it." Vi's mouth formed a stubborn line.

"But those who are lost are human beings. One cannot leave them to die."

"I didn't say no one should help them," responded Violetta, a spurious patience in her tone. "Men like Taggert…"

Tavie had met Taggert the day before as plans were finalized. "I would say Taggert was more valuable than many men I've met." Her mother-in-law gave her *such* a look and Tavie's eyes flashed. "Do not read evil where there is none. I love Dom more than I am able to say. I will not be looking for another man when I have the only one who could ever make me happy."

"The only one!" Violetta, upset by her son's departure and ready to strike out at someone, anyone, pounced on the phrase. "You mean of course the only one you'd *ever* met. Period. End of statement. And then to trick him into marriage! Even a Rambourne should have had more honor… Why are you looking like that? Now sit down, Tavie. I didn't mean to make you angry but no one seems to understand how hard it is for me." Violetta sniffed. "No one cares. It has been that way ever since my dearest Miles died. Why did he die? Oh, it isn't fair…" Violetta rose unsteadily to her feet and moved toward the door.

There she turned to stare at her daughter-in-law. "You'll find out. You'll wish you'd kept him safe where you would know what he did. When he is dead then you'll understand why I cannot quite find the energy to live again." She moved into the hall, followed by a shawl dragging from one hand. "You'll see. Oh, my poor son. Why did he have to be so impulsive? Why did he have to *marry* her? Why… Oh, Rambourne." There was a moment's silence before, in a totally different tone, Violetta asked, "Are you going to stroll in the gardens? May I join you?"

Tavie, wondering at the slightly breathless note in her mother-in-law's voice, unclenched her fists and returned to the window. The boat, she discovered, was out of sight in the mist whispering and whirling over the water. Quietly, Tavie used a few of the words at which Dom laughed but, at the same time, warned her they must never be used in polite circles. Venting her spleen verbally didn't help. Nor did the tears that followed.

Tavie spent much of an hour with her eyes covered with a cologne-soaked handkerchief to reduce the swelling and redness. With any luck, no one would notice how she'd weakly indulged her emotions.

In actual fact, no one did. They were fully occupied with the newest arrival—except for those doing their best to avoid the lady. Lady Sarah Sands, having traveled long hours each day, arrived shortly before teatime and made certain no one was unaware of her feelings on the subject of her nephew's marriage and her animosity toward the bride.

Chapter Seven

ஐ

After raging about Dom and Tavie, Lady Sands recalled a more recent insult and turned on her son. "How dare you forbid me the use of a carriage?" demanded Sarah. "How dare you?" She beat at his chest and Owen grasped her wrists. He winced, embarrassed by his mother. She'd already said far too much about Tavie and his cousin and Owen wished he could think of some way to make her be still.

Not only Owen was embarrassed. Rambourne had disappeared at Sarah's first words, pretending he'd not heard the insult to his daughter. Vi, overhearing her raving from a position at the top of the stairs, changed her mind about joining Rambourne for their usual stroll by the lake and retreated to her room.

Deblon and Mrs. MacReady pressed their lips tightly closed to restrain their desire to defend their new mistress against this shrew. They too found they had business elsewhere. And of course every other servant in the house kept as far from the hall as possible.

Sarah's nasty words made kindhearted Ally's eyes fill with tears and Elf suggested her sister go up to her room. Then she herself approached Owen and Tavie. Elf placed her arm around the latter's waist, giving her a hug and silent support. Sarah would run down eventually, a thought Elf voiced in an undertone to Tavie, who, though suffering from the insults, agreed.

"I believe you've said that already," scolded Elf a bit later. "You are repeating yourself and that is enough. More than enough."

"*Enough*?" Sarah raised her fists and shook them. "I haven't begun to tell the world of the iniquities I've been made to suffer."

And she hadn't. Words spewed from her, her voice rising to near hysteria and falling to such a soft pitch it was difficult to distinguish individual words. She paced. She beat at the walls. She threw the tantrum to end all tantrums.

Then, suddenly, she stopped, saying she was tired and hungry and calmly asked why no one had shown her to her room.

An exhausted Owen went to bed that night, once again wondering if his life would not be better if his mother were put into restraints. He slept badly, tossing and turning, and woke not much more rested than when he'd laid himself down to sleep.

* * * * *

The morning after Sarah's tantrum, the day Dom was due to return from Helvellyn, Tavie woke very early and requested her breakfast be served in her room. Every time she thought of Sarah's hatred for nearly everyone, even her own son on one occasion, Tavie felt her insides quiver. It was difficult to believe one could feel that much bitter emotion and retain one's sanity.

Tavie stared toward the invisible, mist-hidden mountain and fretted, not only about her newest guest but even more about Dominic's safety. The day matched her mood, gray with a light drizzle falling, despite the shepherd's prediction of good weather. Everything had a dreamlike, silvery cast, a world in which nothing moved.

Except something did move.

Idly toying with a slice of cold toast, Tavie wondered who had taken out the dogcart in such miserable weather. The pony, trotting around the curve from the carriage house, neared the turn where the service drive joined the one to the gates. Tavie rose and swung the telescope around but had trouble refocusing to the nearer view. By the time she could see clearly, the stiff-backed, dumpy figure handling the reins was turned away. There was, Tavie noted, something lying in the rear-facing seat.

Tools? She decided one of the estate's carpenters must have left them there.

But why, wondered Tavie, *is Lady Sands bowling along like that in weather fit only for ducks?*

It *was* Lady Sands, was it not? How could she be sure? The drizzle obscuring her vision, Tavie followed the little utility carriage until it disappeared into the overgrown shrubbery. Dom had told her the rhododendrons bloomed each year, forming piles of red and white, and because of the annual show, were tolerated the rest of the year. But just now Tavie wished them to the devil. Their existence interfered before she'd managed, for a certainty, to identify the driver.

A knock at the door caught her attention and Tavie told whomever it was to come in. Elf entered, closed the door quietly. "My dear child, you cannot possibly see Helvellyn in this weather."

Tavie ignored that. "After she calmed down, did Lady Sands not say it was imperative she not be disturbed this morning? That she needed rest?"

"Calmed down? Is that how you describe it? But, yes, she wished to be undisturbed. Why?"

"Because," Tavie spoke slowly, "I would swear she just disappeared down the drive in a dogcart."

"Nonsense," said Elf.

Tavie turned and met Elf's eyes, her own steady.

Elf frowned. "Surely you are mistaken. She was, as you know, worn to a thread by her, er, *exertions*."

Tavie's eyes laughed at Elf's euphemism.

"She brought it on herself of course," chuckled the elderly woman. "Tavie, it could not have been Sarah. Last night I gave her a dose of laudanum that would keep her quiet for hours yet. You must have seen one of the maids."

Tavie was not convinced but invited Elf to join her for some breakfast. Elf took the chair across the table from Tavie. Though Dom was gone, two cups sat on the tray in the usual way. Tavie filled the second before refilling her own. Elf thought the new bride looked pensive.

"Dear Tavie, you mustn't take to heart the ravings of one I begin to suspect a lunatic."

"I know, Elf, dear. You did warn me how she'd be but the reality was far worse than I expected."

"Worse than any of us expected. I never liked her mother. She wasn't Dom's grandmother but our brother's first wife. He met Sarah's mother when he was seventeen and filled to the brim with the family heritage that each heir married his one true love. He mistook infatuation for that love. Knowing the family would not accept her in the normal way, he eloped with her. Luckily Sarah's mother died of pneumonia soon after Sarah's birth because, by then, our brother had met Dom's grandmother, who *was* his true love, and, once his mourning ended, they were free to marry. She was Miles' mother and Dom's grandmother. Our second sister-n-law," she added, attempting to clarify the relationships.

Tavie digested the information. "What do you know of Sarah's mother and her mother's family?"

"What family?" Elf spoke derisively but sobered instantly. "I shouldn't speak of her that way. I detest snobs. But she was a nobody, a shopkeeper's chit or some such. I remember her as one of those who are briefly attractive but lose their looks very quickly. She was an intense young woman with moods, which often became tiresome. Poor tabby. She was so out of place and tried so hard to adapt." Elf sighed. "I am not usually intolerant, Tavie, but there was something about her I could not quite like. The poor woman had the whole world against her, except for our brother who tried to stay loyal to her. Even he failed her in the end. He met Dom's grandmother when Sarah's mother was enceinte. He couldn't have his true love but he could no longer tolerate his wife." Elf shook her head at remembered misery. "Very sad. So very, very sad."

Tavie tried to convince herself the woman she'd seen in the dogcart was not Sarah but couldn't quite succeed. As soon as she was alone again, she'd go to the north wing and see if her newest houseguest had all she required. That would be appropriate behavior on the part of a hostess. No one could suspect it was an excuse to see if Sarah still slept as Elf believed.

Tavie listened to Elf with half an ear. She couldn't get it out of her head Sarah was off making mischief, but what it could be she didn't know. Still, she couldn't rid herself of the prickly feeling that something was wrong.

Before her plan to spy on her husband's aunt could be put into effect, a maid knocked on her door and, given permission, sidled into the room. Blushing, her hands wrapped into her starched apron, she said, "M'lidy," and stared respectfully toward Elf, "and m'lidy—" she bobbed a quick curtsy toward her mistress, "do please come. Bessie, er, Cook's helper, that is, upset a pan of hot oil all down her, m'lidy, and she's screaming the chimneys down, so maybe you could help please? Mrs. MacReady said to ask."

Tavie preceded Elf down into the kitchens but with far less of a lead than might have been expected, given Elf's age. They were occupied for some time, doing what they could for the burns, giving the patient laudanum and, once the poor woman was quiet, calming the other servants.

"I apologize for my staff," said Mrs. MacReady when the three women seated themselves in the housekeeper's cozy sitting room in order to indulge in a soothing pot of tea. "Bessie can be awkward but this is the first time she's caused a disaster. She's Cook's cousin, you see, and he's very attached to her and insists on having her as his assistant. He calls her his good luck charm." The housekeeper shook her head. "I admit I'm worried about how this will affect the meals for the guests."

Tavie met Elf's eyes and sighed. Elf, reading Tavie's mind, chuckled. Tavie, knowing her duty, set down the cup of tea she'd barely sipped. With one last half-despairing, half-humorous exchange of looks with Elf, Tavie returned to the kitchen.

Twenty minutes of tact, praise and something very close to bribery assured Cook he was a great chef, one who could overcome the difficulties of working without his prized assistant. In the end, he vowed, he would exhibit his expertise and, although the world might never know, *he'd* know how much her ladyship admired him for accomplishing all under such adverse conditions.

Tavie had just related the tale and still not finished a single cup of tea when the doctor was announced. She accompanied him to where the sufferer lay, heavily dosed with laudanum against the pain.

"Well, now, Lady Brightwood," said the doctor, polishing his glasses. "Well, I don't know what one can do more than you've done. Not a thing more. Dressings of unsalted butter are best, I think, but must be changed often of course. I'm a demon, a real demon, I say, for clean dressings—and clean hands doing the work. Don't understand why it is, my lady, but when a nurse is clean and neat I find the patient far less likely to take infection. Far less likely. I'll just come along each day and check, but you understand she'll need a lot of nursing. A lot of nursing. You have someone with gentle hands you can release from their own work to look after Bessie?"

"Can *you* recommend someone?"

The doctor blinked, disbelieving his ears. "Are you meaning to hire a *nurse*? For a *servant*?" he asked cautiously.

"That servant is as much in need as you or I might be, Dr. Hayhoe," said Tavie, impatient with the man. "She deserves the best care we can provide."

"I like you," said the doctor with sudden intensity. His eyes gleamed behind the round lenses of his glasses while a flush reddened his plump cheeks. "Yes, I really like you. I'll just send along my best nurse, will that do? My very best." The doctor pushed his glasses up his nose and repacked his bag. "I'll just be giving Nurse my instructions. She'll be here, be here, I say, before our little patient needs anything. But you might assign someone to sit with her until Miss Rivers arrives."

The doctor shook his head as he left. The burns were bad. Whether she'd ever again be good for hard work was a question he wouldn't attempt to answer. And now that he'd met her, he almost believed the mistress of Brightwood Hall would find such a question impertinent and irrelevant. 'Pon rep, he liked the new marchioness. He'd just tell those gabsters passing on all that silly gossip a thing or two.

Gossip was such a dangerous thing, thought Dr. Hayhoe sadly. He brightened. He could now give firsthand information contradicting what he'd heard. It was probably one reason he was called out so often, this ability to pass along the latest news with accuracy. No gossip for him, he thought proudly.

Well now, just who was he to see next, he wondered, as he climbed into his mud-spattered gig and set his old horse to trotting down the lane. He nodded to the dumpy, little woman whose cart he met and wondered why she scowled so. He put it from his mind and continued on to the Miss Bramsets, who were suffering a bit of colic. What, with the brambleberries not quite ripe but the ladies indulging themselves anyway. They'd be very interested that he'd met the new marchioness! Oh yes. Very interested. So would old Mrs. Evershed, who was suffering her palpitations once again. She'd like hearing what he had to say. Oh yes.

Dr. Hayhoe expected to enjoy his day very much indeed.

* * * * *

Thanks to the problem with Bessie, Tavie forgot her suspicions of Sarah. And, as the day passed with no sign of the climbers, Tavie wandered around Brightwood like a lost chick. Every time she reached a window overlooking the lake, she would stare toward Helvellyn where, presumably, the four men were enjoying themselves so hugely they'd forgotten they were expected home. Every time that thought crossed her mind, Tavie gnashed her teeth and said a few forbidden words.

Actually she didn't become overly concerned until afternoon tea was served—and cleared away—without their reappearance. When the men didn't come in the next hour, she became distracted and harder to pin down on the multitude of details about which Mrs. MacReady wished to consult her.

"Oh, go ask Lady Elphinia," Tavie exclaimed, uncaring of anything but what Dom was doing and where he was and why he wasn't safely home where she could scold and berate him for worrying her so.

Tavie ignored Mrs. MacReady's startled expression as she turned on her heel and headed for the nearest window. Then, realizing how rude she'd been, she said, "I apologize, Mrs. MacReady, but I cannot think about silly things like what flowers are needed in the upstairs hall when Dom is out there somewhere, doing heaven knows what..."

The housekeeper shook her head, a fond smile creasing her usually sober face. Dear Lady Tavie, as the staff had taken to calling her amongst themselves, she'd soon discover that Master Dom, the name the older servants still used for his lordship, was like a cat and always lit on his feet. But it made a body feel good to see the bride worrying about her husband. In far too many *tonnish* marriages, the one spouse didn't care a fig what happened to the other. Yes, she'd just go ask Lady Elf about the flowers and which rooms were needed for tomorrow's arrivals.

It was no help to Tavie that, every time their paths crossed, Violetta looked at her with reproach in her eyes, an undeserved censure, which pinched at Tavie's temper. Vi had, after all, admitted she'd no notion how Tavie might have stopped the expedition.

At least Vi expressed her irrational thoughts silently. Sarah Sands wouldn't hold her tongue. "They'll have run into fog," she said smugly, her fingers deftly stitching seams in one of the cheap cotton shifts she made for charity. No useless but ladylike embroidery for Sarah. "It is always foggy on the fells just when you wish it to be clear. I don't think you need worry" she said, suppressed excitement obvious. "They'll hole up somewhere of course. It'll be cold and damp and uncomfortable, I suppose. Chill them to the bone probably but *that* won't kill a healthy young man, will it?"

The last was said in a tone that didn't quite hide a wistful note. When Sarah added more doom-saying, her reasoning came close to making Tavie lose a temper already exacerbated by her own active imagination.

Luckily Owen was nearby and heard his mother's ill-omened words. "That is enough. If you can play no part but that of Cassandra then I suggest you be still."

"Who, pray, is Cassandra? I know no one of that name," vowed Sarah, a bored expression belied by a sharp look in her eye as she wondered what woman her son knew that she didn't. An almost acceptable alternative—given Owen's total lack of interest in the female sex—crossed her mind. "You haven't finally lost interest in your books and taken up with the muslin company, have you?"

"*Mother*." Owen drew in a deep breath and ignored the heat in his scarlet cheeks. "Cassandra is a Trojan character in a Greek tragedy who predicts... Oh, never mind. You wouldn't understand."

"Cassandra!" said Tavie, much struck. "Of course. Her moaning and groaning and those prophecies of disaster that no one believed! I have been trying to think all day of whom I was reminded."

"You know the story?" asked Owen, amazed.

"Yes." A diffident note entered Tavie's tone. "Greek was not my strongest subject and it took forever to translate Aeschylus' tragic trilogy but I had a governess who made studying such things so interesting I persisted in the effort."

Sarah looked from one to the other. "A bluestocking! I might have known." Sarah cackled. "No wonder you are falling in love with your cousin's wife, Owen."

"Mother, you have such a twisted mind there is no listening to a thing you say. I like and admire Cousin Octavia. I admit it. But that is far different from what *you* suggest."

He stalked from the room before Tavie could add words of approval. All she could do was glower at Sarah who smirked like a cat that fell into the cream.

Somehow, something in Sarah's triumphant smile made Tavie shiver and she too removed from Sarah's presence, leaving her husband's aunt in sole possession of the salon. She went to her rooms where her maid was laying out a change of dress. The idea of making polite conversation during dinner while her mind was preoccupied with Dom was not to be thought on.

"Please put that away, Janey, and, if it would not be too much trouble, I'd like a tray here in my room. I don't believe I'll go down to dinner."

Like all Tavie's servants, the maid thought nothing too much trouble for a lady who always remembered one's name and always thanked one even for the most trivial of service. The evening dress was whisked away and Tavie was alone. She walked toward the window but before she could turn the lens on the water she noticed a farm wagon approaching, several riders behind it.

"No!"

Not Dom. She swung the telescope around and focused on the approaching cavalcade.

Tavie found first one rider—Geoff—and then another. Taggert, she thought, but he had his head turned to speak to the last rider. It wasn't until she focused on the third that, for a moment, she felt lightheaded with relief. Dom was safe.

She mastered her weakness. Dom and Geoff. What of Bert? Unwillingly, she turned the lens to the bed of the wagon but the driver was in the way and she couldn't identify the supine figure. Dead? Her heart paused for a beat. Surely not… Ah! A leg moved, bent, the foot braced flat on the bed of the wagon. A dead man couldn't do that. But someone was hurt and most likely it was Bert.

Tavie raced down the hall and took the shallow steps two at a time, one hand bundling her skirts up out of the way and the other grasping the banister to control her headlong rush down to the hall.

"Deblon!" she called as she reached the landing. "Deblon! Come at once!"

But a frowning Deblon was already hurrying across the polished oak floor. He flung open the double doors before turning to speak to his mistress. "It is a farm wagon, my lady. A gardener's lad ran up to the kitchen to inform us of its approach. Mrs. MacReady is preparing for whatever trouble might come, my lady, and I ordered a boy down the lane to see if we should send for the doctor."

Tavie was thankful that Dom had such a well-trained staff. She had been prepared to give such orders but it was unnecessary. She moved down the last few steps to the hall just as she heard Dom's cheerful voice.

"Tavie, my love? Where are you?"

She hurried forward and was just in time to see Taggert and two other men gently carry Bert from the wagon. Tavie bit her lip, feeling guilty because she was relieved it was Bert and not Dom. "Is he badly injured?"

"Just a wrenched knee. Nothing to fuss about," called Bert but Tavie could hear the pain in his voice that belied his optimistic words.

Husband and wife exchanged an understanding look and Tavie turned to the waiting butler. "Deblon, find Lord Darling's valet, if you'd be so kind, and send him up to my lord's bedroom. And that message to the doctor? Ask him to hurry please." Tavie stepped aside as Bert was carried in and pointed toward the stairs. A hand on Dom's arm detained her husband. "You, my lord," she whispered to Dom, "deserve to have your ears boxed. Could you not have sent word so I'd not be dreaming up horrors the way I've done for the past few hours?"

Dom looked startled and grasped her by the arms. He frowned down at her. "But I did. I sent someone off as soon as I found a messenger. You mean no one arrived?"

Tavie blinked at his obvious perturbation, her irritation fading. He *had* thought of her. "When?"

"I saw Manny Porson out collecting flowers for pressing. He's the local school teacher, Tavie, a cousin of the Miss Porson you met? Anyway, I sent him ahead to the boat, which was the quickest way to get word to you. He was to row across and tell you what happened so you could have Bert's room prepared and have the doctor here when we arrived."

"You might have chosen a more trustworthy messenger," complained Tavie, as they followed the others up the stairs.

"But he is." Dom's frown deepened. "Tavie, is the telescope still in our sitting room?" But he didn't await an answer, taking the shallow steps three at a time.

She followed as quickly as she could but Dom was focusing the glass toward the lake when she entered the room. "Dom? Why are you frowning so?"

"The boat was gone from the mooring we traditionally make in an inlet south of the village of Thirlspot. I checked that Manny had gotten off all right. He'd already been gone for half an hour or so."

"But he didn't arrive."

"Exactly." Dom scanned the water, moving the glass slowly, first one way and then another. "I can't imagine Manny would capsize but… Ahhh."

"You see him?"

"I see him." Dom sounded grim as he ran from the room.

Tavie went to the telescope and, careful not to move it, peered through it. For the second time in less than an hour, her skin paled at what she saw. "Unless Mr. Porson is a very good swimmer," muttered Tavie, "he is in grave difficulty." She watched as the beleaguered man bailed furiously, never taking her eyes off him. It was superstitious to believe that if she stopped watching he'd disappear under the surface of the lake, but Tavie could not help herself.

How long before Dom can reach him? she wondered. Tavie wished she dared move the glass in order to see Dom but she had to watch Manny. What a strange name. Manfred perhaps? The boat seemed deeper in the water. Was it? Yes it was. Oh dear. Manny must be tiring.

In that odd way time has of stretching, it seemed hours while Tavie kept an eye on the boat. At one point, she thought all was lost when the man drooped for long, heartrending moments and she found herself praying he'd not give up, not when help was finally on its way. Then, rested, he dipped even faster and Tavie breathed again. She knew when Dominic came into view because Mr. Porson lifted his hands to his mouth and yelled.

From then on, it was as if she had excellent seats in a theater, the dumb-show performance somehow unreal. The second skiff nosed into view. Dom looked over his shoulder, approaching carefully. Manny watched as intently as Tavie did. When the two boats nearly touched, Manny, overanxious perhaps, tried to board Dom's craft. Suddenly the water-filled boat swung away from Dom's and—Tavie screamed softly—Manny fell between them. He disappeared.

"Oh no. Not when things are almost accomplished. Not now. Don't," prayed Tavie, "let anything bad happen now."

* * * * *

Dom heard the splash and shipped the oars before twisting to lean over the side. Oh blast. Manny must have bumped his head or he wouldn't be floating at a depth just beyond reach. Yes. That dark streak was blood. Dom scanned the equipment in the bottom of the boat. Damn. This would not have happened if he'd had someone along to give the exhausted man a hand.

There. A gaff. Carefully Dom lowered the hook into the water and, very carefully indeed, hooked into the back of Manny's shirt. The worsted material ripped a bit and Dom's heart beat faster. The hook set, held and Dom pulled Manny's head out of the water, close enough to grasp under Manny's arm. It all took moments but seemed forever, both to Dom and to Tavie who watched from her room.

Dom heaved. Manny was half over the side of the dory and Dom, one hand making certain the teacher didn't slip back into the water, breathed deeply a few times before making a last effort, pulling Manny into the boat. Now what?

Dom pushed his hand flat against Manny's chest. The heartbeat was slow. Too slow. Something was wrong. Breathing. *Manny wasn't breathing.* In a panic, Dom rolled Manny over one of the thwarts and thumped him on the back. Hard. Water gushed from Manny's mouth. Again. A groan and weak movement.

Dom said a prayer of thanksgiving and turned Manny over. The man slumped against the seat, his head hanging and his hands clutching his chest. A harsh spasm of coughing cleared his windpipe and gradually his color returned. Dom pressed a handkerchief to the cut and spoke soothingly. More coughing followed but finally, breathing more easily, Manny looked up and grinned wryly, if weakly, at Dom.

"All right, Manny?" asked Dom softly, still pressing against the sluggishly bleeding head wound.

"Damn fool thing to do, wasn't it?" Manny's voice was hoarse. "So close to safety and then pull a stupid stunt like that." A healthy red flushed the teacher's face. "I guess—well, the truth is I panicked a bit."

"Anyone might. You must have been hoping for rescue for a long time. Manny, do you feel like explaining what happened? To the boat, I mean? Did you hit something?"

"Bedamned if I know." Manny held the handkerchief now and pulled it away to see if he still bled. "I'd swear I didn't. Hit anything, I mean. I was rowing strongly. Rather enjoying it, you know?"

Dom nodded. Manny wouldn't have too many opportunities to take out a boat. He must remember to give his old acquaintance permission to borrow one whenever he wished. Assuming that, after this experience, the man ever wished to go out on the water again.

"I noticed there was water sloshing around in the bottom. Didn't think too much of it until it increased rather faster than I liked. Then I began to worry. Unfortunately, by that time, I was very nearly halfway across and too far from either shore for me to swim. I plugged the hole with my coat, which helped but couldn't get it stopped enough to row on. The thing that kept me bailing was the surety that as soon as you realized I'd not gotten to Brightwood, you'd come for me."

Dom looked at the foundering dory, which had nearly killed Manny. It should not have. There had been nothing wrong with it the preceding morning when he and his friends unloaded it. Dom decided to pull it to shore with him, discover exactly what had gone wrong. Manny must have hit something even if he hadn't been aware of it at the time. But how could he not have noticed something that would hole a boat?

It was a mystery. As he reached for the rope in the bow of the sinking dory and tied it to his, Dom realized he'd no taste for mysteries. Towing the boat would be a drag and slow their return but he must discover what had happened. It might have happened when he and his friends were in it. Dom shivered as he recalled he and Bert and Geoff would have crossed to Brightwood in the boat if Bert hadn't hurt his knee.

* * * * *

Tavie gave orders that still-another room be readied and more water heated for a bath for Mr. Porson. Also, that dry clothes be found for the man. She searched her mind for anything else that might help and almost grinned at an idea.

"Deblon?" she asked, her head tipped to one side.

"Yes, my lady?"

"Do you think you could assemble the ingredients for a punch? I suspect a good hot rum and lemon mixture would go a long way toward warming up Mr. Porson after such a terrible experience. Perhaps Dom might like some too?"

Deblon nodded. "Yes, I know a recipe, my lady. It calls for rum, sugar, lemons, marmalade, calf's-foot jelly, water and—if required—more rum."

Tavie blinked.

"It is usually, hm, *required*," said Deblon, his features perfectly solemn.

Tavie grinned. "It sounds remarkably suitable, Deblon. I believe Mr. Porson will be revived by it and perhaps, if any is left, Geoff and Bert will find it…um…refreshing?" She turned away but the mention of Bert reminded her. "Has the doctor arrived for Lord Darling?"

"Not yet, my lady. I will send him up immediately when he does."

Tavie dithered. It would take Dom and Mr. Porson some time to arrive. She didn't think she could bear waiting in her rooms alone. She couldn't face Vi, or worse, *Sarah*. A smile crossed her face and she nodded. She'd just go see how Bert was doing. "Well, really," she said, at the open door to his room, "this looks more like a party than a sickroom."

"We thought we might take the edge off Bert's pain before the doctor came poking and prying." Geoff raised his glass to her. "Would you care to join us?"

"In a strange man's bedroom?" Tavie pretended outrage.

The two men laughed and Elf poked her head around the small wing chair by the bed. "You'll be well chaperoned, my dear. Do come in."

"Oh, good. I'm glad you are here, Elf. Have you discovered what happened to our hapless hero?"

"He's been avoiding a round tale but he is," said Elf sternly, "about to explain all."

Tavie took the chair Geoff moved to a place near the bed but refused a glass of what she guessed was brandy. She settled herself and looked expectantly at Bert.

"Here's how it was," he said confidingly. "We must have been only twenty yards from the top, scaling this cliff face you see when—"

"Bert!" interrupted Geoff, no longer amused by Bert's prevarication.

Bert's face reddened. "Well, I can't tell them the *truth*, can I?"

"I don't see why not," responded Geoff.

"It's too embarrassing." Bert pouted.

"You mean it wasn't a fall?" asked Tavie, mystified.

"Obviously not," inserted Elf.

"Oh, I fell all right." Bert closed his mouth but Tavie could see a twinkle in his eye.

"What my mountainous friend is not saying is that we had reached the bottom of Helvellyn and were returning to the field where we'd left the ponies. Dom and I were moaning about how out of shape we must be to be so tired from such a simple climb and Lord Big-breeches of Showoff here had to say he wasn't tired at all."

"And that I'd prove it."

"Which was a step toward folly. He ran toward the field, hopping sort of sideways as he did so, half turned back toward us—"

"And," interrupted Bert, "found myself up to my calf in a hole. I twisted as I fell and this," Bert waved his glass at his knee, "is the result. I'll be maimed for life of course and become an interesting invalid, trading on my weakness whenever I cannot get my own way and—"

"And I think you've had enough of that brandy, my lad," said Elf, removing the glass from his hand. "Any more and you'll be unable to answer the doctor's questions. Tavie, love, where is Dom?"

The question reminded Tavie of what she'd seen on the lake, which had temporarily faded from her mind as she listened to Bert and Geoff. She vividly described what had happened and both men fell silent.

"You know, Bert," said Geoff quietly, "if you had *not* fallen, we'd have been in that boat."

Bert, suddenly and obviously stone-cold sober, nodded and reached convulsively for the brandy Elf had set on the table by his bed.

Chapter Eight

ഇ

Bert and Geoff, the latter's complexion pale, stared at each other. Bertram gulped more brandy.

"Here I was, cursing my foul luck to have a bad knee just when Tavie and Dom were giving their first ball," said Bert in a tone that was supposed to be jesting. It didn't convince his listeners.

"Naughty, naughty, Bert," said Geoff, equally inadequate at pretending humor. "You should have been praising the powers that be that a bad knee is all that is wrong." He swallowed. Hard. "To say nothing of the fact that there will *be* a ball."

"Whatever do you mean?" Tavie's voice held a sharp note.

The men exchanged looks. Bert's waving hand suggested Geoff answer. "Dom swims like a fish, my dear. Bert can swim after a fashion but not well enough to reach shore from any distance into the lake. And I…I cannot swim at all." It was not necessary but he made the conclusion anyway. "I don't believe Dom could have saved the both of us."

Tavie's eyes widened. "You'd have *drowned*? One of you?" she asked in a hushed tone. She thought of how difficult it would have been for Dom to choose between his friends. Her voice rose. "*Perhaps all three of you*?"

When she got a solemn nod in answer, she began to shiver, the avoided tragedy the final straw in a day of one weighty straw after another. The shiver turned to shudders at the horror of what might have happened to Dom while attempting to help his friends, the fear that all three might have been lost. Her skin turned an ashen color.

Elf rose to her feet and pushed Tavie's head down. "No, don't fight me. This is a better cure for a fainting fit than all the smelling salts in the world... There." She allowed Tavie to sit up. "You feel better, do you not? Remember," she scolded, "*it didn't happen*. They are all safe, except for a bad knee, which at worst will leave Bert with an interesting limp. Think how the women will act when he comes into a room leaning on a cane. They will cater to his every whim and push cushions behind his back and bring footstools. Do not grin, Bertram, or they might guess it is a sham and not oblige you with their attentions."

"But it sounds a delightful program, Elf. Do you promise all the young ladies will react that way? Especially the most beautiful?"

"I don't know about the Incomparables. They are often so spoiled themselves, they have no time for spoiling anyone else. But trapped in a chair, as you'll be, I promise you one thing. You will have the opportunity, at long last, to look over a handful of young ladies and discover if any of them suit you. You will be forced to stay still and, for once, will be unable to disappear just as you feel tempted by some nice, sweet girl, a sensation I've heard frightens you into running for your life."

Bert's cheeks flushed a deep red as Elf's half-scolding, half-serious lecture worked an itch under his skin. *How,* he wondered, *can a little old lady read me so well, especially when she's had so little contact with me in recent years?*

"You are wondering how I know, are you not?" asked Elf. "I have a multitude of correspondents and I keep up with most of what happens in London and about the goings-on at house parties. Besides, Bert," she added kindly, "I am an old woman and have known many a young man running from his fate."

"What about me?" asked Geoff, generously attempting to distract Elf from embarrassing his friend still more.

"You? You are not ready to settle down. When you are, you will choose the first woman you see, whether she is suitable or not, just to get it over and your life back to normal. The best thing your friends can do for you is to have the *right* young woman available when that time comes."

"Now it is my turn to find a rock under which I may hide."

Geoff doesn't look embarrassed, thought Tavie. But she had learned he could camouflage his emotions to a greater degree than either Dom or Bert.

"How do you do it, Elf?" he continued, curious.

"Live half so long as I have and perhaps you too will have gained a modicum of wisdom."

"So you really believe I would choose a wife in such a harum-scarum fashion only to have the chore over and done?" he asked with what sounded like purely intellectual curiosity.

"Yes. The word you use is suggestive, is it not?"

Geoff looked confused.

"You called it a chore," explained Elf. "You will think of no more than settling some woman, any woman, in your mother's place and putting children in the nursery. The fact you will have to live with the lady for the rest of your life will be irrelevant to you since you will assume you may go on pretty much as you please and live separated from her as much as possible. And perhaps you will. If you choose *badly*. If you find the *right* woman, you will discover a new joy in life."

"Prophecy, Elf?" Geoff was not quite certain but he thought perhaps he'd been insulted. "I like women," he added. "Why should I expect to dislike my wife?"

"You like women in small doses. Wives do not come in small doses."

"I thought," said Tavie, "that he liked *me*, Elf."

"Oh, he does. But you are an unusual young woman, capable of entering into the men's interests and, still rarer, knowing when you should leave them alone." Elf rose to her feet. "I think I hear the doctor's approach, Tavie, my dear, and it is time to dress for dinner. Yes, I know you ordered a meal in your room but I cancelled it. You and Dom and Geoff must be at the dinner table tonight."

"I meant to eat here with Bert," objected Geoff.

"No. No one must suspect the incident with the boat is anything other than an accident," said Elf. "You will come to dinner and laugh and jest and ignore the fact *none* of you might have been eating dinner tonight."

Before Geoff or Tavie could think about the implication behind her comment and ask what she meant, she whisked herself out of the door and down the hall.

Tavie exchanged a look with Geoff, then with Bert and then stared at nothing at all. "But…it *was* an accident, was it not?"

Neither man answered. They were each turning and twisting Elf's cryptic comment this way and that way. No matter how one looked at it, neither liked the conclusion one reached.

Tavie gulped. As nonchalantly as she could, she said, "We have our orders, I guess. I'd forgotten I ordered a tray in my room. Look at the time," Tavie glanced at the porcelain clock on the mantel, "I'd better hurry. Bert, will you be all right?"

"Oh, right as a trivet, Tavie. The doctor will undoubtedly berate me…" he said, coming out of his mental fog as he spoke. He finished more briskly, "For having drunk so much, I mean, but I dislike laudanum, you see. Do not worry, Tavie. My man will be here to see I've all I require." He watched a bit wistfully as Geoff offered his arm and led Tavie from the room.

Alone except for his unobtrusive valet who slid into the room when the others left, Bert pushed aside Elf's suggestion of sabotage about which, at the moment, he could do nothing. Instead, he thought of her words concerning his fear of getting too close to some woman, a comment that had bitten a bit too close to the bone.

If only there were another Tavie in the world, he'd go gladly to his fate. He sighed. It was too bad one was required to marry for such reasons as name and family and dowry. Especially when one watched a pair like Dom and Tavie and saw how wonderfully close two people *could* be.

Bert turned a wary look on the chubby-faced doctor who stood in the doorway polishing his glasses. Oh well, it was no use moaning about the future when there was a much more immediate problem. The problem of facing, with fortitude, the doctor's manipulations of his poor knee!

* * * * *

Two days later, Lady Clavingstone arrived at Brightwood. She climbed down from her carriage feeling every one of her fifty-two years. Age, she decided, was the devil. It was not of course the most original of views, as she discovered when talking *tête-à-tête* with Elf and Ally after meeting the new bride. Her considered opinion on the latter subject, unprejudiced by her liking of Dominic, was that, "She's as delightful as I'd guessed she'd be."

"We knew people could not help but like her," said Ally.

"Sarah's here," said Elf. It was not so much a *non sequitur* as the uninitiated might think. She added, "*She* doesn't like Tavie," just in case Matilda missed the point.

"And Vi?" Matilda didn't explain. She knew the sisters would understand what she was asking.

The question was followed by a moment's thoughtful silence. "Vi cannot make up her mind," said Ally, a sad expression blurring her already-soft features. "Most of the time she's perfectly agreeable. Then she'll pout and one cannot predict her behavior toward dear Tavie."

"I'll do what I can," Matilda promised.

* * * * *

Whatever Lady Clavingstone did, it was not enough, as Elf discovered several days after the rest of the company arrived. She was shocked by just how badly her plan was failing when she overheard a conversation between Lady Sefton and Sarah.

And gossiping on a Sunday too, she thought in a wry, if fruitless, attempt to ease her mind.

Lady Sefton was known to be kindhearted to a fault and if *she* were wondering, at Sarah's prodding of course, how long Tavie could hide her "true" nature then it was time for stronger measures. She'd just have to put her mind to thinking what measures they might be.

Elf was not alone in her eavesdropping. Not that Tavie had *meant* to do it. Using the early afternoon hours for her household duties, she'd finished checking the upstairs maids' work and discovered she had nearly half an hour before she needed to be anywhere or do anything. After four and a half days of feeling constantly on view, it was an amazing relief to have a few minutes in which she could be alone.

At the end of the hall, there was a deep-set window with a window seat. Impulsively she seated herself, pulled up her legs in a hoydenish manner and drew the drapes so she'd be hidden. She'd sit right here, she thought, and stare out the window and dream of when she'd have Dom and Brightwood all to herself again.

Unfortunately Tavie had no sooner settled herself than she heard voices. Her sigh might have been detected by the two just arriving at the top of the secondary stairs serving the south wing if they'd not been so involved in their own conversation. Tavie's proper, if reluctant, intention to join them disappeared as she heard a voice she didn't recognize say, "I tell you, Lady Brightwood is just like her mother."

"How can you say so?" asked a second, also unrecognized, voice. "Her mother was beautiful, as I recall. No one could call Lady Brightwood beautiful exactly. Also, you will recall that her grace was not so outlandishly tall."

"Nor is Rambourne, which is suspicious, is it not?"

It took a moment for Tavie to understand the implication and, when she did, she gritted her teeth at the insult to her mother.

"But I do not refer to Lady Octavia Brightwood's *looks* but to her *behavior*."

There was a moment's silence. "You mean…"

"I mean the way Lady Brightwood is always surrounded by men. First she tricks Lord Brightwood into this marriage…"

"Brightwood is very much in love with his wife. You can tell that at a glance."

"Yes. Absolutely besotted. Disgusting, is it not?"

The voices approached and passed the window as they spoke. The women now stood a few doors down the hall. Tavie wished she'd let them know she was there. Now, not only to save herself embarrassment but also to save *them* from equal or worse embarrassment, she could not reveal her presence.

The first voice went on when the second had no answer to what was, after all, a rhetorical question. "Not only Brightwood is befuddled. Lord Darling is also caught in her web. My maid says that, before his accident kept him to his room, he was always hovering around her. And then that perennial bachelor, the Honorable Geoffrey Martin! Unbelievable *any* woman could attract *his* attention."

The unknown tormentor's next words very nearly brought Tavie to her feet. "I wonder which one she sleeps with."

The second, slightly kinder, lady tittered, "Come now. You cannot believe that. Such a new bride wouldn't…" The voice trailed off, delicately avoiding the obvious. "Besides," she continued more briskly, "you are aware, are you not, of the Brightwood family's most infamous eccentricity?"

"What eccentricity?" asked the harsher critic avidly.

The second voice lowered to a confidential tone. "They have *one* bedchamber and sleep *together*..." There was a pause. *"All night, every night."*

"Good Lord in heaven preserve us!"

"I have heard it has been going on like that for generations. So, unless Brightwood is in on such an arrangement and complacent about it, she cannot be giving him horns. Yet."

Again the silence dragged. Tavie discovered she was biting her lip and that her hands shook with a mixture of anger and horror. How could anyone think such awful things about her?

"I still say she is exactly like her mother."

And just what, wondered Tavie, and not for the first time, *was Mother like*? *Exactly?*

The same voice continued a bit querulously. "I was certain Lord Darling had an eye for my daughter. He was, for him, very attentive last spring during the season. But this morning when I took my little flower to visit him in his sickroom, he made his disinterest totally obvious. Then *she* came in and he brightened considerably. Brightwood's uncaring wife stole my daughter's future with just a snap of her fingers. It is not fair." There followed half a snort, half a laugh. "And it isn't only Lord Brightwood's friends, is it? Even your very own husband," the voice became sugary sweet, "seemed unable to keep away from her last night."

"Oh, my William has always liked to *look*," said the second woman complacently. "That is as far as it goes with him. I understand that *you*, poor dear, have had to put up with so much *more*? I do commiserate."

"Sir William? Merely look?" There was a stifled laugh as if the harsher-voiced matron knew something William's wife did not. "Well, well. I really must check on my little dear and see if she is ready for tea. More than likely," an exasperated note escaped her, "she will have her nose in a book of poetry and have forgotten the time. I do not know what gets into the dear girl."

A door opened and closed. Shortly another did likewise and very carefully Tavie peeked into the hall. Her heart throbbed like a drum as possibilities spun through her mind. Some of them Tavie recognized as ridiculous, but just what *had* her mother done that was so awful that her father had done the unthinkable, the nearly impossible, and actually divorced her, thereby putting her mother beyond forgiveness? Tavie burned with the need to know.

Elf would tell her. She'd go to Elf's room and finally set to rest fears, which had, off and on over the years, given her nightmares. Tavie knocked on Elf's door and almost despaired when she got no response. Desperate, she moved on to Ally's.

"Yes? Tavie, dear. Do come in. Whatever is the matter?" asked Ally, pulling the distraught, slightly wild-eyed, young woman in and pushing her into a chair. She hovered around her. "Whatever can have happened? No. Do not say a word," she added when Tavie opened her mouth to respond. Ally went to the wall by the bed and pulled the bell. "We'll have tea and then we'll talk. No," she insisted, "not a word."

Tavie blinked, losing the edge of her anger in hearing Ally speak in a firm way that seemed very out of character.

Ally drew in a deep breath and went on in her usual kindly fashion. "Compose yourself, my dear, and we'll speak of whatever is worrying you once the tray has come."

When the maid left, Ally arranged the teapot and plates to her liking and looked up. "I don't know what it is but I am willing to listen. You must treat me as a dear friend, Tavie, as well as a caring relative and you *will* let me help, will you not?

You understand how much I love Dominic, my dear. He is like a son—or should I say grandson? I have become so very fond of you, as well, my dear. I'll do anything I can to make life easier for you."

While waiting, Tavie had had time to pull herself together and no longer felt quite so nervous but she needed answers. "I *knew* you would help." Then she couldn't think how to go on. It was easier to talk of Dom. "Dominic *is* wonderful, is he not?"

Ally, ready for she knew not what, blinked. "Oh, the very best of our many relatives. I am so glad you agree."

Tavie, knowing she was on the verge of learning the truth of her past, found herself relaxing. She'd expected to be very tense and perhaps fearful, but was not. On the other hand, she was not quite ready to begin so she continued with her favorite subject. "You know, when I discovered with whom I'd become entangled, I recalled all I'd read in the society columns. The tittle-tattle one cannot avoid, you know? I wondered if he'd been dissimulating and pretending to be a gentleman in order to—um..."

"To mount you as his newest mistress?" Ally smiled gently at the red making Tavie's cheeks rosy. "There is no use mincing words when one is with friends, Tavie. Roundaboutation takes so long and so often, in the end, one is misunderstood. Dominic *has* been wild but he has never, to my knowledge, offended against propriety by offering a slip on the shoulder to a gently bred female. Nor is he forgetful that he was raised a gentleman."

"I am not certain about that. Would a gentleman," asked Tavie, "swear roundly at an innocent young lady only because she refused him her name?"

"Innocent?" asked Ally with a teasing look.

"Oh well." Tavie waved the hand not holding her teacup. "Yes. Technically. Quite innocent. My father, you see, wrapped me up in so many layers of lint it was quite unbearable. I've fought all my life for every tiny bit of freedom I've managed."

"It amazes me you have any spirit at all."

"It did not amaze *him*." For once Tavie's voice revealed some of the pain she'd suffered in the past. "It was the *spirit* to which my father objected."

Ally nodded her head so hard a strand of hair fell from her rather haphazard coiffure. Quite accidentally, she gave Tavie an opening for the questions she'd come to ask. "I remember your mother. Such a lively lady."

"What I just overheard…why I came to you…" Tavie drew in a deep breath and plunged in. "Ally, I must know. Was my mother so very bad? I know my father divorced her, which is utter ruin forever, but…"

"Oh dear. What *did* you hear?"

"Only that I am just like my mother and," Tavie's brows lowered and her eyes flashed, "it was *not* a compliment."

Ally laughed. "I am so glad to see you can be angry about it, Tavie. You are not like her in any way. You neither look like her nor do you have her character. You are, needless to say, a much better woman than your poor, delightful mother."

"Delightful?" asked Tavie a bit doubtfully.

"Oh yes." Ally nodded her head several times in emphasis.

"You knew her?"

"Yes of course, my dear." Ally's hair came down a bit more at still-another vigorous nod. "Everyone knew her. So much in need of love and so desperate for excitement and gaiety—and so misunderstood. It was a disaster when her father arranged her marriage to your father. Everyone predicted it. And, in quick time, it all came true and in the worst possible way for you. I am so sorry, my dear."

"My father would tell you it is he who should be pitied."

"So he should. A tragedy, my dear. A tragedy for all of you."

"But what did she do which was so bad?"

Ally's eyes widened. "You truly know nothing?"

"Lady Alvinia, my father ranted and raved and coddled me and loved me—oh yes, I believe that in his way he loves me—but he'd not under any circumstance do more than say I am just like my mother and must be protected from my own willful nature." Tavie scowled and pursed her lips. "I got so tired of it."

"Oh dear. So would anyone," said Ally faintly. "How very silly the poor dear man has become. Oh dear, oh dear." She waved her hands in rueful denial. "Do forget I said that, my love. I am sure I did not mean to insult your father."

Unexpectedly for both of them, Octavia's delightful laugh burst out. "Oh, do! Please do! I've said such things for years and it is a delightful change to have someone agree with me instead of telling me I must show proper respect for my father's wishes and must not—oh, not do this or not do that or do the other because."

"Because?"

"Simply *because*." Tavie nodded. Her mouth compressed tightly before she relaxed it and went on. "Never a reason, you see."

"The reason, I suspect, was that you might kick up your heels and rebel as did your mother."

"Oh, but I did rebel. I found myself a position and ran off to become a governess. I know now how foolish I was and would never do it again but I still do not know how *she* rebelled."

Ally nodded. "And you wish to know. How understandable that is. At first it was merely trifles. Racing in the park and dressing in the extreme of fashion and collecting around her all the wildest sparks on the town—nothing which would have caused more than a ripple, if first *her* father before her marriage and then *your* father after it had not taken strongly against it all."

"Just as he did with me. Why is it, Aunt Ally, that people do not learn from experience?"

"One would have to admit one was wrong in order to decide to change, I think. Admitting one is wrong is a very difficult thing, is it not?"

"I see. I never thought of that. Will *you*," said Octavia, her eyes holding Ally's, "tell me what happened? In the end?" Tavie rose, poured away dregs in her cup and refilled it with hot tea. She shifted her chair closer and settled herself. "Aunt Ally, you cannot know how much I appreciate the fact that I am about to learn her history. I have dreamt up horrors and then told myself not to be fantastical—but occasionally, oh, only once in a great while, they still creep out to haunt me and I wake in a sweat."

"She didn't commit murder or treason, so forget those nightmares."

Octavia laughed a bit weakly this time. "Oh dear. How sadly lacking in imagination I am. I never once thought of treason."

"But murder? Oh, you poor dear child." Ally sighed, a commiserating sound, and patted Tavie's hand with her own plump fingers. "Well, with no frills or furbelows, it is quite simply that she set up her own household in London right across the square from your father's townhouse."

"A London house?" Tavie blinked in confusion. "Does he *have* one?"

"He did. Then. Once the dust settled, he sold it and retired, with you, to the country. He hires rooms—in the Albany, I believe—on those occasions he is forced to visit London for more than a day or two."

"Was it so very bad? Separating from him and setting up an establishment that way?"

"Oh yes. At least the *way* she did it. A quietly arranged agreement where the couple takes care not to be in the same place at the same time—that is one thing. But a wife must *appear* to support her husband. Georgianna said there was no bearing your father's constant lectures and disapproving manner. She needed *love* she said. Love and gaiety and parties and new gowns and, most of all, she needed witty people around her."

"Father is the least witty man I know, if you refer to the easy *bon mot* and quickly paced exchange of thoughts. Not that I've known all that many men of course."

"But I have known a great many over the years and I agree. He's intelligent but not at all clever." Ally nodded firmly. "Your mother had money of her own and, under your grandmother's will, she could use it as she wished. That alone was an unbearable insult to a man of your father's nature, a man who needs to control such things himself."

"I can see that."

"She was young and impatient and unwilling to compromise in any way."

"Are you excusing her?"

"What I am trying to do is show there were faults on both sides."

After a moment, Tavie sighed. "So. We have them living apart."

"Yes. I said your mother had money but it was not a large fortune. Ladies snubbed her of course, so she found herself with only men for friends and some, my dear, were quite unscrupulous. They thought her delightful but they also found her generous to a fault. All too soon, she was in the hands of the moneylenders. By the time anyone with an honorable bone in his body realized what was happening, it was too late. The cent-percenters had come to your father, you see." Ally paused when Tavie frowned. "*Moneylenders,* Tavie. Your father foolishly refused to pay. It seemed he meant to teach her a lesson."

Tavie absorbed the information Ally had given her, feeling a measure of pity mixed with exasperation for a woman she'd never really known and still more for her father who had put up with so much. Exasperation won. "Drat it, Aunt Ally, my parents may have made salmagundi of *their* lives but they made a mess of mine. That must have been about 1785?"

"His refusal to settle her debts came, if I have not confused the dates, a year or so before. She was saved, once, by inheriting from her father but became wilder and more uncontrolled—determined, she said, to teach your father a lesson." Ally sighed. "It was sad really. *Her* father was initially at fault for forcing her into an unsuitable marriage. *Your* father was at fault for trying to change the very things about her that, *before* the wedding, he'd found delightful. And your mother had no sense at all when it came to finances. She'd always had all she wanted so could never see that she no longer had unlimited funds. Nor would she bend to any of the restraints which would have allowed forgiveness and, after a time, reinstatement into the *ton*."

"So her death when I was six or seven was a release for both of them?"

"But she didn't die. Not *then*, I mean," blurted Ally, then covered her mouth in horror at her blunder.

"She didn't?" Tavie rose to her feet, her knuckles white where her fingers bent around the back of her chair. "I was told—"

"Oh dear," interrupted Ally, "I should not have let that particular cat out of its bag. But it slipped out and is done. You see, I assumed you knew that much. She *did* die of course. Eventually. Perhaps five years ago? Six? Time has a way of passing without notice when one is as old as I've become. No, it must have been all of seven years."

Tavie stared at her and Ally, hoping to get the young woman's mind off the fact she'd been lied to, hurried on. "What she did do—when threatened with debtor's prison—was run off with her current love to Italy. There they joined the most raffish set imaginable."

Tavie's blank look sharpened.

"Since she was such a delightful companion, she never lacked a protector, my dear. Do not think she died in poverty and neglect."

"She joined the demimondaine?" asked Tavie in a hushed, truly shocked voice.

"I suppose one must call it that," said Ally hesitantly, her manner suggesting she wished she could think of a more acceptable way of viewing the matter. "But I remember her with such fondness I cannot bring myself to blame her. I have heard that, for the most part, she enjoyed herself very much. She was such a pleasure-loving little butterfly, you see. My goodness!" Ally's soft features sharpened. "Seven years ago you'd have been eighteen, would you not? And ready for a season? Oh dear. Oh yes. *Now* I understand."

"Understand what?" Tavie had herself well in hand but her voice would have betrayed to an observant soul how much tension she felt.

Ally, unfortunately, was bemused by her discovery. "I have wondered," she said, "why your father continued so adamantly to withhold you from society, but don't you see? Her death, just when you should have been presented, reminded people and the gossip started up all over again. Dear Morty could not have borne to be in London at that time."

Tavie's eyes flashed, her temper edging out of control. "What *I* see is that she deserted me. How could she leave me with my father? Locked up in her tower in her place, so to speak? How terribly selfish of her."

"Shush, child. Ask your father about her jewels someday when you've accepted this information. There were rather amazing rumors about them after her death and I believe you'll be pleasantly surprised to learn they are yours."

That did it. "Jewels? Jewels! Of what use are *jewels*?" Tavie's voice deepened with barely suppressed emotion. "What I *needed* was her love and support."

"Oh dear. I see I should not have told you."

Tavie released her death grip on the chair and paced, the westering sunlight streaming in Ally's window making flames of her hair.

"Please dear, calm yourself. Dear Elf will be so angry with me for upsetting you."

"*Elf will…*" Octavia broke off a laugh, which held a harsh note. "My dear Aunt Alvinia, do not disturb yourself. I will never tell her you explained why the high-sticklers think me unacceptable. But one cannot take in so much new information without reordering one's mind." She paused and actually looked at Ally. "Do not be perturbed, Ally, dear." Controlling her own feelings, she gave her husband's great-aunt a warm hug. "If you do not mind my deserting you, I truly feel a need to be alone for a bit."

Ally, dithering, nodded. Tavie whisked out the door, closing it with special care.

The elderly lady stared at her door, a frown creasing her usually placid brow. She rose to her feet and pulled her shawl closer around her plump shoulders. "I was so certain telling her was the right thing to do. Oh dear, I fear I was much too frank… If only Elf had been here to help. Elf is so much better at such things."

But Elf was setting into motion unwise plans of her own. Unknowing of the latest gossip making Tavie out a flirt if not a siren, Elf had Bert helped down to the formal apartments where he was tenderly placed in a bath chair and, when Tavie next appeared, she was designated to wheel him around wherever he wished to go.

With Bert raising her spirits and making her laugh, Tavie was less likely to lose her temper. Also, with Bert there, the ladies were less likely to make sly comments to Tavie's detriment. But of course with Bert in constant attendance on their hostess, the two young people obviously on the easiest of terms, the newest round of gossip raced through the house like fire in tinder.

It was a day or two before Elf heard it. *Is there,* she wondered, *no way to stop Sarah's mouth*?

No one with a grain of sense could believe Bert was entangling Tavie—or vice versa—in an *affaire*. Not only was that bit of idiotic gossip in circulation but *Owen* was believed to be under Tavie's spell as well. To say nothing of Geoff, who had long ago been labeled the complete misogynist. Unfortunately *all* the male guests found their hostess delightful—which was enough for jealous tattlemongers to judge her guilty. Tavie was touted as the embodiment of all her mother's more self-destructive traits.

In desperation, Elf and Ally took over the entertainment of the older women. Giving in to her worst nature and lowering herself to Sarah's level, Elf reminded several old friends of Sarah's jealousy and desire to see Owen in Dom's position. This was thought-provoking and there was some easing of tension.

Released from duty to the older generation, Tavie delighted in getting acquainted with the younger females in the party. She'd been allowed no friends during her childhood and one might have assumed this would make her standoffish or shy, but not a bit of it. Discovering the likes and dislikes of her contemporaries, discussing fashion—something she'd of necessity learned about but never realized was a topic for hours of interesting conversation—organizing short walking tours with picnics for the young ladies... It was all new and delightful and Tavie threw herself into it with joy.

The younger matrons and girls, after a few days of wary watchfulness, accepted her wholeheartedly and, loyally, began defending her to the older generation whenever she was maligned in their hearing.

Something had begun to go right.

* * * * *

"Tavie?" Dom called out in the empty entry hall. He raised his voice when he got no response "Tavie, my love! Where are you?"

"Tavie, Tavie, Tavie!" Geoff added his voice, cupping his hands around his mouth and turning on his heel to project in different directions. "The presence of Octavia, Marchioness of Brightwood," he intoned, "is required at the main entrance to Brightwood Hall. At once if you please."

Curious, several people emerged from the salons. Other public rooms emptied as more arrived. Sarah Sands kept herself toward the back of the largest group.

"Tavie, love?" Dom turned in a circle, his excitement and impatience obvious to all. "Ah," he said, his smile broadening. His hand extended toward his bride who appeared from behind the baize door to the service area. "Come, love. My wedding present to you has arrived."

"Present?" Tavie flushed, her eyes sparkling. "Well?" she asked when a glance around the hall revealed nothing new.

"Outside. Come along now."

Dom pulled her hand through his arm and hurried toward the doors which Deblon threw open with dramatic intent. Framed in the sunlit view was a modified version of a lady's phaeton, its major innovation that it had been constructed with a dainty crane-neck perch. The perch hung gracefully above a body built along slightly sportive lines but without the extreme height so popular with the great whips of the day. Its body was beautifully treated, different woods inlaid in geometric designs and varnished to a brilliant shine. The wheels were picked out in sun-catching copper—a compliment to Tavie's hair. Poled up to the carriage was a pair of perfectly matched black geldings, about fourteen hands in height.

Tavie's eyes widened and her grip on Dom tightened. "For me?"

He looked down at her shining face and nodded. He leaned nearer and whispered in her ear. "I love you, my darling."

Tavie, forgetting her audience, put her hands on either side of his face, drew Dom's head down for a kiss of thanks. The applause brought her back to her surroundings and she blushed, her eyes traveling around those people crowding up behind them in the hall. She dropped her gaze and took a deep breath. For the most part, the faces revealed amusement at her *faux pas* but, here and there, some registered disgust at such a public display of affection.

Will I never learn to behave in a conventionally ladylike way? she wondered.

"Do you like them?" Dom led her out and down the steps toward the team. "My agent took forever finding just what I required but I wasn't about to go looking myself and leave you here alone."

"He did very well, my lord," said Tavie politely, adopting her most social façade in an attempt to compensate for her impulsive, but underbred, response to the gift. "What are their names?"

"Naming them is your privilege, my love."

Tavie thought for a moment. "Romulus and Remus," she decided, smiling carefully, concealing her feelings from all but Dom who was near enough to read her shining eyes.

Dom walked her around the pair, discussing the animals' finer points and, eventually, arrived at the driver's seat. "Want to take them in hand?"

"Our guests," she demurred and added in a low voice, "You know I don't know how to handle a team, Dom."

"One has to begin somewhere. Don't be missish, Tavie. You can do it."

"Well..." She gave in to temptation. "Just around the circle and then we must put off lessons until we are alone again."

"I don't see why," he argued. "We will plan some of our jaunts to be short and slow and I can give you a lesson on the way. Our friends will understand and not object." Hands at her waist, he lifted her up and followed her onto the narrow seat.

"If only we could."

Tavie wished they might have spent the morning with Dom teaching her the finer points of handling a team as compared to the single horse with which she'd first practiced. But she knew, if Dom did not, that she'd rarely be able to take the time for lessons, however he tried to fit them into the party's schedule.

When she returned to the point of departure, the younger people surged forward, startling the animals. They reared. Dom's hand closed simultaneously over the reins and Tavie's hands, helping her pull them down and calm them. He was proud that she hadn't panicked. In fact, he wondered if she needed his help, both her voice and her intuitive handling of the reins correct for the situation. The horses settled quickly—a well-behaved pair just as he'd ordered—and the most rambunctious of the young women, worried, apologized for having caused the brief tempest.

"That's all right. Dom has a lot to teach me about driving—I've only begun to learn, you know—and every new experience helps me understand what I must do. All's well that ends well, as the bard says."

"Oh, did you see the play last season?" asked one young, still naïve lady.

"No," said Tavie, her eyes meeting Dom's briefly. "But my governess, um, *made* me read it."

Tavie was obviously becoming more socially adept. One did not, after all, admit to a love of learning. Or that reading a play was a delightful pastime for a cold winter evening. Especially reading them aloud with others, each reader taking one or more parts.

Near the open doors, Sarah watched and plotted. She smiled slyly and then looked around to see if anyone had noticed an expression she realized must have revealed her gloating. She retreated into the house where she met Elf just coming to see what all the excitement was about.

"That hussy once again made a spectacle of herself—kissing Dominic right here in front of everyone." Sarah allowed herself a smug smile, happy to have been able to insert that little needle into her much-disliked aunt's skin. She continued on up to her room where she could be private with her plans.

Chapter Nine

ᘓ

Elf ignored Sarah's insult to Tavie and moved into the sun. Blinded, she blinked, her old eyes slow to adjust to the brighter light. "What is going on?" she asked. The crowd parted and let Elf through.

"Tavie's present arrived and I could not wait for her to try it. What do you think, Aunt Elf? Would you trust yourself to this carriage? Miss Alnwick says it is far too dangerous a carriage for a lady to drive, but it is not, is it?" Dom's eyes pleaded with his great-aunt for approbation of his gift. "I designed it myself and my agent saw to the construction. Tavie likes it, do you not, my love?"

"It is very lovely, Dom. I just hope I am capable of learning to drive it properly."

"Of course you are."

"It isn't a high-perch phaeton of course," said Elf judiciously, her hand stroking her chin. "It looks a trifle more raffish than I would like at *my* age. However," she added, with something that, in someone of lesser breeding, might have been called a grin, "twenty years ago I'd have liked nothing better than a go at the reins." Elf shook her head. "Even *ten* years," she finished on a wistful note.

Laughter rippled through the crowd as Elf had hoped it would and one sensed a relaxation among those watching. Matilda and Violetta appeared around the side of the house and had to have the whole explained to them. "Very dashing," was Matilda's decision. Violetta, however, frowned. "You will be careful, my dears, will you not?"

"I would never let anything happen to Tavie." Dom's features expressed his hurt at his mother's comment. "You know I would not."

"Well, see that you don't," she scolded. She turned away only to bump into his grace. "Oh. Rambourne, do see what Dom has bought Tavie. It is his wedding gift to her." She watched various expressions cross the duke's face. "What do you think?" she asked, a question no one else dared raise though they wished to do so.

"I think," he said, after carefully inspecting the team and carriage, "that your son has a very good eye for horses but that he has bats in his belfry when it comes to choosing a proper carriage for a lady. Look at it. It is obviously unstable. Octavia, I forbid you to ride in that thing. Come down at once."

"I cannot."

"What do you mean you cannot? Of course you can."

"No, I can't." Tavie's eyes twinkled. "Not until Dom helps me. You may believe, Father, that I will not be taking it out by myself. I cannot get on or off the seat without help. Not and maintain my dignity!"

The crowd laughed and, after a moment, his grace joined in. "I see you will not be guided by me. So be it. My lord, I demand you see she comes to no harm. My lady?" he asked, turning to Violetta, "will you do me the honor of a stroll through the rose garden?"

Violetta ignored the fact she and Matilda had just made a thorough inspection of the roses and, blushing prettily, told Rambourne there was nothing she would like more and that he had the very nicest ideas of anyone she knew.

The rest of the group wandered off as well. Some, like Rambourne, wanted short constitutionals. Others, those who ate at midday, wished to freshen up before a luncheon was served, al fresco, on the south terrace.

Several discussed the entertainment planned for the following day, an expedition to Castlerigg Stone Circle and then into Keswick for tea at the local inn. Dom suggested he and Tavie ride there in her new carriage and Tavie anticipated the coming day more than she had already.

The remainder of the guests dispersed. The team was led away by a groom and Dom and Tavie entered the house where the housekeeper pounced on Tavie. Dom listened to Mrs. MacReady explain a problem in that evening's menu. He grinned at Tavie's patient expression, told her he'd be in their room when she was done and finished with a whispered, "Where you can give me a proper thank-you for my gift."

Mrs. MacReady chuckled softly when Tavie's complexion deepened to a rosy hue but continued her explanation of why they would be unable to serve escallops of veal and requesting that Tavie make suggestions for a substitute that would balance that particular course.

Dom, guessing it would take time to reach a solution, went to his office where the mailbag awaited his attention. He unlaced the flap and poured the contents onto his desk where he sorted out the dozen or so items into those directed to guests and his personal post.

Nearly the last piece to come to hand was one he recognized instantly. The anonymous letter writer had sent another missive. Dom's insides curdled. Using a great deal of willpower, he relaxed. He waited another moment or two to still the trembling in his fingers before lifting the seal and unfolding the cheap paper. It took a great deal of resolution to focus on the words—not that there were many.

She is a witch. Witches must die. She will die. Soon.

A cold chill ran up Dom's spine as he absorbed the threat. A threat against Tavie. Even though his wife was not named, he knew it was against her. For a moment, he wanted to rend the paper into tiny bits as he'd done before, but common sense overcame that urge. Elf had ordered him to show him any new note.

Dom gritted his teeth, a growling sound welling up in his throat. How could anyone threaten his wife? Anyone who knew her must know she was a delight, a very special human being. So did the letter come from a stranger? But would a *stranger* wish Tavie harm? It made no sense. None at all. Dom's thoughts swirled as he climbed a secondary staircase to Elf's room.

She opened her door, took one look at his face and backed up so he could enter. "Oh dear," she muttered.

"Several *oh dears* are required, my dearest of relatives," responded Dom, the expression in his eyes bleak.

"Another letter?" she guessed.

"Yes."

Elf held out her hand and Dom placed the note in it. Elf read it, blenched and sat. Luckily a chair was just behind her since her knees weakened immediately she'd scanned the words. "Witch?"

"Die?" he countered. "Why?"

Elf waved a hand dismissively. "That part's easy. The bible, Dom. One isn't to allow a witch to live or some such thing. But why would she be thought a witch?"

"You are taking that seriously?"

"You mean do I think the writer believes her to be a witch?"

"Exactly."

"I don't know. How can one tell what is in the mind of the sort of person who would write such stuff? I suppose the why is irrelevant. What I *do* take seriously is the threat."

"So do I." A muscle twitched in Dom's jaw. "I am announcing that the house party is over and everyone is to leave."

"What reason will you give?"

"Because I said so?"

"It won't do. You would have to give a reason."

"The truth then. My wife has been threatened and I want no one here who might be a danger to her. That I have to protect her and how can I when we have guests, their personal servants, extra help, some of whom I do not know personally, tradesmen making deliveries and—"

"You cannot tell them the truth," interrupted Elf. "You must not do that, Dom. It would cause more talk just when talk is dying down."

"Talk!" sputtered Dom, the whites of his eyes showing. His voice rose. "What do I care for gossip when Tavie is in danger? I must keep her safe."

"But, Dom, will making everyone leave actually help you do that?"

They battled back and forth for another ten minutes, neither giving in. Finally Elf asked, "Dom, the letter came in the mailbag?"

"Yes."

"Then we need not arrive at a decision on the instant. The person who sent the letter cannot be here in the area, am I correct?"

The notion relaxed Dom and he breathed more easily. "It would seem a reasonable suggestion," he said a bit cautiously.

"Then humor me, Dom."

He tensed up all over again. "Do nothing?"

"Of course you will do something. You will tell Bert and Geoff to watch over her and tell Tavie herself so she may be on guard."

"No." Dom's chin struck a stubborn angle. "Not Tavie. I will not have her upset. There are a couple of servants I would trust with my life. More importantly, I will trust them with hers. They will keep their chaffers muffled and attend her when she is out." At Elf's bewildered look, he smiled for the first time since opening the letter. "Chaffers muffled? A cant term you don't know? It means to keep their mouths tightly shut, Elfie, dear. I'll have them on guard along with Bert and Geoff and myself."

Elf muttered the word as if memorizing it and then said, "And Ally and myself of course."

"Aunt Ally? Do you think you should tell her?"

"Do not underestimate Ally," said Ally's sister. "Her soft ways hide a great deal of courage."

Dom nodded. If Elf said it then it must be true. He drew in a deep breath and let it out. "I told Tavie I'd meet her in our room. She'll be suspicious if I do not arrive soon. Dear Elf, please do not tell her about this. I'll protect her. Somehow. And do it without worrying her. I don't want her worried about anything ever again."

Elf watched him go down the hall and shook her head. Silly lad. Just how did he think he'd keep his wife in a state of permanent bliss? It was human nature to worry! She removed to her sister's room where, silently, she passed over the note.

Ally read it and shook her head, a slow and sad motion. "Oh dear."

"Yes," nodded Elf. "Oh dear, indeed."

* * * * *

Three carriages set off for Castlerigg. A closed carriage held the few older women who wished to view the stone circle. The second, the top down, bristled with parasols as young ladies protected their complexions from a sun that was shedding golden light over the fells. Most of the men rode near that carriage, laughing and talking as they passed through the wonderful scenery.

The third carriage was Tavie's present. She held the reins with some trepidation, having little experience with a team or with extended trips. But the miles passed smoothly, thanks to the coach-maker's recently invented springs. Those springs eased the jounces over the whinstone with which the road was paved and, finally, she relaxed and began to enjoy herself.

Castlerigg Circle itself was all she'd hoped. It was easily accessible, the surrounding fells one of the most dramatic prospects she'd yet seen. The stones were not particularly high, but someone counted thirty-eight in the pear-shaped circle and one of the guests, who knew about such things, told those who were interested that the ten extra stones forming a rectangle near the eastern edge were an unusual feature for such antiquities. When Tavie and Dom walked amid those oddly placed stones, she felt a frisson up her back and a chill that made her shiver.

"I don't think I like this place," she said quietly.

"It is rather eerie, is it not?" Dom seemed to welcome that odd feeling and Tavie shook her head in rueful amazement. "Ready to return to the carriage?" he asked, more sensitive than she had realized to her less than positive reaction.

"I am, but quite obviously the others are not."

"We will leave Geoff and Bert in charge and go on to the inn to arrange for our tea. An acceptable excuse, you see. Besides, no one will miss us."

Others followed as they willed, collecting on the tree-shaded lawn behind the inn. It was a cheerful group, old and young mingling freely and enjoying the treat. But Tavie could not feel at ease. *How odd,* she mused. *The feeling is reminiscent of my feelings the day Bert returned, injured, from the Helvellyn climb.*

With tea out of the way, some of the guests wished to explore Keswick. Each of the young ladies had purchases she wished to make and several of the men offered to squire them to the shops. Still others, people who were acquainted with Southey, wished to stop by Greta Hall to pay their respects to the hardworking poet.

The sun had dipped close to the tops of the western fells when everyone finally gathered for the return journey so it would be very nearly full dark before they reached

Brightwood. As they started off, Tavie thanked God for the long summer dusk that would add an hour or so to the evening light.

"Well done, Tavie," Dom praised. She'd held Romulus and Remus well together east of Keswick at the turn onto the road along the west side of Thirlmere.

As they continued, a companionable silence fell. They'd gone over a mile when Tavie spoke. "It's been a lovely day, has it not?" She had decided to ignore the obviously ridiculous impression that disaster hovered over them.

"Hmm," he agreed, keeping a relaxed but watchful eye on her handling of the team. "I am so proud of you, Tavie. You are a natural whip and doing fine. Really fine. You'll gain confidence and pick up speed in time, with more practice…of course you will."

His innocent tone drew her eyes in a brief, suspicious glance. "What is the matter, Dom?" Then, guessing, she laughed. "Itching to get your hands on the reins, are you not?"

A tinge of red colored his ears. "Well…"

"Well?" she teased. Their eyes met in momentary understanding before she looked back to the road.

He heaved a rueful sigh. "I must admit I'd like to see what they can do, check whether they have the turn of speed promised. I didn't have them in hand when they were purchased, you know, so I'd like to confirm they are all they are supposed to be."

"Must you sound like a wistful little boy?"

"How should I sound?"

"Like my Dominic. You should tell me to pull up, that you want a turn."

"That would not be at all polite. They are your team and it is your rig and I cannot very well order you what to do with it."

"How virtuous you sound. One might even say smug!" She softened the words with another quick smile.

Tavie waved her whip as the closed carriage filled with the older women passed and disappeared around a gentle curve. Three men on horseback trotted along beside Tavie and Dom, complimenting her on her technique, but then they too picked up speed and left Dom and Tavie behind. Tavie slowed to fall behind their dust. The second carriage with the younger women passed, their bouquet of parasols folded away and the sides of the landau fully open to the lovely evening. The rest of the men on horseback accompanied the young women's carriage and, once they'd gone by, Tavie pulled up under a convenient tree and stared out over the lake.

"Tired, my love?"

"Tired? Yes, I think I am." She thought about it. "I don't mean physically," she added. "It is just having so many people constantly underfoot. Dom, I have had to conclude Father succeeded better than he knew in making me other than my mother. From all I have heard, she would have reveled in this house party. I, however, find a little socializing goes a long way. Dom," she began in a more urgent tone, "what I've heard of the season..." Tavie shuddered, drew in a deep breath and continued. "Are you aware that some women are never home a full day the whole of a season? For three solid months, they go hither and thither and never sit quietly at home with a book or even indulge in a simple entertainment with just a few close friends? Dom, is that the way *you* live during the season?"

"One needn't," he responded, evading her question. Then, noting her determined expression, he answered honestly. "I do not suppose I thought of my rooms as much more than a *pied-à-terre* in which I slept and kept my clothes. I was so restless, always searching for something. *You*, Tavie," he said as she straightened. "Now I've found you I feel complete. For the first time in my life, I am *whole*. I too prefer a few close friends to huge social crushes. I've an idea." He'd found a solution he thought she'd like—and come to that, so would he. "We will make ourselves a reputation as that eccentric couple from the Lakes, choosing only a few of the more important events to grace with our presence and, for the rest, we will give intimate little dinners. Such elite little dinners that people will fight for invitations. There is, after all, nothing forcing one to rush around from morning to night while in town."

"But your clubs and gaming and…the Fives Court and…" She waved her hands. She had run out of things she knew gentlemen did in London, since it was ineligible to suggest he might visit a mistress. Which he'd better not do in any case.

"What," asked Dom, when he'd controlled his chuckles, "do you know about the boxing at the Fives Court?"

"Only that it is in St. Martin's Street," said Tavie, much on her dignity.

He laughed. "There will be time for our own interests. When you are comfortable, you'll attend musical evenings without me or perhaps a literary soiree. You'll visit museums and galleries and, much as I know you'll be impatient with them, there will be fittings for a new wardrobe each time we are in town. You too will be much occupied with things you'll do alone or with friends, Tavie, and I will do my sort of male thing—the boxing and visiting my club—when you are otherwise occupied. Worry not, my love, we'll work it out. But now we'd better change places and be off or they'll have to hold dinner while we dress. Which would be very odd behavior in the host and hostess. Outside of enough, I'd say."

Rather than climb down and go around, Dom rose to his feet, leaning his calves and some of his weight against the splashguard. He held himself as far away from her as he could so Tavie could slide across the seat. Her knees rubbed against his and he leaned still farther away from her—

There was a loud cracking sound and he felt himself tipping backward—

Tavie grabbed for his coat, pulling him toward her and holding just long enough that he managed to find enough balance to leap down and land on the pole—

Tavie breathed again.

But then the pole cracked, broke and threw him off to the side.

"Dom."

Tavie tugged on the reins when the carriage jerked forward, forcing herself to steady the uneasy horses before scrambling down over the high wheel. In her anxiety to reach her husband, she was totally uncaring when her skirt ripped or that she showed far too much leg. Dom was stretched out on the ground to the side, frighteningly still and pale.

"Dom, oh, Dom!"

She knelt beside him, feeling around his head for lumps, feeling for broken bones. Finding none, she sat and pulled him up onto her lap, clasping his head to her bosom.

"Dom," she sobbed softly, "oh, Dom."

"Ouch."

Tavie lifted her head to look into his face but didn't let go.

"I don't think you should hug my head quite so tightly, love. It hurts like the very devil. What happened?" Dom groaned softly and tried to sit up only to lie back, quickly, against her thighs. "Don't worry," he said when he saw tears running down her face. Reaching up, he brushed her cheeks softly. "Don't cry. I'm all right."

"You hit your head," she accused.

"Yes. But not badly," he responded, feeling for the lump beginning to come up at the back. "What happened?" he repeated.

This time Tavie answered, having decided he wasn't quite as badly hurt as she'd feared. "The splashboard broke, you dropped down, the pole snapped and you pitched off to the side. Thank heaven you did not fall under the team's hooves."

"Yes, do thank heaven for that," he said quietly. Dom took a few deep breaths and sat up. Holding onto the spokes, he climbed to his feet where he wavered for a moment. His head throbbed and his vision felt a trifle out of the way but he didn't think he'd cast up his accounts, which was a danger the first time he'd tried to sit up. Slowly he bent toward the broken part of the carriage to check the damage.

"Tavie, am I right in thinking something is wrong here?" Almost as soon as the words were out of his mouth, he wished them unsaid. If there had been tampering, he didn't wish Tavie to know. "I mean, Romulus has not scraped that hock, has he?" *Quick thinking*, he told himself—but with none of the smugness he'd have felt if totally himself. He simply hoped he'd been quick enough.

Tavie checked first one horse and then the other. "I don't find anything wrong with either of them, Dom." She threw a suspicious glance his way but he didn't see it since his eyes were closed. He again felt wobbly. "Do you think we can ride them, Dom?" she asked, wondering if he could stay on an animal's back the several miles to Brightwood.

"I don't know if they were trained for riding, Tavie," he answered after a moment. "They were wanted as a carriage team so I didn't think to ask." He thought of trying to ride and winced, thought of the possible danger to Tavie if the horses were *not* trained and asked, "How long do you suppose it will be before someone comes looking for us if we just remain here awaiting them?"

Worried, Tavie thought, *Too long*. "I could walk back to that cottage we passed and get help."

"No." The word exploded from him and he grabbed for his head. Taking a deep breath, he added, "You aren't going anywhere without me, Tavie." He was as convinced as he could be that tampering had caused the accident, although he hadn't determined just how. Aware of the danger to his wife, he wasn't about to let her go off by herself. In fact, perhaps he *should* tell her of her danger, put her on guard…

"Dom, someone is coming."

He straightened carefully and looked down the road to where a horse and rider approached. He blinked his eyes into focus. "That's Geoff."

"I wonder why he returned. We're not so late anyone should have begun to worry about us."

Dom didn't answer. Geoff had undoubtedly guessed he'd try the reins on the way home, testing the team's paces, and the fact they hadn't caught up with the slower cavalcade ahead was a clue there'd been trouble. Geoff was not stupid and, thank God, they'd had that chat about the letter. Sure enough, his old friend was frowning as he reined in beside them.

"If I am *de trop*," he drawled, "simply inform me of the fact and I'll leave." His eyes went to the carriage and widened briefly. "If not, what can I do to help?"

"You can get Dom back to Brightwood where we can call the doctor to look at his head." Tavie put her hand over Dom's mouth when he would have expressed his outrage at the notion. "He was unconscious and didn't rouse for some minutes. I'm worried it might be concussion."

"Hmm." Geoff rubbed his chin. "Transport's a problem, is it not?" He glanced at his friend. Almost sharply, he said, "Dom, sit down before you fall down, you idiot."

"I hate to admit it but I must have hit harder than I thought." He slid down the wheel and leaned against it. "The devil! I feel a fool."

"Feel one if you must," said Tavie, scolding gently, "but do not, under any circumstances, *play* the fool as well."

Dom chuckled at her oddly phrased scold and decided he must warn his wife of her danger. She was too unconventional. He could not predict what she would do next, as he might of a young woman with less spirit and less independence of mind. "Tavie." He stopped her by the simple expedient of clutching her skirts. "Tavie, when we get back to the house I want to talk to you. Do not go off by yourself for any reason until I do, please."

"By myself?" Tavie stared down at him. "All right. If it is important to you," she added when he didn't release her.

"Promise."

"I promise not to go off on my own."

Dom closed his eyes and nodded, wincing as the movement did nasty things to his aching head.

Once the horses were freed, Tavie checked the carriage but found she didn't know enough to tell if there'd been tampering. *First the boat – the boat which might have killed all three of the friends. Now the carriage. A brand-new carriage. A carriage Dom designed.* It seemed unlikely the splashboard should have fallen away from the front that way. And should a new pole shatter as this had?

"Something the matter, Tavie?" asked Geoff casually.

"Why did the pole break, Geoff?"

He checked it over, poking and prying. "Tavie, this is the carriage Dom had built for you, is it not?"

"You know it is."

"Then why is there an old and rotten pole on it?"

"Rotten? Let me see." Even to Tavie's uneducated eye, now she knew what to look for, the wood appeared odd. "Would the carriage maker try to save money by—"

"No," interrupted Geoff, waving away the notion. "Very reputable man, Obadiah Elliot. You noticed he used his elliptical spring, did you not?" Tavie nodded, having been educated on the subject by Dom. Unaware of that, Geoff went on to explain. "He invented it. It makes it unnecessary to build the old-fashioned heavy frameworks and results in a much lighter and speedier carriage. But never mind that. I'd say this tongue was put in after it arrived at Brightwood."

"But who would do such a thing? And why?"

"Someone who didn't like you perhaps?" asked Geoff casually but watching her reaction carefully.

"But why would someone, anyone, dislike me? Until this house party, I'd never been in society. Where would I have made an enemy who hated me enough to want to hurt me? Or see me dead? No. It is unthinkable."

Geoff had his own theory about who was behind the letters, the threats and the accidents. But he had no proof that the obvious candidate, Dom's heir, was the villain. Besides, he *liked* Owen. Given the style of the accidents, he had reluctantly dismissed Sarah, a still more obvious candidate for the role, out of hand. These were not the sort of projects a woman could handle.

He had, moreover, an alternate notion. Tavie was an only child and someone might wish to remove her from her father's will and particularly might wish to do so before she had children who would inherit after her. But *who,* and how would one discover discreetly what her father would do with his wealth if Tavie were no longer alive to be his heiress? Coming out of his reverie, Geoff noticed Tavie was staring at him with wide, painfully open eyes.

"I do not see any more reason to delay," he said, a doleful expression making his thin face clownlike. "I must go to my fate sooner or later and it might as well be sooner."

He led Romulus toward the carriage, stepped up on a spoke on the wheel and pulled himself onto the bare back. Romulus shifted his weight from one foot to the other as Geoff settled and the ears moved back, but the horse didn't offer to forcibly remove the burden of Geoff's weight. Geoff leaned forward and patted Romulus on the neck.

"Good boy. Romulus will do, Tavie. Now for Remus."

He'd deliberately tried the more patient, slightly less spirited animal first. Remus eyed him and he eyed the horse. Remus stamped a hoof and twitched his tail. "Well, boy, are you going to cooperate?" Somehow Geoff didn't think the second gelding would tamely submit to the indignity of a rider.

Hearing hoofbeats, Tavie turned toward the road. "Wait, Geoff. A gig is coming."

Geoff, careful to make it silent, let out a long breath. With any luck, he wouldn't have to attempt the second horse. Remus had a mischievous look Geoff had seen in the eyes of other horses. Now, if there were a saddle, it would be different. He'd have enjoyed the challenge if the odds had been a little more even. But bareback? He didn't like those odds at all.

Dr. Hayhoe pulled up at Geoff's call. "What? What do you say? An accident?" The doctor's eyes traveled from Geoff to Tavie and wondered where his lordship might be. Had he been wrong about the young marchioness? Was she no better than she should be? Only just married and playing her husband for a fool with his friend?

Tavie approached, looking up at him with concern in her eyes. "Please, doctor, will you look at Dom? He hit his head and was unconscious for some minutes. I'm worried about him."

The doctor felt himself flush and told himself it was the last time he'd jump to conclusions about the bride but reminded himself, in his own defense, that one heard *such* stories. They made it difficult not to think the worst. He climbed down from his gig and moved around the phaeton. They found Dom stretched full-length on the ground, the back of his hand pressed to his forehead.

"Here now, here now! What's to do, my lord?"

Dom opened one eye, decided the question was rhetorical and closed it again. Gentle hands touched the back of his head but, even so, Dom winced when the doctor found the lump. At the doctor's orders, he opened his eyes and focused on Tavie who was leaning over Hayhoe's shoulder, a worried look on her face.

"Eyes all right," muttered the doctor. "Quite all right. That's the best test," he added, speaking more loudly. "Yes, my lady, the best test in the world. He'll do. He'll do. Just needs quiet and time to rid himself of the headache."

"Thank heaven," breathed Tavie.

"I wonder, doctor," said Dom's friend, coming forward, "if you'd be so kind as to take Lord Brightwood up in your carriage and transport him home. It is an imposition, given the distance you must backtrack, but, with this carriage broken and his head the way it is, I don't like to see him trying to ride so far."

Hayhoe chuckled. "It'll be quite a squeeze, with my lady on one side and me on the other, but we'll get him home, that we will. Yes we will."

It *was* a squeeze. Tavie twisted sideways to make herself as small as possible and put her arms around Dom to hold him steady. The doctor found it a trifle difficult to handle his horse but he managed, driving slowly so as to avoid as many bumps as possible. He, after all, didn't have patent springs under his carriage! Geoff rode behind, leading the team, and the cavalcade made slow progress back to Brightwood, arriving just as searchers were about to set out looking for them.

"*Another* accident?" Bert's eyebrows rose until nearly hidden under the carefully contrived Brutus styling of his hair. He leaned both hands on the head of the cane to which he'd graduated that morning. "Well, that's two. Things come in threes, do they not? What do you suppose will happen next?" he asked on a cheerful note that had Tavie wanting to hit him.

He moved forward, limping, to help first Tavie and then Dom out of the gig. Dom allowed his huge friend to take much of his weight. He'd been silent on the trip back to Brightwood, his mind going in tail-chasing circles. He wondered if he'd been wrong. Perhaps the letter writer *was* in residence and had contrived to make it appear as if the letter came with the mailbag by adding it once the bag was placed on his desk.

If such had been the way of it, it might be wise to pretend to be worse than he was. If he were thought to be hurt, he need not play such an active role as host, need not go off from Brightwood and leave Tavie alone. Yes, that was just what he'd do. So he leaned on Bert, who leaned on his cane, and then, once inside, he pretended to need help up the stairs.

Hayhoe tipped his head to one side and wondered about Dom's condition. *Is there more wrong with his lordship than I thought? Is there now?*

Tavie, knowing her husband thoroughly, was seriously concerned. Dom would have to be at death's door to lean on Bert that way. His pride was such that allowing the whole world to see his weakness was, in the normal way, unthinkable.

Geoff, knowing Dom even better than Tavie did, was thinking similar thoughts. He took her arm and they followed the doctor up the stairs. Behind them, Deblon cleared his throat.

Tavie turned on the landing, the frown not leaving her face. "Deblon," she ordered, not waiting to discover what he wanted, "if you have not yet announced dinner, please do so. Ask Lady Brightwood and my father to act as hosts, if you will be so kind. This evening I must see to his lordship." She scurried on up the stairs.

Dr. Hayhoe, much against Dom's vocal dislike, made a thorough examination. "Because," he said to Geoff, "his lordship must have hurt himself more badly than he is admitting. Yes he must."

The doctor would not leave until he had probed and prodded and tortured Dominic almost to the point where the marquis nearly decided he'd let the doctor in on the plot he'd hatched. Enough was enough.

But before Dom gave into the urge, the man left. Shaking his head that he'd found nothing, Dr. Hayhoe frowned all the way to the front door, giving rise to all sorts of surmise amongst those servants who saw him leave, and later, amongst the guests who were given a description of the doctor's concern by maids and valets. All of which was a serendipitous addition to Dom's plan to fool the villain.

Once the door closed, Dom threw off the bedclothes, reached for his robe and, hopping out of bed, shrugged into the brilliantly colored silk. He paced, worrying away at what had happened. He looked up to find his friends and Tavie scowling at him. Geoff lounged against the mantel. Bert slouched in a chair, his bad leg resting on a hassock. Tavie stood near the door, which she'd closed behind the doctor, hands on hips and mouth pursed. When she saw she had his attention, she scowled more fiercely than ever.

"I think," she suggested in a judicious tone, "you had better have a very good reason for worrying us so."

"I do." When the scowl did the impossible and deepened, he asked, "Don't I?" When she still didn't agree, he looked from Geoff, who nodded thoughtfully, to Bert, who hadn't quite caught on. "I am injured. I cannot possibly go off anywhere."

"Why not?" asked Bert.

"Leaving Tavie alone?"

"*Alone*?" asked Bert. He now understood Dom's trick but his voice revealed hurt at Dom's lack of trust in their ability to care for Tavie. "She wouldn't be alone!"

"I'd not have a moment's peace, worrying about her."

"Worry about *me*?" Tavie blinked, shaking her head in bewilderment. "But it is *you* who is in danger."

Dom's eyes widened. Husband and wife stared at each other as Dom absorbed Tavie's obvious knowledge that something was wrong. "Is it?" he asked. "Me, I mean?"

In the ensuing argument, each stubbornly denied his danger. Each insisted it was the other's. They squared off and glared at each other. It was obvious to their friends that, no matter how they argued, neither Tavie nor Dom changed his mind one iota about who was the target of today's villainy.

Bert cleared his throat. Geoff coughed softly. Dom's features relaxed into a grin and Tavie smiled in response. He opened his arms. Dom's look beckoned her to him and, despite the fact Geoff and Bert were there, she went. Then, after a mutual hug, she turned in his embrace, adopting her favorite position by leaning back against his chest, and looked from Bert to Geoff, the two men obviously, if silently, questioning Dom.

"I wish someone would explain what is going on," she said plaintively, finally breaking the silence.

"Have you decided to tell her?" asked Geoff.

"I must. Today proved the letter writer is more immediately dangerous than I'd believed. She must be on her guard."

"Letter writer?" Tavie looked from one to the other. "What letter writer?"

"You know we'd watch her when you could not," said Bert, his hurt that Dom did not trust him to see to Tavie's safety not yet soothed.

"I would trust either of you with my life. It is Tavie I find I can trust to no one but myself. Until you fall as deeply into love as I have done, you cannot possibly understand how I feel."

Tavie, looking gratified by his intensity, nodded. "I feel the same way about Dom. Whenever he is gone from me, I cannot seem to do anything but worry about him. I wish this silly party were over and all those awful people would go away."

"You do not mean that," said Bert. "You have assembled a delightful house party."

"You refer perhaps to Lady Sands?" asked Tavie, her tone wry. Then her mood shifted to mischievous and she added, "Or perhaps Lady Broughton? She thinks you would be perfect for her daughter. Then there is Miss Pytchley who delights you with her attentions whenever you cannot escape and Lady Eloise and—" Bert's groan interrupted her and she chuckled. When Bert stopped blushing, Tavie sobered and once again asked, "What letters?"

Geoff, however, wasn't paying attention and when he spoke changed the subject to the one occupying his mind. "Dom, did you check the damage to that pole?"

"I looked at it but, except that it seemed more shattered than I'd have expected, I felt too sick to decide what was wrong."

"I poked at the wood with my penknife. It was rotten, Dom."

"Rotten? Elliot would use only well-seasoned timber!"

"True. But the pole could have been changed. Last night. You house your servants too well, Dom. No one sleeps over the carriage house, do they? It is quite unprotected, assuming one has access to a key. And anyone knowing the workings of this house *would*. Or a picklock could open those old-fashioned locks in a trice. I could myself."

"You could?" asked Bert, his interest caught by the novel idea.

"I could. And do not ask where I learned because I cannot tell you."

Neither Bert nor Tavie missed the look Geoff and Dom exchanged. The two left out of the secret silently commiserated with each other. Bert suspected it had something to do with Geoff's work for the government about which he spoke as little as possible. It was an open secret among the three friends that Geoff occasionally took on jobs for Castlereagh under direction from the War Office. Tavie had guessed at something of the sort by putting together one or two clues Geoff had dropped before the party began.

"But that is not relevant." Geoff waved away their curiosity. "What is, is that we've no notion where or how the villain will strike next."

"First the boat..." Bert said.

"I checked that. It was an accident," Dom said.

"How can you be certain? Someone who understands the construction might have known how to weaken it so it would come apart under pressure."

"All that happened was that a plank loosened at one end. It could have happened at any time. Rot around a nail for instance..." Dom shrugged.

"A removed nail would do the same then," Geoff suggested.

Dom drew on his memory for a mental picture of the relevant plank. Had there been marks in the wood around the holes? He could not remember.

"We don't need to argue it," said Geoff. "We don't know which of you is the target but we do know we have had at least one case of attempted murder and very likely two. We also have those letters."

"What letters?" asked Tavie for the third time.

Geoff went on as if she hadn't spoken. "We must come up with a plan to protect—"

"I forbid," interrupted Tavie in a penetrating tone, "any of you to say one more word until someone tells me about those letters."

Chapter Ten

"Tavie, if we are forbidden to speak, how can anyone tell you about the letters?" Geoff asked in a teasing tone meant to put her off.

"What letters?" asked Bert. "Oh," he added at Geoff's exasperated expression, "*those* letters."

Knowing her stubborn nature, Dom told her as little as possible. "Anonymously written threats, Tavie. Nothing you need worry about except to know you are threatened."

"What do they say?"

"You don't need—"

"Dominic."

The three men looked at each other helplessly. "Tavie, really, you do not want to know," soothed Geoff.

"Don't ask," said Bert ominously. "Geoff's right. You do *not* want to know."

"Besides, I've destroyed them," finished Dom as if that settled the matter, ignoring the one Elf had placed in the bottom of her modest jewel box.

"*Destroyed* them?" Tavie looked from one to the other. "You should not have done that."

"Because you wish to see them?"

"Because if something *does* happen, there would be no proof of the threats."

"Nothing is going to happen to you," Dom said.

Once again Tavie squared off with Dom, her clenched fists waving under his nose. "While you are protecting *me*, you great lummox, who will be protecting *you*?"

Dom's chin jutted dangerously. "I tell you it is you who is in danger."

Geoff shook his head in rueful amusement. He walked between the antagonists. He put a hand on Dom's chest and stopped just short of treating Tavie likewise, realizing just in time what he was about to do. He flushed slightly at his near *faux pas*, but he *had* managed to get their attention.

"Dom, she is right. We do not know for certain…exactly who is in danger," he said when they stared at him. "Or, coincidence that it would be, perhaps your marriage has set off *two* murderers. Your son would cut out your heir, Dom, but," he went on to Tavie, "your potential offspring would be additional heirs to your father's fortune, which someone might find a worry. Do you have any notion who inherits if you do not?"

"Why have I not thought of that?" asked Dom before Tavie could do more than shake her head. But whether she was denying knowledge or denying the idea, no one knew. Thoughtfully, Dom continued. "Yes, that might explain why someone wishes Tavie harm."

"Or perhaps you all have holes in the head. I am all of a quarter of a century old. Why would a greedy heir wait so long to put me out of his way? The idea is idiotic."

"Perhaps the murderer had not thought of it before. Perhaps your marriage put it into his head. Or perhaps so long as you remained a spinster, he didn't care, believing he or his heirs would eventually inherit."

"I prefer the idea it is Dom's heir rather than my father's." Tavie bit her lip, her eyes narrowing. "But that is Owen, is it not? Owen would not hurt so much as a fly. Besides, he'd not know how to change one pole for another, would he? Or could someone hire the job done?" She went back to leaning against Dom and pulled his arms more tightly around her, trying to dissipate the chill the discussion induced. "Oh, but it is all so very silly. There is no one who wishes either of us such ill they'd resort to murder." She frowned again. "Except Sarah perhaps, but women do not know about making holes in boats or changing poles and things of that nature. Besides, if Sarah wished to murder someone, she'd poison them or stab them in the back or something equally certain." She looked up over her shoulder at her husband. "Wouldn't she?"

"Sarah..." Dom frowned fiercely, a wisp of a thought teasing him. "Something about Aunt Sarah..." He shook his head. "I cannot recall. Never mind. It'll come to me." He hugged his wife and then gently placed his hands on her shoulders to set her aside. "I do not know about these idiots but I am starving. Ring for a maid, love, and order us up some dinner, will you?" He crawled into bed, pulling the covers up to his waist. "I'll just wait here for my invalid tray and then join you in the sitting room for real food once it is set out, all right?"

"No, it is not," said Bert instantly.

Dom frowned at his friend. "Why not?"

"Because you'll cause talk if your tray goes back to the kitchen uneaten," said Geoff with patently false patience. Then he grinned. "Far more important there won't be enough for *us* if *you* eat a share." Geoff always ate more than Dom despite being a much smaller man.

Tavie forced a chuckle at the men's attempt to lighten the atmosphere. "The servants know how hungry you get, Geoff. They'll bring up a generous dinner, enough for all."

"Good. If we are going to be playing guard dog, I need to keep up my strength. Can't stay alert and wary if I am thinking of my stomach, now can I?"

As he'd intended, Geoff's words drew a real laugh from Tavie. For the remainder of the evening, the men, understanding each other very well, worked in tandem to keep her laughing.

Much later, Tavie joined Dom in the huge bed where countless Thorntons had been born and died. The thought of the continuity of family line was comforting. The idea the direct line might be broken by Dom's death was unthinkable. He, with her help—or that of some other woman—would provide an heir to carry on the next generation. She could bear anything so long as she believed that to be true. Even her own death would be better than that Dom might die. Snuggled up to her husband, she closed her eyes and, after a fashion, slept.

* * * * *

The days sped by and the date of the ball approached. Tavie was always busy but glad to have her mind occupied. She was working when Dom opened the door to her little office. He didn't think he'd been particularly quiet but his wife did not look up from the lists she studied, adding a note as he watched.

What, he wondered, *if I were a murderer? I could walk up behind her*—which he did—*and put my hands around her throat*—which he did.

When she twisted within his fingers and smiled up at him, he sighed. "You are dead," he said sorrowfully. Then he bent and kissed the side of her throat above the ruffle of her morning gown.

"Dead? What do you mean Dom?"

"Such innocence. Have I not asked that you never be alone? And did you not promise? Is this the way you keep your promises?"

Tavie frowned. "But I thought you meant when I go somewhere. How could I be in danger in our own home?"

He sighed dramatically, an exaggerated expression of exasperation, before explaining.

"Fiddle. Dom, I cannot have someone around, talking to me and interrupting me, when I am working." She pursed her lips into a moue. "Think. How would *you* like someone around when you go over your accounts?"

"You are correct. I would not like it. But, my love, I'd die too if something happened to you, so you *will* be careful, will you not? For instance, you won't stay in a room alone without remembering to lock the door?"

"Won't people think me a bit strange?"

"You may tell them you wish to avoid interruptions. Please, Tavie."

"Oh, all right. I will feel the fool and I still think..."

Dom scowled and she drew in a deep breath, letting it out in a whoosh of disgust before she continued.

"It is nonsense *but*," she held up her hand, "I will lock the door."

"Good." Dom picked up a handful of papers and glanced at the headings. "I hadn't a notion how hard women work to organize a ball. I wonder if it is worth it."

"I am very likely doing more than I need. It is my first effort and I am so afraid of forgetting something or doing something wrong. Even with Ally, Elf, your mother and Lady Clavingstone to consult—well, how can I be certain I've asked all the right questions? Most girls have had the opportunity of seeing what their mothers do. Even if they have not paid much attention, they have a notion of what goes on. I've never *been* to a ball, let alone been in a house where one was organized."

Dom pressed forward over the top of her chair and Tavie leaned against him. She luxuriated in the feel of his hands kneading her shoulders, tension and worry seeping away under his attentions.

How was I so lucky as to have married this wonderful man? It isn't possible I might lose him now.

Tension rushed back despite his continued touch. The week since the carriage accident had passed without incident but everyone aware of the situation believed they had not seen the last of the horror. Until they discovered who was trying to kill one or both of the victims, none of them dared relax one iota.

"What is it, Tavie?" asked Dom.

"How do you remain so calm, Dom? I am in constant expectation of further disaster."

"You are afraid?" He frowned, his fingers digging more deeply into tight muscles, trying to undo the knots he felt there. "But, my love, Geoff, Bert and I are here. We won't allow anything to happen to you."

"To *me*? Dom, I am not worried for myself. Or, in a way, maybe I am. Do you not understand that I feel just as you say you do? Having found you, I think I'd lose my mind if I lost you and you are so *careless*. I am always in a quake for you, Dom."

"We are even, are we not? You can understand how I felt when I came in here and you didn't notice until I had my hands on your throat. It might have been the murderer, Tavie, except Bert and Geoff and I have been in the billiards room, one of us at the hall door with an eye on you, ever since you came into this room." He chuckled at her look of disbelief but shook his head at her stubborn refusal to worry about herself. "While you worry about me, I worry about you. But right now, this instant, neither of us need worry about the other because we are together." After a short silence in which his hands stayed busy, his tone changed to the suggestive. "Do you think that chaise lounge over there would be long enough for—"

"Dominic Thornton," Tavie interrupted, "don't you dare suggest what I think you are about to suggest. We couldn't. Not possibly…here…where anyone might come… Dom, you mustn't…" She gasped at the sensations his roving hands roused in her always-needy body. "Dom, the door…"

"Is locked," he whispered into her ear and then nuzzled the side of her neck. "How do you think I can be certain we are safe?" he asked softly.

"But…here?"

Tavie thought she'd become used to Dom's style of loving, having discovered under his tutelage and to her delight, it was not something one indulged only in the dark of the night. But…here? Here where anyone wishing to discuss some aspect of the ball with her might interrupt? Her breath came in gasps and her pulse raced.

Tavie discovered, as others have, the ancient rule that the danger of discovery added a touch of spice to what they were doing.

Later, when Dom played lady's maid and helped her adjust her clothes and pin up her hair, she giggled. "I am rather glad you were a rake long ago in your *old* life, my beloved husband."

"What an odd thing for a wife to say," he responded, his voice as calm as suppressed laughter could make it. He found another hairpin and pinned up another curl.

"If you had *not*, you would not be so handy at putting me to rights, would you?"

"Ah, but if I had *not*, perhaps there would be no need to, er, put you to rights? We'd have a conventionally cold marriage where I visited you a few minutes each night until you were *enceinte* and then avoided you until there was need to repeat the process."

"Oh." Tavie blinked. "Is that the way of it?" She thought of some of the houseguests and decided that, indeed, for some couples, it very well might be. Poor things. "Well, *another* reason for being glad," she said.

"Oh?" Finished with the pins, Dom smoothed one curl after another over his finger, an excuse to continue playing with her hair.

"Of course. I would have hated to miss that," she said and gestured toward the chaise. "You are the most wonderful lover a woman could have, my lord," she added just a trifle shyly.

"I want to please you, Tavie." His fingertips stilled against her shoulders, a barely felt touch. "It was never so important before. I was pleased if the woman I was with found satisfaction, but it wasn't something I cared about as I do now. With you, it is so very different."

"So I should hope!" Tavie didn't know whether she was jealous of the women who had been in his life or happy he felt differently about her. Self-understanding led to the wry thought that she was both jealous *and* smug and that it was not a particularly comfortable combination. Perhaps it would be best if they didn't discuss his past.

"Think you might take time off from all that," he waved at the desk, "and come riding?"

Tavie, about to say no, changed her mind. She knew Dom would not go if she did not. She knew he no longer had the excuse of a bad head to keep him home but, somehow, he still managed not to go out without her. She also knew he missed his daily exercise. As did she.

"I'll make time, Dom. When do you want to go?"

His lips twitched slightly as he checked his fob watch. "The horses," he said, his mouth prim but his eyes dancing, "will be at the front door in fifteen minutes."

"Fifteen minutes—not half enough time for changing!"

"I was coming to suggest a ride when I…hmm…was distracted."

She cast him a wry, half-shocked, half-funning look. A glance at the desk, a shrug of her shoulders and Tavie threw up her hands. "I don't suppose I've forgotten anything. Elf is forever telling me to relax. I'll just go up to change… Coming?" she added with that odd shyness that occasionally overtook her when the subject turned intimate.

They strolled toward the stairs, stopping to chat a moment or two with any guests they passed on their way. They behaved as proper hosts should, properly attentive and asking all the right questions. If there was an extra glow to Tavie's complexion, if Dom kept a proprietary hand on his wife's waist, none were so rude as to mention it. And most were glad to have discovered their original notions about the bride were inaccurate. Only a very few remembered that Lady Sands had started the rumors. And only Lady Sefton mentioned it.

"My dears," she said, "I am so glad you invited us. That we have had this opportunity to become acquainted with your darling wife, Lord Brightwood, has been a delight. When you come to town this fall may I hope that I am the very first hostess you honor with your presence?" She smiled at Tavie's obvious pleasure. "I do not understand how Lady Sands could have been so *wrong*," she said and then nodded. "I have written all my friends that I mean to add you to my guest list, my dear child, just as soon as I return to London."

Tavie ignored the "child", which seemed odd since Lady Sefton was not *that* much older than herself. She and Dom thanked her ladyship. Dom smiled down at his wife, pride in his gaze. Tavie, looking up at him, had a rather rueful expression on her face. She had been so wrong about how she'd be treated by those who had taken to themselves the right to determine who was and who was not *someone* in society.

Not, she thought, *that we are out of the briars.*

Not all were as generous as Lady Sefton when it came to a true understanding of Tavie's character and the threats to their safety remained. But even Tavie had to admit Elf's idea of a house party had been an ingeniously simple means of contradicting the content of rumors that, otherwise, would not have been easily countered.

* * * * *

The night of the ball, the ballroom chandeliers glittered and gleamed. They had been removed from protective swathing and cleaned and the candlelight, through the cut-glass baubles, sent broken shafts of multicolored light down over the swirling figures of the dancers. It added a fairy-tale beauty the guests appreciated.

Sarah Sands, however, did not notice. She was having far too much difficulty keeping track of Dom and Tavie. At first she believed it would be easy. The reception line kept them together long into the evening. Then they led off the dancing. She felt some concern at that point, but for a time it appeared all would be well. Dom promenaded Tavie around the perimeter of the room, stopping often to talk to their guests. Sarah followed. Discreetly. Eventually, she told herself, they would pause to rest and then her chance would come. And in such a crowd, no one could be suspected more than another. She'd be safe.

It was not of course that simple. Someone asked Dom for permission to dance with Tavie. After a rueful glance at his wife, he agreed and turned to ask a nearby matron for the honor of leading her out. So it had gone. The music would end, Sarah would think her time had come. And it would start all over. Another man would take Tavie onto the floor and Dom would follow with a female guest.

With growing anticipation, overlaid with an irrational fear the two would *never* stop dancing, Sarah continued stalking them. She was only feet away when, *finally*, Tavie and Dom strolled to where Elf stood.

Surely now, thought Sarah.

"It is going pretty well, is it not?" Tavie asked Elf.

"Tavie, my dear worrier!" scolded Elf. Her eyes twinkled. "You were told over and over you need feel no disquiet."

The mention of worry brought to Tavie's mind her responsibilities. "I'll just check the dining room one more—"

"Oh no, you will not!" Dom took her arm and tugged her around. "Except for opening the ball, I have had not one opportunity to dance with my wife." He bowed over Tavie's hand in a formal request, his gaze never leaving hers. "This, I believe, is ours?"

Playing his game, Tavie curtsied demurely. "Let me see, my lord." Ostentatiously, Tavie opened her fan and tipped it so she could pretend to read the names supposedly written on the spokes. "Why, what an excellent memory, my lord. This *is* your dance."

Sarah ground her teeth and faded back beside the window drapes. She fingered the tiny vial that she'd once stolen from an acquaintance's laboratory and, this evening, hidden in a secret pocket in her gown.

The gentleman scientist had lectured for a boringly long time on the dangerous properties of the chemical. It had seemed at the time that it might someday become useful. And now it would.

Eventually.

Sarah fretted about where the two would, this time, come off the floor.

Tavie, meanwhile, waved the fan under Dom's nose. "Now I look at this thing more closely," she said, her eyes gleaming with mischief, "I see you have *all* the remaining dances, my lord. Is that not strange?"

Dom chuckled and led her out to join the nearest set. "Not only is it odd, Tavie, it is going to shock all the high-sticklers and make the gossips busier than ever. It is not done, you know," he said, attempting a stern expression he could not maintain.

"To dance so often with one's husband, you mean?"

"But of course." His eyes gleamed with laughter. "How unfashionable it would be."

"Did we not agree to be the eccentric couple from the Lakes?" Tavie tipped her head in query, faintly anxious. The anxiety faded when Dominic nodded. She relaxed. "Then we should begin as we mean to go on. *All* my dances, Dom," she ordered. He grinned at her. She misunderstood. "Surely you cannot think I wish to endure half hour after half hour with men I neither know nor care to know."

"It wasn't that of which I was thinking but of the way you were ordering me to obey. Am I to live under the cat's paw, my love?"

"Only when it is for your own good."

His grin widened. "All your dances?"

"All. All we actually *dance* anyway. Otherwise," she said, tongue-in-cheek, "I might find you soliciting a dance from one of these delicious young ladies and be tempted, or *worse*," her eyes widened in pretended dismay, "you might find a mature woman who does not enjoy such felicity in her married life as I do in mine."

He sobered instantly. "No one will ever again tempt me but you."

His eyes promised that and much more as he swung her into the romping galop the musicians struck up. Tavie's breath raced, her pulse beating.

"I wish," he said softly at the end, as he slowly released her and bowed over her hand, "that I might tell all these people to go home and leave us and I might be alone with you for the rest of our lives." His eyes never left hers as he raised her from her curtsy.

But no one would have known he wished his guests to the devil when, Tavie's arm tucked under his, he strolled around the room, stopping to chat with this guest and then that, subtly reintroducing Tavie to strangers who had passed them in the receiving line earlier and whose names she might have forgotten.

"This," he said finally, "is very thirsty work. Would you like a negus or a lemonade, love?"

She tipped her head in pensive thought. "I've never tasted champagne, Dom." She batted her lashes at him. "I think I'd like my first glass in your company."

"You've never…"

"Never. My father did not believe women had a head to sample wines. Or, for that matter, any drink stronger than negus."

"That," said Elf, who happened to stroll up just in time to overhear, "was because your mother became rather quickly lightheaded if she had so much as a glass. I often felt it had nothing to do with the wine. She could become equally gay with none at all. I believe she grew drunk on nothing more stimulating than pleasure, Tavie."

Dom had, meanwhile, signaled a footman who carried a tray with glasses filled with everything from lemonade and negus to cups of punch and of course glasses of the required champagne. As the young fellow neared Lady Sands, she stepped into his path, her back to Dom and Tavie. She took her time choosing her drink, pointing and asking which was what. The footman answered impatiently, his gaze going to Dom, to whom he apologized silently for the delay. Dom reassured him just as silently. Seconds later, Sarah allowed the footman to move on.

"Here, Tavie. Champagne for my lovely wife," said Dom, lifting the last two glasses. "Thank you. That will be all." A fragment of manners returned to him. "Except…Aunt Elf?" He looked at his great-aunt's glass that was half full of some darker fluid. Sherry, he thought. "I see you are not yet in need of a refill. Yes, that will be all, Martin."

Sarah tensed at the delay. Her heart pounded in anticipation. She watched out of the corner of her eye, pretending to be interested in the dancing. Someone stopped to speak to the bride and groom and she grimaced at this further delay to her revenge. She wondered if one thing after another would interfere and if she'd *never* achieve her goal.

Sarah pooh-poohed such fancies—but a faint dewing of sweat moistened her brow as she waited anxiously. Then Dom circled Tavie's wrist, raising her arm so he could loop his through her elbow. Sarah gritted her teeth. Why did they not drink? But they would. It must be soon. *She couldn't breathe…*

Tavie stared into Dom's eyes and tipped her glass toward her lips. Sarah held her breath and then…let it out in a sigh as still-another couple stopped to speak to the two and they lowered their still-linked arms to respond.

The gentleman, who was slightly tipsy, spoke at length and Sarah wondered if she were fated to lose still-another opportunity to gain her proper place in the world… But finally the couple moved on and Dom turned back, raising his arm again. Their gazes locked, neither seeing anything but the other. Again the two lifted their glasses toward their lips.

Sarah stared. Now. It would be *now*…but it wasn't. She sighed. What could Dom possibly have to say to the witch? Why could he not be silent? Why didn't they *drink*?

A rather wild movement in one of the sets brought the dancers far too near the couple. Sarah's eyes were drawn to one particularly nimble young man whose jumps and spins were so exaggerated that his partner appeared rather embarrassed.

Sarah looked back at Dom and Tavie. They still had not sipped, their gazes still locked together in that odd, blank way of lovers that Sarah had always found inexplicable. And Dom still murmured words no one but the enraptured Tavie could hear.

And then it happened. The young man lost his footing and backed into Tavie. Tavie fell toward Dom. Her champagne slopped. So did his. She shrieked lightly at the sensation of cool liquid splashing down her neck, dripping down to soak into her low-cut bodice.

Sarah swore softly but no one noticed.

It was not possible she was fated to fail. Always. No. It could not be. She *would* achieve her proper place in the world.

Obviously, however, not tonight.

* * * * *

Dom's free arm went around his wife to save her a tumble. He glared over her head at the tipsy, red-faced gentleman whose overly enthusiastic dancing had tumbled him against Tavie.

"Blast it, Redfern, do look where you are going. You've spilt our wine."

The man mumbled something, becoming more flushed with every word. "Sorry," Tavie deciphered from among the jumble of words. She touched him lightly on the arm and smiled.

Young Redfern blinked. "Angel," he said much more distinctly, which had his partner pouting. "Died and gone to heaven. Must have…"

"I think you've just retrieved yourself for life, Lord Redfern," said Tavie, laughing. "That must be the nicest compliment anyone ever gave me. Dom, do see to Lord Redfern's, um, *comfort* while I run up and change. I cannot remain in this gown, wet as it is." She touched the bodice. It was draped from pale golden muslin, which the champagne had darkened to an ugly old-gold color, and now revealed the exact contour of her breast in a most distressing fashion. Tavie plucked at it, deeply embarrassed. The dampening of a gown was a "look" a notorious flirt might adopt or, still worse, the *other* sort of woman looking to attract a protector.

Sarah, fairly shaking with disappointment and half-made plans, oozed herself into the circle of sympathetic onlookers. "Why, Tavie, dear, what happened to your lovely gown? How sad. Is it ruined do you think? Why do I not come with you and help you and perhaps we may save it?"

"Thank you very much, Lady Sands, but," began Tavie, her eyes flitting among the nearby guests, "I don't believe that will be necessary. Elf will come." The last person Tavie wished with her was Sarah and her eyes begged Elf to understand that she felt the need of protection from the gossips she'd meet on her way to her room.

Elf tore her eyes away from Sarah's profile and nodded. She'd already determined to go with Tavie but had her own reason for attending to Dom's wife. Could she really have seen what she thought she'd seen? Had Sarah looked as if she wished to murder Lord Redfern? Surely not?

Besides, *why* would Sarah look daggers at the hopeless man? He was a creature of no account, who lived on the fringes of the *ton* and, pockets to let, loved to be invited to parties where he enjoyed himself immensely as he slowly drank himself silly and ate as much as two other guests—assuming dinner was served before he passed out.

But Sarah had looked so very strange, and what sort of mischief would require murdering poor bumbling Redfern? Elf's gaze drifted to the glasses. Dom's hung from two fingers, the last drip about the fall to the floor and Tavie's...

Gently, Elf took the glass Tavie still clutched and, with a sly glance around, sniffed it. Almonds? How very odd. She'd never had champagne that smelled of almonds. Carrying it carefully, she followed the embarrassed, young woman. Their progress was slow because several people stopped them to ask about the accident, which Elf took time to explain. They needed no more rumors about Tavie and certainly not that she *drank* and *just like her mother*—a phrase Elf had overheard far too often during the house party—*couldn't hold her wine.* Things had gone very well the last week or so and Elf didn't want this latest *contretemps* interfering with the progress they'd made in establishing Tavie in the *ton.*

Once Tavie was in the hands of a maid, Elf trotted along to her room where she chose a small bottle. She emptied the perfume out the window and rinsed it until it no longer smelled of lilies. She poured the dregs of Tavie's champagne into it and capped it securely. Were those few drops enough that someone, a doctor perhaps, could discover if there was poison? And why was she so convinced Sarah had attempted to murder either Dom or Tavie or both while under the eyes of well over a hundred people? It would be the action of a madman.

The thought did not bring the comfort it might have done had anyone other than Sarah been involved.

Dom awaited Tavie at the foot of the stairs. "Has supper been announced?" she asked.

He nodded. "Shall we go before everyone has found his way to the tables? If we are lucky, we'll be in time to choose some lobster patties."

"I'll be very distressed if Cook didn't make enough. I ordered what sounded sufficient to feed the British army and half the French as well."

"Ah. But they are always the first to disappear. I doubt tonight will be different."

Tavie's lips compressed and then she sighed. "If they *have* run out, I recommend the mushroom fritters as a substitute. Cook has a way with them, you must admit."

"Yes, and a delicate hand with the sauces he serves with them. Perhaps," said Dom, seating Tavie beside Ally at one of the round tables, "I should bring both?"

"You know what I like, Dom." Tavie smiled up at him, got a wink from him and realized what she'd said. She felt the blush rising under her skin and pursed her lips tightly to control a desire to add another suggestive remark to the first inadvertent one.

While Dom entered the fray at the loaded serving tables, Tavie glanced around the room, checking on her guests. It had gone well. A new sort of pride stiffened her tired back and she looked up with a smile at her mother-in-law. "Will you and Father join us?" asked Tavie.

"What a delight to get off my feet for a while," sighed Vi, once Rambourne limped off to get their supper. "I do not believe I have danced so much since," her eyes widened and her mouth drooped, "since," she continued more quietly, "before Miles died. Aunt Ally..."

"Shush, Vi. You are doing nothing of which Miles would disapprove. You know you are not."

"Yes. I know that. Which is why I determined I would enjoy myself tonight and I have. I had forgotten what a pleasure country balls can be."

"Are they different in town?"

"Oh yes, Tavie. This would be a failure in town."

Tavie blenched, her eyes swinging to Ally, who looked just as bewildered as Tavie felt. "You did say you were enjoying it, did you not?" asked Tavie cautiously.

Vi looked at the white-faced girl then turned to look at Ally. "What have I said?"

"That this would be a failure in town," Ally reminded her.

"Well, of course it would." Neither woman responded. "But, Aunt Ally, you *know* it would."

"Why?" asked Tavie.

"It is not at all a squeeze. One actually has room to dance, one can find one's particular friends amongst the guests, the chairs are not always full so one can never find a place to rest," Vi waved a hand gracefully from a rather limp wrist, "oh, any number of things."

Ally laughed. "Now I understand, Vi, but Tavie does not. She thinks she has been insulted."

Vi blinked and gathered her scarves more closely around her. "I certainly didn't mean to insult her." She looked at the younger woman. "Truly. The evening is very much a success. Surely you know that?"

"But—"

"Oh, it wouldn't do in London. Things are quite different there. In the first place, there would be many more people that you could and should or *must* invite. You would wish your rooms as full as they could hold. It would be deemed a failure otherwise. Often I've gone to parties and not seen a soul I wished to see. That's what I meant about being able to find friends in this group. One expects that in the country of course."

"It sounds absurd."

Ally chuckled again. "Oh, Tavie, what a delight you are. It is very silly indeed but it is the way of the world, as you'll discover."

"Must I?"

"Must you what, love?" asked Dom as he settled beside her and studied his plate with satisfaction. The lobster patties had not run out. Yet.

"Discover the London your mother and Ally describe."

"You mean the squeezes and boredom of doing the same thing over and over?"

"I am not certain what I meant."

"I'll be with you and," he lowered his voice but not enough, "remember, our decision will make it possible to avoid much of it. We can endure the rest."

"What decision?" asked Vi. She looked from one to the other, suspicious.

"Does it matter?" Dom reached for the bottle of champagne Martin handed him and deftly popped the cork. He poured into the six glasses on Martin's tray and, setting down the bottle, took two, one for Tavie and one for himself. When the table had been served, Rambourne and General Whalley having returned to it with Vi and Ally's supper, Dom raised his glass for a toast. "May Tavie enjoy her first sip of champagne!"

Despite her father's obvious concern, Tavie did.

Chapter Eleven

ꟃ

Tavie and Dom stood on Brightwood's steps and waved off another cavalcade. Two couples had climbed into the first and most opulent carriage. The next held maids and valets. Following them were two utility carriages, each loaded to capacity with trunks and boxes. Trailing all were grooms leading the gentlemen and ladies' hacks.

When the dust raised by the multitude of hooves made it impossible for anyone looking back to see them, Tavie allowed herself a brief grimace. "What a parade. Does everyone travel that way?"

"You wish to know if most travelers have at least two carriages on a long journey? Yes. Those who can afford it do. One wishes some privacy and would have none if a maid and valet were in the same carriage every day, all day. I don't know of course but I suspect the servants are equally pleased not to be in constant attendance."

"I see." Tavie looked thoughtful. "We'll be expected to transport our whole wardrobe everywhere we go?"

"Why, Tavie." Dom pretended shock. "You do not think they carried merely clothing, do you?" he exclaimed. He continued with equally pretend patience. "One takes one's wardrobe, to be sure, because how can you guess just what will be wanted? And jewels and other gewgaws of course. But you will also carry sheets so you need not worry about damp or dirty linens at the inns at which you halt. You take an assortment of plate, not trusting those same inns to have dinnerware of sufficient grandeur off which you may gorge," he grinned a quick grin, "I mean *dine*. And you carry along a large assortment of medicines, enough for the army that sailed for Portugal a few weeks ago. If you ride, you pack your personal tack and take a groom and—"

Tavie interrupted what threatened to be a lecture on how to travel in style that was only half an exaggeration. "Dom, is England really going to move more strongly against Napoleon on the Peninsula?"

Dom sobered, abandoning his teasing. He'd learned early in their marriage that Tavie was seriously interested in such things. "The government had to give such orders once Ferdinand was forced by Napoleon to abdicate. When the Spanish rose in rebellion," he shrugged, "it was too great an opportunity to miss."

"Will *you* go?" she asked. She blenched at the momentary excitement she saw in his eyes. "Dom?"

Excitement faded and a rueful look replaced it. "I'm too old, Tavie. War is a game for young men, unless you are bred to it. If I had bought a commission a dozen years ago or more…" He sighed. "Well, one cannot always be prescient, can one?"

"You would *like* to go?"

Dom thought about it. "No."

Tavie whooshed out the breath she'd been holding.

"Like I said, I'm too old. I know too much. I think of the dirt and heat and forced marches and bad food and pain and the horror of seeing friends die. I think of all those mundane things instead of high principles such as patriotism and honor and heroism that justify going to war in the minds of young hotheads."

He tipped his head, continuing in a more serious vein. "Not that I believe we can or should avoid this war. Nor," he said, as intense as Tavie had ever seen him, "do I believe it will be easy. Napoleon may or may not be a monster, as some insist, but he is a military genius and he has brilliant men loyal to him who will fight like demons for his cause. I fear it will be many years before the war with France is ended and, if you think back to the so-called Peace of Amiens, which lasted such a short time, then you will admit there is no certainty that, when a new peace is announced, it will last."

"Oh dear—as Elf would say."

"An Elfish oh-dear indeed, or even two," he responded, his tone a trifle grim. Then he forced a smile as Lady Clavingstone approached them. "Ah. My dearly beloved godmother, are you too deserting us?"

"Not today, assuming you are willing to have me around longer."

"As long as you like," responded Dom promptly, pinching Tavie's little finger when her mouth drooped to the slightest degree. Tavie instantly agreed that Lady Clavingstone should *know* she was welcome for as long as she wished to stay.

"That is a plumper if I ever heard one." Matilda chuckled. "Nor do I blame you. You wish for your home back and all strangers to the devil. You would like to continue your interrupted honeymoon. But," Matilda frowned and looked from one to the other, "even if I haven't a notion what I can do," she said rather cryptically, "it will be more than if I were not here."

She nodded briskly and they watched as, with a stately tread, she moved on into the gardens. Tavie and Dom eyed each other in heavy silence.

"Dom," said Tavie carefully, "just how many are aware that something just a tad out of the ordinary appears to be happening around here?"

"Obviously," responded Dom just as thoughtfully, "several more than we knew."

The next two hours saw the backs of the last of the guests who were leaving. The household was reduced to Elf and Ally, Rambourne, Vi, Bert and Geoff, Lady Clavingstone, Owen and of course Sarah, who was the only *unwelcome* visitor still under their roof, although Geoff occasionally eyed Owen with a jaundiced eye.

Extra bedrooms, opened for the party, were put back under covers. Tavie devised simpler menus that left Cook a prey to contradictory feelings. He could no longer gloat over the complex meals produced under adverse conditions but, on the other hand, he needed a rest after a month of intensive work and was relieved he could cease supervising everything going on in his domain.

Cook's cousin was recovering from her burns but it would be some time before she was back under his thumb where she belonged. He often wondered how he managed without his human good luck charm. In future, he'd see his awkward cousin stayed well away from boiling oil, hot water, sharp knives and every other danger she might find in his kitchen. Charms of proven efficacy were too hard to come by and, if he could avoid it, he'd never again be without his.

* * * * *

The next few days passed quietly enough. Bert suggested taking Tavie for her first climb but for one thing or another—mostly Tavie's subtle, delaying tactics—nothing came of it. They rode, resumed Tavie's driving lessons and played cards and billiards. Dom introduced Tavie to that strange Scottish game called golf. He had a small, well-maintained course, an area of the gardens Tavie had once discovered, wondered about and then forgotten in the hectic preparations for the house party and ball.

"Gulf? I have never heard of it."

"Golf. It isn't the most popular of games but I've found it fascinating. My father and I were on a tour that ended near Prestwick where I discovered my lord father was a fanatic. Tavie, we were out on the course at dawn. If it rained, as it did nearly every day, he did not cease cursing until it stopped. It was embarrassing. I suggested we put in a course here at home and Father calmed down, returned to normal and we left for Brightwood soon after. But in the meantime," added Dom sheepishly, "I guess I too was infected with the disease." He watched Tavie critically. "No, no, Tavie, that's not the way. You hold the club like this." His arms went around her so he could demonstrate.

Tavie discovered an aptitude and she too began to understand why the Scots had banned the game back in the 1400s.

"Because," Geoff, who knew such odd tidbits, explained, "it interfered with archery practice, which in that century, was considered essential to national security."

"Perhaps," suggested Tavie some days later, "we could extend this course?"

"I've planned several ways of doing that very thing. Now I know you too like the game we will choose one. We'll have a few trees cut through that plantation and put another hole just over the rise and then another behind that beech grove to the right. From there we'll make a line back to this hole and, including the first hole as the end, we'll have eight. It is fun, is it not?" he added, kneeling to mound a pile of dirt to hold his ball.

"Fun," exploded Tavie, just as he swung. "Dominic Thornton, how can you call it fun? I have wasted several strokes attempting to free my ball from that rough grass, which I am certain should not be there at all, and you tell me I am having fun?" She scowled and turned to face her own ball. Once she'd swung, she grinned and jumped up and down. "I did it! It went right where I wanted it to go." Tossing the club aside, she turned and hugged Dom tightly. "It *is* fun, is it not?" Then she scowled because everyone laughed at her.

Dom enjoyed their life. Teaching Tavie new skills, a hand or two of whist in the evening and, after the tea tray, when the older guests went up to bed, he and his friends and Tavie could play billiards or adjourn to the library for conversation.

Yes, it was very enjoyable indeed. However it had been a long time since he'd had his Tavie all alone to himself—anyplace other than their bedroom, that was.

He wanted her company for a whole, long, lazy day and went about planning a kidnapping with great secrecy. He'd steal her away. It would be as it was before Elf and Ally arrived. He stood on ceremony with no one remaining at Brightwood so there was no guest who would be offended if host and hostess disappeared for the day.

Except Aunt Sarah perhaps.

But Sarah's feelings didn't count. He wished she would go home. He could tolerate everyone else, even when they interfered with his time with Tavie, but not Sarah. Dom frowned. He wished he could remember what it was about Sarah that teased at the back of his mind, the question popping up over and over at the oddest of moments.

He pushed it away again as he talked with his shepherd concerning the weather. The old man was rarely wrong. True, he'd been mistaken about the climb up Helvellyn but Dom counted that all to the good. The old man had made his mistake for this summer. The result of their consultation was to settle on a date two days hence.

Having the day, Dom needed a destination. The maps he and his friends used were brought out again. Supposedly they were choosing their next climb. But while the others pored over the region, arguing over mountains they'd not yet ascended, Dom searched out places he loved. Places that were beautiful and peaceful and not far off and, above all, secluded.

He organized food. He wanted something special and consulted with Mrs. MacReady, swearing her to secrecy. The housekeeper understood perfectly. After all, she'd been first housemaid, training for her current position, when Dom's father married his mother. She well remembered how Thornton newlyweds behaved. In any case, even without those memories, she would willingly abet Dom and Tavie in an escapade. She liked the young couple.

Dom's suppressed excitement grew barely contained and became obvious to Geoff. "Just what have you up your sleeve now, old friend," he asked.

"Nothing that need concern you."

Geoff's brows snapped together. "You are not planning something dangerous, are you?"

"Heavens, no. To the contrary," said Dom, his face softening with anticipation. "Don't bother your head about me, Geoff. You'd approve if you knew but no one is to know."

Sarah, who had paused just beyond the door, moved away. To the contrary, he had said? That was a clue for anyone with a mind with which to think. Sarah had no trouble at all reading the situation. Dom obviously had plans to sneak away with Tavie. It was a chance she must not miss. But when? Sarah's only fear was that Dom might get away before she knew and she'd be unable to find them.

* * * * *

Dom had a qualm the night before they were to leave early the next morning. Tavie knew that Dom planned a surprise, something she'd like, but he'd told even her no more than that. Now Dom pulled on his robe and cinched the cord around his middle.

"Where are you going?" asked Tavie sleepily.

"Just something I want to discuss with Geoff. Go to sleep, love."

"Don't be loo-ong," she said on a yawn.

He chuckled. "No, love, I'll not be long at all."

Geoff's room was dark and Dom entered quietly. He tiptoed toward the bed and leaned over to shake Geoff, only to find himself choking, Geoff's hands around his throat. He backed away, half dragging Geoff from his bed before the fingers let go their hold.

"Dammit, what do you mean by it?" asked Dom, outraged.

"Oh lordy." Geoff ran a rueful hand through his hair. "I thought the murderer had decided on other prey. Don't you know better than to sneak up on someone that way?"

"I didn't want to startle you," said Dom, very much on his dignity.

"Didn't want to…" Geoff stifled guffaws in his pillow. When he sobered, he shoved the pillows into a pile and leaned against them. "Light a candle, Dom. I prefer to see people with whom I'm talking."

Dom lit a spill in the coals in the fireplace and used it to light a candle. From that, he lit others on the mantel. He turned, a glower still marring his features.

"You can," said Geoff, "come down off your high horse as well. How was I to know it was you?"

"Did you have to be quite so rough?" Dom felt his throat.

"I was to ask, politely of course, if my intruder had murder on his mind before defending myself?"

"I see where that might not be wise but if it had been someone else's throat, I would find it a lot more humorous."

"Since you did not come to murder me, why did you come?"

Dom pulled a chair near, turned it and straddled it. He leaned his arms on the top. "I've decided to confide in you. Someone should, maybe, know what I'm up to. Other than Mrs. MacReady, that is."

"Oh. MacReady knows? You do trust someone around here then?"

"Now who is riding a hobbyhorse?"

"Sorry." Geoff yawned. "Get on with it, man. Before I fall asleep."

"Mrs. MacReady only knows I'm taking Tavie off for a day. It isn't that I dislike having you here or the others for that matter, except Sarah of course, but it has been too long since we've had a day alone."

"You didn't have to explain that. I've watched you grow more and more possessive of her. So where are you taking her?"

"West. It isn't important exactly where. What I want you to do is keep an eye on things here. Sort of keep track of everyone. See if anyone does anything suspicious or asks too many questions or—oh, you know the sort of thing."

"And if someone disappears altogether?"

Dom frowned. "Following us, you mean?"

"Exactly."

"No one knows we are going, so how could anyone follow?"

"Be prepared. If *I* guessed you were up to something, and you must admit I did, someone else might have guessed and, as a result, you'd best be on the watch."

Dom's frown deepened. "Maybe I should cancel the whole thing." Geoff waited. Dom shook his head. "I am sure you are dreaming up horrors. We are off at first light. No one will be awake, let alone prepared to follow."

Once the candles were out and Dom left, Geoff laid back, his hands behind his head, and stared toward the unseen ceiling. He wished he didn't have this vague, nagging sensation that Dom was wrong. He moved his head against his hands, rubbing at an itch there. If only he knew why he felt that prickle at the back of his neck. Most of all, he wished he could go to sleep and forget the whole thing.

Under such influences, it took a long time to nod off. As a result, Geoff overslept and, when morning arrived, was late rising.

* * * * *

"Wake up, love," laughed Dom, hugging her harder with the arm that had held her against his side for the last few miles.

Tavie raised her head and blinked sleepily. She looked around to see where they'd gotten to but recognized nothing. She yawned, snuggling back into Dom's embrace.

"Now then, sleepyhead," he said with a laugh, "it is time to begin our day."

"That," she yawned a still wider yawn, "is what you said when you forced me out of bed before the first dove cooed and practically dressed me yourself."

"Yes, but that was to get you to the gig. Now we have to walk."

"Walk?" Tavie lifted one foot and looked at the awkward, ugly shoe Dom had shoved over several layers of stockings. "Now I think I understand the footwear. You are," she accused, "going to teach me to climb whether I wish it or not."

Dom blinked. "You don't *wish* to learn?" He didn't wait for an answer to what he believed an absurd question. "Climbing is for another day. Not what I had in mind for now. We are following that stream for a mile or so and then you will be pleased you made the effort. I promise you. It is a tiny bit of the world that must have escaped from Eden when Adam and Eve were expelled. Nothing could be so beautiful if it were not a piece of paradise."

Tavie, finding Dom's poetic description intriguing, allowed him to help her down from the gig. She watched him unhitch the mare and hobble her before turning her loose near a stream that burbled merrily toward the River Derwent.

"She'll be safe enough until we return," he said. "No one comes here but sheep and a shepherd now and again. Come along," he ordered, swinging a pack onto his back.

"What is that?" asked Tavie, tagging behind as he strode toward the narrow end of the valley.

"Our breakfast and lunch and enough for tea if we decide to stay so long." He turned and faced her on the narrow track beside the water. "Tavie, do you mind? I know I practically kidnapped you and brought you here without a word as to where or why. Do you understand?"

"Of course I do. I've wanted to be alone with you too. Lead on, my lord. I, your faithful helpmeet, will follow."

He grinned and Tavie grinned back.

Her grin faded when he turned to lead the way. *If only,* she thought, *he doesn't expect me to climb anything then I expect I'll manage to survive.* She looked beyond him up the stream. So far as she could see, their way lay along a narrow path obviously made by the hooves of many sheep. *If sheep manage it,* she thought, *then surely I can.*

But a glance at the hills rising steeply to either side had her shuddering. Firmly she closed her mind to the possibility she might find herself at the top of one of them. Dom had said he was taking her to a place of beauty, that some other day they would begin her climbing lessons. Again she shuddered. Why hadn't she found the courage to tell him she simply could not do it? That she could not bear even the thought of being that far up? She had even dismissed her silly notion of having the guide teach her to overcome her fears.

They neared Dom's secret place half an hour later. The valley had narrowed, the stream burbling at their side. The trail had been going uphill at a reasonably steep angle but, so far, it hadn't bothered Tavie because the sides of the valley rose even higher, evening out her emotional reaction. The noise of the tumbling water had been a constant companion and made conversation difficult. Now Dom halted where the stream disappeared around an outcrop of rock, which hid whatever was beyond.

The trail, thought Tavie, *has ended. Where is the promised beauty?*

Dom's roguish smile warned Tavie he was up to something, but she was hot and tired from the trudge, despite the mist and cool morning air, so she only smiled, a trifle warily, back at him.

He stood very close to her and, raising his voice over the raucous noise of the water pouring through the rough stone channel ahead, asked, "Tired, love?"

"Yes," she responded equally loudly. "I hope it is worth it."

"You've guessed we are there? Almost?"

The "almost" chilled her. She drew in a deep breath. "Let us say I hope we are there?" She was getting her breath back. "I've concluded I am not cut out for hiking. I am spoiled. Too soft. We should have ridden, Dom."

"Perhaps another time we shall." He took out a Belcher neckerchief and told her to turn around.

"Why?" she asked, suspecting what he intended and not happy about it.

"Please, Tavie? I'll guide you. I want the scene to come to you in all its glory all at once. Indulge me?"

When he looked at her like that, she'd have cheerfully cut off her right hand for him. Turning her back seemed simple enough by comparison. With her eyes bandaged, Dom eased her around and ahead of him. His voice in her ear guided her every footstep and it wasn't as difficult as she'd thought it might be. At one point, he warned her the path was slippery from the spray and that she should hold tightly to handholds he helped her find. A few moments later he stopped her, his arms going around her and his warmth seeping into her.

"Tavie, love, you are the most perfect woman in the whole world. Look now on one of the most perfect settings the world can provide you."

He flipped off the blindfold and Tavie, stunned, gazed her fill. Ahead, not quite a quarter of a mile, was a waterfall. It was a double fall actually as the stream split by a rock projecting from the top of the cliff. The two narrow streams fell nearly thirty feet with no obstruction. From there, water tumbled down a series of short rapids into an almost perfectly round pool from which it overflowed to burble its way along the exquisite little valley to where it disappeared through the gorge behind them. But the falls held Tavie's eye. They sparkled in the early morning sun, rainbows forming and shattering and reforming in the mist rising from the bottom.

"Cat got your tongue?" asked Dom, close to her ear, a laugh in his voice.

"Awe, more like," she retorted. "Dom, it is a thing of beauty for certain. How did you ever find this place?"

"As a boy, I was all over these hills. I spent every hour I could steal from my tutor out and about, exploring. I know a dozen places like this. Well," he amended, "perhaps not quite like this. I chose the one I believe the most beautiful to show you first."

"I love it." She turned in his arms for the first loving kiss of the day. It very nearly got away from them but Dom, a rueful look in his eye, set her from him. "Let us get comfortable, Tavie. And eat. I do not know about you but I am hungry." He gave her a peck on the nose and an affectionate hug. "We've the whole day. Let us not rush things, hmmm?"

* * * * *

Sarah swore softly. She turned her hack and retraced her steps. How could she have lost them? True, the fog had been heavy as they'd come down from the pass, but how had she not caught up with them? She'd even seen them once, the gig trundling along like some prehistoric animal through strands of vapor. She'd been so certain Dom was taking Tavie across the fells into Borrowdale to the inn there. So certain she had not worried at all—until she'd come to the last rise before the village and looked ahead.

There was no carriage in view and there *should* have been.

She backtracked, going up every possible trail a man of Dom's skill might have taken his gig. Each time she reached a point where a carriage could go no further with no sign of them.

Back on the main track, she flipped her reins over the roan's rump and, startled, he jumped away from the pain. Sarah swore more savagely, controlled her mount with a vicious twist of the reins and settled to watching for the next side trail. It wasn't long before she found one and directed the horse's feet onto it.

* * * * *

"Full?" Tavie grinned at Dom who lay back against the thickly woven, woolen blanket, his hands behind his head. He shook his head, opening his mouth, indicating she was to give him more. She popped in another bit of bread and cheese before taking another bite herself. They chewed as contentedly as cows with cuds, as Tavie pointed out when they both swallowed and washed all down with a swig of tea from one of the flasks.

"Am I crazy to feel so content, love?"

"I hope not, Dom. I feel the same way. Except for one thing."

"Hmm?"

"That track around that stone where we came into this little valley. Is it as narrow as I think it is?"

"Over the water just there? It is barely wide enough to squeeze around, yes. Which is why this place is secret. Not many have the courage to try when they don't know it is worth the trouble."

Tavie shuddered. Coming around blindfolded with Dom telling her where to put her feet and hands, she hadn't thought about the fact she was doing the impossible. She glanced back to where the water cut through the narrows, falling several feet in the process. The path must have been as much as eight feet above the water at one point. She'd been that high and hadn't known it. But now that she did, how was she to get back? Well, that was for later. She'd done it once. Perhaps the trick was to use the blindfold and have Dom guide her. If she could not see, then perhaps she would not fear?

But that was crazy. *Awareness* was the problem. And now she *knew*.

"Come here, love." Dom motioned her to him and she lay down, snuggling close. They'd cut short their sleep and now, tummies full, the sun warm, the roar of the falls, the muttering of the stream, Dom and Tavie dozed.

* * * * *

Sarah wasn't sleeping. She was, once again, cursing the fact she'd wasted yet another half an hour riding up the wrong track. It had wound way back into the fells, ending at an abandoned farm. Sarah, hot, tired and hungry, dismounted, grabbed the reins too close to her hack's mouth for its comfort and led it to the well. She tied it and, letting the bucket fall, listened for the splash. None came. She unwound the ratchet. Still nothing.

Dry well, she decided when a thump indicated the bucket was at the bottom. In the watery wealth of the Lake District, a dry well was an improbability but it had happened here. Sarah swore loudly as she climbed onto the wide lip of the well and, from there, back onto her horse. The nervous gelding made mounting as difficult as possible by sidling away. Again she jerked the bit viciously and again she snapped the reins across the animal's rump. The roan had never been treated so roughly. He didn't like it and tried to tell his rider so in the only way he knew. His attempt to unseat Sarah only led to more pain and, cowed, he gave it up.

Given the opportunity, Sarah suspected he'd show her a clean pair of heels. She must not forget to tie him well if she had to leave him anywhere. In the past, horses had left her in the most difficult of places because she'd forgotten to tie them. She did not understand why they tended to run back to their stables. No one else seemed to have that problem.

Ah. But it would not happen today. Once she found Dom and Tavie, she must have a way back to Brightwood. With loving fingers, she smoothed the hunting bow slung on her back. All those hours she'd spent perfecting her aim by tracking rabbits would pay off. But she would not dare lose her horse, not so far from home as they'd gotten, not when returning in good time with a good excuse was so important.

* * * * *

Geoff found Bert in the billiards room. "Seen Lady Sands?"

"No, and I thank the Lord for my good luck." Bert lined up his next shot. He straightened without taking it. "Where are you going?"

"I've got to find Lady Sands."

"Come on, Geoff, no one in their right mind would be looking for that woman. Let her be."

"Dom and Tavie are off by themselves."

"I know that. We all guessed something was up with them."

"Including Sarah?" After a significant pause, he added, "She's the only one missing, Bert." He stared at his huge friend.

Bert stared back, his hand tightening around the cue stick. He swallowed. Hard. "Where have you checked?"

"All over the house. I even asked her maid. Mary, I believe her name is. Lady Sands was gone when Mary went in with her morning chocolate. Such a mousy woman that one is. I think she's afraid of Sarah. I wonder why she stays with Lady Sands."

"Who cares? I'll take the gardens to the east."

Geoff put Mary from his mind. "I'm heading for the stables."

"Transport!"

"Yes."

Bert didn't bother to rack his cue. He tossed it onto the table. "I'm coming with you."

The men moved with that space-eating stride one used when one didn't want it obvious one wished to get somewhere quickly. Bert's jaw hardened when they discovered that, indeed, the hack that Lady Sands used was out. So was a lady's saddle. Horse and tack were missing when the grooms started their morning work. Which had been at six. It was nearly nine.

Geoff ran back toward the house. Bert paused long enough to order a pair of strong mounts saddled and brought up to the house to await their pleasure. Then he too headed for the house. Back in the hall, Bert tracked Geoff's direction by following a footman's pointing finger.

"Geoff?"

"In here."

Bert headed for the open door and peered in. Geoff stood, his hands on hips, studying Dom's gunroom walls.

"Anything missing?" asked Bert.

"Not that I can tell. You know this collection better than I do."

Bert gave the room a quick check. "I think it is intact."

"Then she didn't take a gun—unless she owns one of her own."

"Do you think she'd try outright murder? So far everything has been made to look like an accident."

"Strange, is it not? Suddenly we have, neither one of us, the least doubt Lady Sands caused those accidents. How she could have done so I cannot think but we now believe she's out to try again."

Bert grimaced. "She's been the only real choice for villain from the beginning and if we could figure out who she has as an accomplice, we'd have done something about it sooner. You know that."

"I don't think," said Geoff, moving from the gunroom to the library in his usual quicksilver fashion, "that Lady Sands has an accomplice. I think she managed those stunts herself and do not ask me how she could. I don't know. I just think she did."

"Sarah? Manage what?" asked Matilda from where she had been nearly hidden by the sides of a leather-covered chair turned to catch the light from the window. She peered at Geoff and Bert.

"We think she had a hand in sabotaging the boat and then the carriage."

"Sabotage? That sort of thing does sound like Sarah, does it not?" asked Matilda.

"Yes, but we cannot think of who she could have had to help her, so I, at least, cannot quite accept she was responsible," reiterated Bert.

"No accomplice," said Matilda. "She'll have done it herself."

Geoff and Bert looked at each other. "Lady Clavingstone," said Geoff with barely controlled patience, "do you think you might explain?"

Chapter Twelve

ꙮ

Matilda blinked at Geoff's intensity but nodded. "Sarah's grandfather was a cabinetmaker, not that she bruits the fact around. Once she was old enough to become snobbish about such things, he ceased to exist for her but, when she was young, she liked visiting him. He taught her to use his tools. I remember she fixed a window at school. Everyone was shocked because she not only knew how it *should* work, she knew what tools were needed to make it work. She'd become impatient, you see, waiting for the headmistress to order it done."

"Then you think she could have loosened the plank on the boat which almost sank?"

"And," asked Bert, "replaced the pole on Tavie's carriage with a rotten one? That's pretty heavy work for a lady."

"Lady," snorted Matilda. "She was born one but the training never quite took. She has the strangest ideas in her cockloft," continued her ladyship, using cant language she should not have known. "She has always thought Owen would make a better marquis than Dom, for instance, and she confuses a title with the person holding it. As if a title made whoever held it someone special! And she has often believed herself ill-treated for the most ridiculous of reasons." Lady Clavingstone put her head to one side. "But why," she finished, "do you ask?"

"Sarah isn't here. We think she's followed Dom and Tavie and has planned another attempt to harm them."

Matilda rose to her feet, clutching the book she'd been reading. Her face turned a funny shade of greenish-gray.

"Why are you standing around gossiping then? Why are you not following?"

"Which direction would you have us go, Lady Clavingstone?" Geoff gestured at the maps still strewn across the table. "I hope to find a clue. Bert, while I study the maps, you question Mrs. MacReady. She's the only one who might be able to help us. Dom hoped to keep secret the fact he was taking Tavie away, but I guessed. Now I believe Lady Sands did as well. Don't just stand there, Bert. We haven't time."

"But I think perhaps I may know where they went."

Geoff breathed in and out deeply. "Then do you not think that, just perhaps it might possibly be a wise idea," his voice rose, "*to tell me*?"

Bert's ears reddened. "That's just it. I can't. I'm trying to remember."

"*What* are you trying to remember?" Geoff clenched his fists, the feeling of urgency so strong he had to restrain his desire to shake the information out of Bert.

"What Dom once said. Remember? He called it the most perfect spot in the whole world. Promised to show us sometime."

Geoff headed for the table. "Now you mention it," he bent over the maps, sliding them around, tossing a couple to the floor, finally locating the one he wanted, "somewhere on the River Derwent..."

"No. A stream that feeds into the river, was it not?" Bert too bent over the map.

Matilda recovered her poise, although anxiety seeped into every corner of her being. "I'll question Mrs. MacReady. And I'll get Violetta. Perhaps Miles took her somewhere like that and she'll remember how to get there."

Geoff tracked the river inch by inch on the large-scale map, beginning where the Derwent opened into Derwent Water and following its path south. Each time he came to a feeder, he traced it carefully, trying to recall something about it from the summers the three boys had explored every nook and cranny in the region.

"No, not that one," said Bert, at the fourth. "The valley ends at that outcrop of rock, remember? Nothing special about the place except that stream comes through a gorge. No one would bother going over that rock, would they? Besides, it would be dangerous for Tavie. She hasn't had the training for it."

Something made Geoff hesitate but no recollection came to mind to explain why. He let his finger trail to the next side valley and the next and the next. They discussed each but came up with no clue as to where they might find Dom and Tavie.

Vi's face was ashen as she followed Matilda into the library. "What do you mean Dom is in danger? How can he be in danger? Why would anyone want to hurt my Dom? You are insane to think such a thing. Dominic is wonderful. Everyone likes Dominic. No one would want to hurt him. No one."

"Did you not explain?" Geoff asked Lady Clavingstone under cover of Vi's spate of words.

"I did. Vi, please try to remember any special places Miles used to take you. Some place so special Dom would want to take Tavie there for a stolen day."

"Please, Lady Brightwood. Think."

Vi blustered for another moment and then, with a look toward Matilda, who was swelling with impatience, she calmed and actually thought about it. "Well," she said after a moment, "there are the falls. In the hidden valley."

"What falls?" Bert said just as Geoff asked, "What hidden valley?"

"Well, you go around this stupid rock which is right in the way and it is dangerous and difficult and one is so afraid of falling down into the stream which is particularly swift and rocky right there, but then, when you manage it, you find yourself in this long, narrow, steeply rising valley with a few trees here and there and a round pool below a tremendously beautiful waterfall." Vi got a dreamy look to her. "Miles always swam there after we'd—" Her eyes focused and she looked from person to person. She blushed rosily and closed her mouth tightly, but the dreamy look, induced by good memories, didn't quite fade.

"You said no one would go around that outcrop, Bert!" Geoff's finger returned to the place Bert believed impossible.

"That can't be it. I tell you that place is a *cul-de-sac*."

Geoff bit his lip while searching his memory but shook his head when still nothing came to mind. "Can you show us on the map, Lady Brightwood, where you and your husband went?"

"Map? Oh, I was never good at maps." Vi put her hands behind her, stepped back a step and shook her head. "My governess despaired of me."

"Then tell us," pleaded Geoff, desperation making his voice hoarse. "Try to explain how you got there."

"That is simple. You take the old track over the fells," Geoff's finger followed along a line on the map as she spoke, "and turn right at the river and then pretty soon you turn right again and go as far as you can and then you walk and then you have to go around that stupid rock and then you are there."

Vi seemed to think she'd explained it perfectly. Once again Geoff's finger traveled up the stream he and Bert believed was the wrong one, but now they stared at each other, wondering how to make the shatter-brained woman give them a more certain clue to their destination. That last right turn, after all, could have been any of several.

Vi's voice was still dream-laden when she said, "Miles always said it was a little bit of paradise."

Geoff groaned. "Yes. Exactly. I remember now. Dom called it Paradise Falls but said that was only his own name for the spot." He and Bert bent to the map, hunting for the name. "Bert, we have to chance something. It must be the place you say is impossible."

"It is impossible," said Vi firmly. "Quite impossible. I could never do it except one way."

"How was that, Vi?" asked Matilda, hoping for more description.

"Miles would blindfold me. Then he'd tell me exactly where to put my hands and feet and after a bit we'd be there."

"Great Zeus!" Bert stared at Geoff. "Would Dom put Tavie into such danger?"

"I don't suppose it is all that dangerous," said Matilda. "Not for a woman who trusts her husband totally and does exactly as she is told."

"She's right, Geoff. We have to try something and it is the only clue we have. We cannot just stand around doing nothing. Let's go."

Four horses stood near the front steps. The head groom and a younger man sat on hacks, each holding the reins of a second. Their identical grim expressions warned Geoff the servants had somehow come to the same conclusion he and Bert had reached. He took his horse's reins, mounted and flashed a quick smile at the grooms who, until then, had held themselves stiffly, obviously expecting to argue about joining the search.

"We'll be happy to have you along, Cozens, but you do understand, do you not? Lord Brightwood and his lady are threatened, or so we believe. And if we go chasing after them, we too may find ourselves facing danger." Geoff looked from one man to the other.

"We understand, Mr. Martin, sir, but we bean't cowards and if his lordship needs us then we want to be there."

Geoff explained where they wanted to go, describing the falls and valley as Vi had done. Neither man had heard of the place, the one merely shaking his head but the other explaining, "Don't hold with all this climbing nonsense. Seems like a waste. What do you do after all? Why, first you climb up to the top, am I right, sir? And then what? Why, you climb right back down again. Seems a mite foolish—" The man suddenly recalled his master's passion for the sport. His ears reddened. "If'n you'll pardon me for saying so o'course." He fell into abashed silence.

"I suspect it is a mite foolish, Cozens. But whoever said the aristocracy had any sense?"

The stablemen chuckled, their embarrassment eased by Geoff's banter, and fell back, allowing Geoff and Bert to take the lead with a gait that wouldn't tire the horses too quickly but covered the ground steadily and surely. Both men wished to race off as fast as they could but both knew that killing their mounts would do no one the least bit of good.

Definitely not Dom, whom they must find and find as soon as possible.

* * * * *

Sarah had gone a fair way along the trail she now followed before she realized she'd absentmindedly strayed onto the track back over the pass to Thirlmere. She swore. The words echoed from the fells around her. She twisted the reins, thinking furiously. How had she missed them? Where had they gone? Forcing back her need to rant and rave and the need to relieve her feelings by beating her horse, Sarah forced herself to think.

She'd trailed the pair at some distance, fearful that Dom might look back and see her. From the top of the pass, she'd seen them ahead of her.

"About right here," she murmured. She glanced around. "Yes. Here."

The track curved and she'd lost sight of the gig. Believing she knew where they were going, she'd let her mount pick its way until she could safely increase its gait to a canter.

"Where am I?" Sarah reviewed her thoughts. Her quarry had gone around that curve…

Ahead was the river. So, as the sun rose that morning, she'd come to the river and turned upstream toward Borrowdale where she'd thought to locate herself a good ambush.

It hadn't worked that way. Somehow, after reaching this point, the pair had disappeared. Where could they have gone?

The mere!

Why had she not thought of that? Of course Dom had taken Tavie to the top of the mere where they'd be alone, rather than into the village where they'd be amongst people.

Sarah flipped her reins against her mount's rump and he picked up speed. It must be all of two, maybe three miles to where the River Derwent opened into Derwent Water. Sarah gripped her reins in one hand and the fingers of the other toyed with the feathered ends of the arrows in the quiver hanging from her saddle.

Soon, she thought. Her breathing became fast and shallow as her anticipation grew. *Very, very soon.*

* * * * *

Dom leaned on one elbow, the fingers of his other hand tracing his wife's brows, running down her nose to the tip, touching her kiss-reddened lips lightly. He smiled when she pursed them, kissing his fingers, and then, opening her mouth, she drew one in.

The skin over Dom's cheekbones tingled, an instant response to her provocative act. He grinned. "Careful, wench. At this rate, you'll wear me out before I reach my prime. Are you never satisfied?" he teased, lowering his hand to her bare breast, and discovered, much to his surprise, given what had just passed between them, that perhaps she was *not*. "You are the most passionate woman I have ever known," he said, his voice thickening.

When Tavie's body stiffened, he raised his head, looked down at the angry flush suffusing her cheeks. She glared at him.

"Oh, oh," he murmured and quickly lowered his mouth to hers.

Her hands came up to his chest and pushed. He wished he'd not so impulsively told her the truth. Obviously it was the wrong thing to say.

"I shouldn't have said that?" he asked with pretended innocence.

"You should *not* have said that."

"It is a compliment."

"A compliment with a sting."

"Tavie," he said seriously, "I cannot change my past. I had not met you, did not know you and was not aware you *existed*. Is it fair to hold against me experiences which were not meant to insult or hurt you in any way?"

"I don't hold them against you. In fact, I am often glad you have the ability to make me feel as I do. Nevertheless I cannot help but be jealous of every lady you ever kissed."

"Lady, Tavie?" He touched the end of her nose. "There have been very few of those. I was never one to enjoy the strict rules governing discreet *affaires* between members of the *ton*. I liked my relationships simple and direct and no strings or complications."

She grimaced. "Just a business arrangement."

"Yes."

"I know it is common for men to have mistresses but I cannot understand it. How can you want to lie with a female for whom you have no affection? Dom, I could not bear for anyone but you to touch me the way you do."

"Since I met you and fell in love, Tavie, I feel the same. It is so much more than I had before. I'd feel cheated now I know how it can be." He touched her again, trailing his hand from her breast to her hip but her mood had darkened. Dom rolled over and up. "Do you swim, Tavie?"

"No." Silently she thanked him for his sensitivity to her need for time. She followed his lead. "My governess knew and wished to teach me but we needed somewhere private and there simply was no such place."

"I'll teach you." Dressed in drawers, his shirt and buckskins over one shoulder, Dom reached for her and pulled her to her feet. He looked down her slim body and noted how proudly she carried herself, even naked and out in the open where any other lady he knew would feel exposed, embarrassed and exceedingly uncomfortable. Once again Dom thanked whatever guardian angel had led him to find his Tavie.

"Swim?" She looked uncertain and then shivered. "It is too chilly. I don't think I want to learn today, Dom. I'll just watch you." She reached for her *zona,* intending to wrap it around her breasts, but Dom pulled the wide band of cloth away from her. Holding one arm across her bare breasts, she looked at him.

"Leave it here. Just pull on your shift and petticoat. Maybe you'll change your mind about swimming." He added her dress to the clothes he carried, leaving his coat, vest and cravat lying beside her cloak and bonnet. At the last moment, he picked up their shoes in which they'd stuffed their socks. He looked down at the blanket and laughed. "Look, Tavie. It is as if we are still lying there." He moved a couple of things to increase the impression.

Tavie chuckled and added to the illusion by pushing the pack under his coat. "There. We are taking a nap." They strolled hand in hand toward the falls. "Have you swum here before?" she asked.

"Often. I discovered the valley from up there," he gestured toward the rough cliff beside the falls, "when I'd followed the stream from Hollow Farm which is just over the ridge. I thought it my secret, so consider my surprise when Father took me to *his* favorite place in the entire world and we came in from the end where we arrived today. He and I thought it a great joke but he warned me it might have been rather embarrassing if he'd ever arrived here with Mother on a day I'd decided to climb down from the top."

"So we are not the first to have used it for a lovers' tryst?"

"No. He told me his father showed him the place. I suspect Thornton men have passed the secret from father to son for generations. I know I'll eventually show mine." He stopped beside the round pool and gestured. "There is a shallow area if you wish to paddle, Tavie," he said into her ear. The noise from the falls had increased and it was difficult to converse.

After taking a quick wash in the shallows, Tavie found a suitable rock near where Dom dove in and watched a bit enviously as he crossed to where the rapids tumbled into the calmer water. Watching became boring and, curious to discover what sort of plants grew near the constantly misty rapids, she moved carefully over and around the rock-strewn verge of the pool.

Dom rose up once, waved at her and went back to swimming. When he came out of the water, he shook his head to rid his hair of the excess. He swept it back from his forehead with both hands and then put on his breeches.

Tavie looked back along the valley and felt, for a moment, that awful vertigo. She had not realized the slant of the valley floor was so steep. But it was a slanting rise, not an abrupt drop and she managed to accept it, the dizziness going away. A movement caught her eye and she focused on where the stream went through the constriction around which she'd come blindfolded.

"Dom. Hand me my dress."

He heard her voice but not her words and put a hand to his ear.

Quickly, she moved toward him. "My dress. I fear we have company."

He turned and shaded his eyes. Suddenly he reached for Tavie and crouched behind a relatively high boulder. "Don't say a word," he cautioned.

"Why not? No one could hear over the sound of the falls."

"Tavie, be careful." He gestured toward the woman. "That is Sarah, love, if I'm not mistaken."

"Sarah?"

Tavie stared, bemused, as Sarah crept toward the blanket. The woman moved from rock to rock, her eyes never leaving the spot where Tavie and Dom had made love not so very long before. "Dom, is that a bow she's carrying?"

"Bow and arrows, love. I think Sarah has decided accidents are too uncertain a means of getting rid of us. She is going to try outright, straightforward murder this time." He turned and scanned the rockface behind them. "We've got to get out of here."

Tavie turned and looked too. "Not that way."

"Don't be an idiot, love. This isn't the way I wished to introduce you to climbing but we are forced to it. Now do not argue. That woman is dangerous. I do not know how far she can send an arrow with enough force to do murder, so I want to be high enough it is already impossible before she discovers where we are." He put his hands to her petticoat and pulled it through her legs, tucking it up into the waistband at the top. "Odd-looking trousers, my dear," he said, his voice gruff. "I don't think you'll set a new fashion this way but at least you'll be alive to try."

"Alive." Tavie closed her eyes. *Sarah wanted Dom dead.* He might believe otherwise but Tavie *knew*. Tavie's eyes snapped open. She shook as she contemplated the cliff face. She was going to have to force herself up it. "I'm afraid, Dom."

"Of Sarah?" Worried himself, he ignored the fact Tavie shook her head at his false assumption. "All we have to do is get up there and we are practically home. And safe. The Hollows is not that far away. In fact, a shout," he exaggerated, "will probably bring someone running and not even Sarah would try murder before witnesses."

Working quickly, he tucked her dress and his shirt into the back of his buckskins waistband. He stuffed her shoes into his boots and made them into a bundle with a ribbon from her dress, tying that to his belt. "There. I think we'll make it with everything to hand. Now there is one rule a beginning climber should take to heart, Tavie. *Do not look down*. As long as you look up you won't be afraid of how far from the ground you've come."

Which is, thought Tavie, *very good advice for someone not petrified by the very thought of heights.*

But she *had* to climb. Dom's life depended on not giving in to her fears. She would, she determined, do exactly as he told her to do. It was the way she'd made it around the outcrop over the stream, was it not?

Tavie threw one last look toward Sarah. She gasped. "I told you it was you."

Dom looked too. An arrow, sticking through Dom's coat, vibrated but immediately a second smacked into Tavie's cloak. "We were both right. Let us go. *Now*," he said, his expression grim. "Do exactly as I say, Tavie, and we'll make it smoothly. It isn't a truly hard climb, thank God, and I know it like the back of my hand."

Tavie, keeping her eyes on the ground before her, made the way up beside the rapids with relative ease. When they reached the cliff face, Dom moved to the right for several yards, motioning her to follow. The noise was too loud now for talking and he pointed to her feet and where he wanted her to set them, pointing higher and higher, showing her the route they were to follow.

They took one last look behind, saw Sarah straightening up from the blanket with an expression that, even at that distance, made Tavie shudder. She gritted her teeth and faced the cliff, reaching for the first hold. How high would she have to go before Dom would be safe?

How high, oh God, how high?

Tavie muttered prayers under her breath, looking no higher than the next hold, moving slowly but steadily, with Dom practically encircling her to show her the way, to help her up—and to protect her from Sarah's arrows.

Suddenly an arrow clattered against the rock below them. "Do not," yelled Dom, "look down." He knew he had to keep her climbing. So he mouthed directions into her ear, helping her where and as he could.

"There, Tavie, that's right. Now up you go." Another arrow hit, this one closer. Tavie reached randomly and Dom grabbed her arm. "We cannot hurry this, Tavie. There. Right there. Now your feet. That's right—damn!"

"You are hit." Tavie froze.

"Do not stop. It hurts a bit but it won't stop me climbing. Believe me, it is more embarrassing than dangerous, love. There. Right there. Yes, Tavie. Like that..." Dom talked her up until they could pull themselves over the top.

As he looked back down, he explored the area the arrow had poked through his buckskins. Sarah was *not* following them, as he'd feared she might do. Instead, his aunt was seated on a rock, her back rigid, and a bunch of arrows in one hand. She faced toward the lower end of the valley, not moving.

The pose was one of some ancient queen. Dom frowned. What was the matter with her?

He turned and found Tavie lying on the ground not far enough from the edge for safety. He leaned down to her, wincing at where the arrow had penetrated just enough to draw blood but do very little real damage—except to his pride.

"Tavie?" She didn't move and Dom lowered himself to her side, turning her slightly. "Tavie, you need to move farther away from the edge…Tavie!"

Tavie moaned and Dom pulled her close. Her eyes fluttered. "What…"

"We did it, Tavie. We reached the top."

She opened her eyes wide. "The top? You are safe?"

"We are both safe. Or we will be when I can get you to move away from the edge." He grinned at her. She turned her head toward the valley, her pale skin whitening still more. "Hey," he said, "you won't faint *now,* will you?"

He chuckled at the notion, the chuckle dying as he realized that was just what she had done. Dom swore at the twinge his lifting her caused but he bore Tavie to a safe place up the stream to where a stunted tree maintained a precarious existence in the rocky soil. Wetting a handkerchief, he wiped her face with it. He re-wet it, folded it and laid it on her forehead. He looked down at her, frowning as he pulled his shirt over his head and tied it. Why had she passed out? He dumped her shoes from his and pulled on socks and boots. They were safe now, were they not? A quick check showed his aunt still seated in the same place in the same pose and he returned to where his wife lay, the frown still darkening his brow.

If she'd had hysterics upon discovering Sarah was after them, that would make sense but they were safe, so why…

Dressed himself, he worked Tavie's gown over her head and manhandled her into it. It was all right for him to see her in dishabille but he wasn't giving anyone else the opportunity. Luckily she'd followed his advice that morning and chosen a sack dress that was easy to get in and out of.

Dom headed back to the cliff face and looked down. Sarah still sat there, still stared straight down the valley toward the far end. Dom, looking that way, noted Bert and Geoff staring at the blanket, the two grooms darting looks this way and that. Bert pulled out one of the arrows. The men searched the area, turning slowly. Dom waved both arms and caught Bert's eye. Dom pointed down, signaling where they would find Sarah.

Bert shaded his eyes and scanned the bottom of the cliff face but could not find what Dom was pointing at. "Surely he didn't leave Tavie down there to face Sarah alone."

Geoff spoke through stiff lips. "It isn't possible that Tavie was killed and Dom escaped. If she were dead," his frown deepened, "but, no, I do not think he would leave her even then. But where *is* Sarah?"

"Dom is still jabbing a finger toward the bottom of the cliff. I think we should head that way."

"But carefully. It will do no one any good if we are dead."

"True."

As the four cautiously approached the pool and rapids, Dom returned to Tavie who moaned softly. He sat down and pulled her up into his arms, touching her face gently until her eyes fluttered and she looked up at him.

"You had me worried, love," he said gently.

"You are all right?" Her fingers lifted, curved against his jaw. "Really? All right?"

"More than all right, Tavie. And our right and left flank have moved to the attack, bringing reinforcements." He laughed at her bemused expression and added, "Bert and Geoff are down in the valley with a couple of grooms."

Tavie clutched at his shirt, staring painfully into his eyes. "She won't hurt them, will she?"

Dom sobered, covering her hand. "I do not think she'll ever hurt anyone again, Tavie. I do not understand it yet but she's just sitting. She hasn't moved since I first saw her after we reached the top."

"First saw her?" Tavie frowned. "Was that so very long ago?"

"You've been unconscious for well over ten minutes, love. *Too* long. I don't understand that either."

"I told you I was afraid."

"You were never in that much danger."

"Oh yes I was. I got more than two feet from the ground."

It was Dom's turn to look confused. "You will have to explain, Tavie."

Tavie took a deep breath and, at the same time, took her courage in both hands. "Dom, I cannot stand on a table without getting dizzy. I cannot look out a first-floor window if I look down. Remember that day you climbed up and into the room I was in? I nearly fainted that day."

He blinked. "You mean I am married to a woman who is afraid of heights?"

"Awkward, is it not?" she asserted in a dry voice. "I will try not to interfere with your climbing, Dom, but will you understand I'll never join you in that pastime? It is something you will have to do without me."

He was silent for a time, his eyes probing hers. "You wish I'd give it up, do you not?"

"I must not be so foolish. It is so irrational to be so very afraid."

"I did not ask if it were rational, Tavie, I asked if you wished me to give up my climbing?"

"I refuse to wish any such thing." She set her mouth in a stubborn line, glowering at nothing in particular.

Dom chuckled. "We will discuss it later. I see Bert has come up to discover if we are all right."

Tavie pushed herself to her knees and then to her feet. She walked toward Bert, her hand out. He grabbed it and pulled her toward the cliff edge before Dom could stop him and, leaning over to look down to where Geoff waited, pointed to Tavie. Dom arrived just in time to catch her as she sank gracefully into his arms. He scowled at Bert and carried her back from the edge.

"What in heaven's name did I do?" asked Bert, bewildered.

"Climb down and tell Geoff she only fainted. She'll be all right shortly. Oh, but first tell me what Sarah's up to. All I could see from here was that she didn't move."

Bert, a worried eye on Tavie, said, "She demanded we fall to our knees in obeisance. She's the future queen of England, you see. Prinny means to marry her as soon as he can get a bill of divorcement out of Parliament. Geoff thinks that, having failed to kill you, she knows she's been caught and, having no other choice, has escaped into madness." He knelt beside Tavie who was, again, coming around. "Are you all right, Tavie?"

"What happened?"

"You fainted again when Rock-between-the-ears, here," Dom scowled, "pulled you close to the cliff edge so Geoff could see you were all right."

"But you were not. All right, I mean. You fainted," accused Bert. "What did Dom do to you?"

"He didn't do anything," said Tavie quickly before Dom could explain. "I will be fine if no one takes me near a cliff ever again in my life." Tavie clutched at her crimson cheeks. "Oh, Dom, I feel such an awful fool."

"She's afraid of heights, Bert. She was so afraid that she actually passed out once we reached the top but, when it was necessary, she made every move up that cliff face like a professional. I could not be more proud of her. Now get down there and help Geoff with Sarah. It sounds like my dear aunt is finally ready for a bedlam." He shook his head. "I suppose I should feel sorry for her but I cannot. Owen, thank heaven, will have the responsibility for her future."

* * * * *

"Poor Owen," said Tavie some hours later. Everyone convened in the library, minus Sarah of course who was deeply sedated, and Owen, who was embarrassed. "Poor, poor Owen."

"*Poor Owen*. That woman tried to kill us. *Three times*," Dom interjected.

"Four," corrected Elf. "I'm next to certain she tried poison the night of the ball. Remember that spilt champagne? I saved a tiny bit of it and will have somebody test it."

"Does it make any difference now?" asked Tavie.

"No, not a bit of difference. You can destroy it and forget it, Aunt Elf." Everyone looked at Dom. "We just want to forget," he explained.

"It was generous of you to offer Owen that Northumberland property as a place to keep her," commented Lady Clavingstone. "And I believe you'll have a slave for life, Tavie, hiring Sarah's abigail as you did. The woman, Mary, thought she'd be thrown on the parish, given her tragic history."

"Mary is an excellent maid and her history was not her fault. She did not *wish* to submit to the happily deceased Lord Besselmite."

Dom squeezed Tavie's hand and said, "As for Sarah, she is, despite it all, a lady. It wouldn't be right to incarcerate her in a bedlam and it would be hell for Owen to keep her at his estate. Even if he built a separate house for her, it would be too near. Besides, the family always cares for its own. Owen will of course hire a nurse and guards. She must not be allowed to run free to murder some other fool for some equally twisted reason. Her keepers should be instructed to pretend to go along with her delusion she is Prinny's intended. Maybe if everyone treats her as if she were a future queen, she'll drift along in that dream world and be content."

"I'll suggest that to Owen," said Elf. So far Elf was the only one to whom Owen would talk.

Vi spoke from the couch where she sat very close to Rambourne, her hand firmly held in his. "I do not want to talk about Sarah anymore." She shuddered. "I become quite frightened every time I remember she actually tried to murder my Dominic."

"Or my Tavie," said Dom. "It didn't seem to matter to her which of us she killed, just so long as she made an heir impossible."

Vi straightened. "That is quite enough about Sarah. Dominic, I have an announcement to make."

Faint, red spots appeared on the duke's cheeks and he glanced down at Vi, who smiled coyly up at him and batted her lashes. The spots darkened but he met Dom's eyes and said, "I intend to marry your mother just as soon as we can make arrangements for the wedding."

"Not quite that soon," objected Vi. "I must order my *trousseau* and I would prefer an autumn wedding. Once all our friends have returned to London, you understand, and at St. George's, I think, and—"

"Violetta, we will do no such thing."

Vi looked at Rambourne, wide-eyed.

"We will call the banns right here in the village," he said in a no-nonsense fashion, "and in three weeks we will be married with Dominic to attend me and Tavie to attend you. And then we will go home."

Dom cleared his throat, hesitant to interfere, but Tavie looked horrified and jumped in with two feet. "Father," said Tavie, while Dom stifled the biting words on the tip of his tongue, "before you make the same mistake for the *third* time, will you stop and think?"

Rambourne looked mystified.

"You drove my mother to rebellion. You drove me to rebellion. You are setting out the right way to drive Dom's mother into rebellion. Is that what you want?"

"But why?" The poor man looked honestly bewildered. "I am only telling her how she is to go on. It is the duty of a man when he is responsible for a woman. Women need a strong hand or they become foolish little butterflies." He looked around.

Elf and Ally shook their heads. The men looked at him as if he were hopeless. Tavie glowered.

"But what is wrong? Surely women don't *wish* to be perfect widgeons." If anything, the reaction to that was worse.

"I think I finally understand," said Ally, breaking a stunned silence. "You, my old friend, have been blundering around… I mean," she blushed delightfully and corrected her phrasing, "you have spent your whole life in error as to a lady's feelings and ambitions. *Of course* most females wish to be butterflies." She explained in a confiding sort of manner, "They are raised to be delightful widgeons, they think of their clothes, the parties they will wear them to, the parties they will give, the clothes other women wear to the parties they attend or give," Ally took a deep breath, "and you, Morty, dear, always do your best to change our nature. But you cannot. You must take a woman for what she is." With a worried look, Ally added, "Vi is very much the butterfly. Accept her as she is and do not try to change her or Vi must cry off now before it is too late."

Rambourne frowned. "You mean I have to watch my women make fools of themselves?"

"No, no. You must watch them flitter and flutter and enjoy their brief life," said Elf. "You *like* watching other men's women. It is only once they come under *your* rule you think them foolish. Let Vi fly, your grace. Give her a generous dress allowance and she'll make you proud of her. She has a wonderful sense of style, you know."

Rambourne's frown deepened. "But can *I* change? You imply Vi will wish to be in London, attend all the parties. I hate London."

"Once you liked it very well. Before the scandal."

Rambourne's frown faded and surprise took its place. "Why, so I did. Do you suppose..."

"Why do not the two of you have a *long* engagement?" suggested Elf. "You gallant her around during the little season and see if she does not make you feel proud. And you, Vi," she added sternly, "you stay at Rambourne's country place and the two of you attend winter house parties and you discover if you *really* despise the country or merely *think* you do. You didn't dislike it when Miles lived," she clinched the argument, "now *did* you?"

Vi and Rambourne looked at each other. Their handclasp tightened and they blushed. Silent communion was followed by a nod of each head. "Maybe we both can give a little here and there," said his grace.

Dom and Tavie also looked at each other. They too communicated silently. Their parents would marry. Eventually. Dom sighed softly at the thought of future chaos and hoped the pair would have the longest engagement on record. Another thought struck him and Dom leaned over to whisper in Tavie's ear. "Except...Tavie, is it allowed? Our parents marrying each other?"

Tavie bit her lip. Then she grinned. "I'm not sure. My father may have to get a dispensation but if he's set in his mind he'll manage it."

Dom smiled. "And then, love, each will be our children's grandparent twice over. Once for himself and once married to the other grandparent."

"I do not think they'll think of that and let us not tell them," said Tavie. "I've a strong suspicion we'll have enough trouble with them just the way they are. We mustn't complicate the relationship any further." She adopted a thoughtful look. "Is it not odd how some parents need parenting more than their children do?"

Epilogue

ꟃ

Elf and Ally didn't find Tavie's notion at all strange. They had always known that good sense had little to do with age. They also knew they'd always be willing to step in when the inevitable idiocy arose and someone needed them.

Still, at their time of life, a little excitement went a long way and both were very glad indeed when their coachman arrived back at their little house in Cheltenham. Home again, they could return to the pleasant routine of their life. They could catch up with the gossipy correspondence that took up much of their time and could spend their evenings discussing it thoroughly.

Brightwood had been an interlude in their lives. Saving Dom and Tavie from being a runaway scandal had been exhilarating of course but "Enough," as Elf said more than once, "is very much enough."

Up in the Lake District at the Brightwood estate the party was over and the guests were finally gone. Dom and Tavie were, at long last, free to continue their interrupted honeymoon. To no one's surprise, it was a honeymoon that, with brief interludes of sociability, lasted the fifty odd years of their marriage.

Also by Jeanne Savery Casstevens

ꟼ

House of Scandal

The Ghost and Jacob Moorhead

About the Author

ꟼ

Jeanne Savery began writing when she stopped being a perpetual student. After a long apprenticeship, her first sale came the same year she turned fifty.

She has two kids, three grandchildren, and a wonderfully supportive husband. Hubby has itchy feet, so the family traveled whenever he found funding. Savery has lived at both ends and in the middle of the U.S.A. as well as in England, Australia, Germany, and India and has traveled here and there in Europe.

It goes without saying that whenever she and her husband leave home a laptop travels with her.

Jeanne welcomes comments from readers. You can find her website and email address on her author bio page at www.cerridwenpress.com.

Tell Us What You Think

We appreciate hearing reader opinions about our books. You can email us at Comments@EllorasCave.com.

Why an electronic book?

We live in the Information Age—an exciting time in the history of human civilization, in which technology rules supreme and continues to progress in leaps and bounds every minute of every day. For a multitude of reasons, more and more avid literary fans are opting to purchase e-books instead of paper books. The question from those not yet initiated into the world of electronic reading is simply: *Why?*

1. ***Price.*** An electronic title at Ellora's Cave Publishing and Cerridwen Press runs anywhere from 40% to 75% less than the cover price of the exact same title in paperback format. Why? Basic mathematics and cost. It is less expensive to publish an e-book (no paper and printing, no warehousing and shipping) than it is to publish a paperback, so the savings are passed along to the consumer.
2. ***Space.*** Running out of room in your house for your books? That is one worry you will never have with electronic books. For a low one-time cost, you can purchase a handheld device specifically designed for e-reading. Many e-readers have large, convenient screens for viewing. Better yet, hundreds of titles can be stored within your new library—on a single microchip. There are a variety of e-readers from different manufacturers. You can also read e-books on your PC or laptop computer. (Please note that

Ellora's Cave does not endorse any specific brands. You can check our websites at www.ellorascave.com or www.cerridwenpress.com for information we make available to new consumers.)

3. ***Mobility***. Because your new e-library consists of only a microchip within a small, easily transportable e-reader, your entire cache of books can be taken with you wherever you go.
4. ***Personal Viewing Preferences.*** Are the words you are currently reading too small? Too large? Too... ANNOYING? Paperback books cannot be modified according to personal preferences, but e-books can.
5. ***Instant Gratification.*** Is it the middle of the night and all the bookstores near you are closed? Are you tired of waiting days, sometimes weeks, for bookstores to ship the novels you bought? Ellora's Cave Publishing sells instantaneous downloads twenty-four hours a day, seven days a week, every day of the year. Our webstore is never closed. Our e-book delivery system is 100% automated, meaning your order is filled as soon as you pay for it.

Those are a few of the top reasons why electronic books are replacing paperbacks for many avid readers.

As always, Ellora's Cave and Cerridwen Press welcome your questions and comments. We invite you to email us at Comments@ellorascave.com or write to us directly at Ellora's Cave Publishing Inc., 1056 Home Avenue, Akron, OH 44310-3502.

Cerridwen Press

Cerridwen, the Celtic goddess of wisdom, was the muse who brought inspiration to storytellers and those in the creative arts.

Cerridwen Press encompasses the best and most innovative stories in all genres of today's fiction.

Visit our website and discover the newest titles by talented authors who still get inspired—much like the ancient storytellers did...

once upon a time.